# THE MIDDLE AG[...]
## TO BRING[...]
# THE SISTER FREVISSE MYSTERIES
### by Margaret Frazer

### THE NOVICE'S TALE

*Among the nuns at St. Frideswide were piety, peace, and a little vial of poison . . .*

"Frazer uses her extensive knowledge of the period to create an unusual plot . . . appealing characters and crisp writing."
—*Los Angeles Times*

### THE SERVANT'S TALE

*A troupe of actors at a nunnery are harbingers of merriment—or murder . . .*

"A good mystery . . . excellently drawn . . . very authentic . . . the essence of a truly historical story is that the people should feel and believe according to their times. Margaret Frazer has accomplished this extraordinarily well."
—Anne Perry

"A wonderful historical tapestry."
—*Minneapolis Star Tribune*

### THE OUTLAW'S TALE

*Sister Frevisse meets a long-lost blood relative—but the blood may be on his hands . . .*

"A tale well told, filled with intrigue and spiced with romance and rogues." —*School Library Journal*

"Very pleasant reading. May the series continue!" —*Kliatt*

"Dame Frevisse is well-born, well-educated and not at all afraid to stick her inquisitive nose into anything which just does not seem right." —*Tower Books Mystery Newsletter*

*continued . . .*

## THE BISHOP'S TALE

*The murder of a mourner means another funeral, and possibly more . . .*

"Some truly shocking scenes and psychological twists."
—*Mystery Loves Company*

"Rich period detail, canny characterization and a lively plot should endear Sister Frevisse and her tales to anyone who enjoys historical mysteries." —*Minneapolis Star Tribune*

"Rich in literary quotations and in details. Enthusiastically recommended." —*Kliatt*

"A most interesting addition to the world of whodunits."
—*Rendezvous*

## THE BOY'S TALE

*Two young boys seek refuge at St. Frideswide—but there is no sanctuary from murder . . .*

"This fast-paced historical mystery comes complete with a surprise ending—one that will hopefully lead to another 'Tale' of mystery and intrigue." —*Affaire de Coeur*

"Effectively and realistically brings to life 15th century England." —*Rendezvous*

"Entertaining!" —*The Paperback Forum*

## THE MURDERER'S TALE

*Sister Frevisse's respite at Minster Lovell turns deadly when murder visits the quiet manor . . .*

"The period detail is lavish and the characters are full-blooded . . . an exceptionally strong series."
—*Minneapolis Star Tribune*

"Good tension and high drama . . . Fans of Ellis Peters' 'Brother Cadfael' mysteries will relish a similar setting and atmosphere here." —*The Bookwatch*

**DON'T MISS OTHER SISTER FREVISSE MYSTERIES AVAILABLE FROM BERKLEY PRIME CRIME**

# The
# Prioress' Tale

## Margaret Frazer

BERKLEY PRIME CRIME, NEW YORK

THE PRIORESS' TALE

A Berkley Prime Crime Book / published by arrangement with the author

PRINTING HISTORY
Berkley Prime Crime mass-market edition / August 1997

ISBN: 0-425-15944-2

Berkley Prime Crime Books are published by
The Berkley Publishing Group, a division of Penguin Putnam Inc.,
375 Hudson Street, New York, New York 10014.
The name BERKLEY PRIME CRIME and
the BERKELY PRIME CRIME design are trademarks
belonging to Penguin Putnam Inc.

PRINTED IN THE UNITED STATES OF AMERICA

10   9   8   7   6   5   4

Cosyn myn, what eyleth thee,
That art so pale and deedly on to see?
                    — *"The Knight's Tale,"*
                    **Geoffrey Chaucer**

# Chapter

## 1

THE LATE-OCTOBER days had mellowed back toward a memory of summer, warm and clear all of the week since Monday. Only the golden slant of the early-afternoon sunlight—too long and low for any summer's early afternoon—betrayed how far this year of our Lord's grace 1439 was gone.

But it had been a good year, Alys thought as she watched the last of her nuns hasten along the cloister walk ahead of her into the church for the office of None. It was a short office, thank God. As prioress of St. Frideswide's, she had enough to do without her days being eaten up with time in church.

As Sister Emma's skirt tail disappeared through the doorway, Alys paced forward, closing on her heels to hurry her. Alys' dignity as prioress necessitated she come last to her place, all her nuns standing in their choir stalls waiting until she did. Then she would sit, and when she had, they could. It was a satisfying moment, a reminder to herself and them seven times in every day of who she was and how important, but Alys' impatience moved her almost invariably to hurry dignity along. Sooner begun, sooner done—that was plain enough, but she seemed to be the only one able to

1

see it. Some of them—and Sister Emma was only the
worst—would probably dawdle leaving their graves when
the Last Call to God's Judgment came.

Behind Alys as she passed from the sunlit cloister walk
into the church's cooler shadows, Sister Johane, who had
the duty during the days this week to ring the bell calling
them to church, let go the bell rope, duty done, and the bell
clappered to merciful quiet in the cloister garth. That bell
was among the things Alys had in mind to change. One way
or another, she meant to have as sweet a ringing bell there
as there had been at home in her girlhood, a bell that was a
pleasure to the ear instead of this thud-toned dullard
someone had given the priory fifty years ago, probably as a
penance for a sin that had been as dull as its tone.

She mounted the steps that set her choir stall a little above
the others and took a short, sharp look along the lines of
nuns facing each other in their lower, plainer stalls. Dressed
alike in their black Benedictine gowns, black veils, and
white wimples, their heads bowed so their faces were
hidden, there was no way to tell them apart except in height
to anyone who did not know them well, or else knew
who stood where, each one to her same place, office after
office, day after day, year into year. Alys knew—blessed St.
Frideswide and God in heaven, she knew! After twenty-
three years in this place she ought to know, and more
especially now that they were all hers. She knew not only
one from the other but what each one of them was like and
how each one of them had to be dealt with. Most of them
she had brought to heel since she had become prioress.
Some of them had taken to it readily, grateful to have the
Rule relaxed, the priory made more fit to live in. Others had
had less wit, taken longer to be convinced. Others—well,
they had learned to keep their mouths shut better than they
had, but she was not done with them yet, she knew.

She sat down heavily in her stall. In a rustle of skirts and
veils her nuns followed her. *"Gloria patri,"* she declared
loudly, to set the office on its way, but she had more to deal
with than prayers, and while her tongue turned to the words
her mind kept on about the cursed nuns who still fought her

on seemingly every little thing. Why couldn't they see that things were better now than they had been the last years Domina Edith had been prioress? The priory had been dying then, right along with its prioress. Nine nuns and no novices, that was all St. Frideswide's had been left with when Domina Edith died. That was all there had been for years. With Domina Edith dead and then Sister Lucy, who, God knows, had been more than old enough to die long before she finally did, the place would have been down to seven now, except the poor fools who were left had managed, by God's grace, to have sense enough to elect her prioress instead of that soft-wit Dame Claire who had been Domina Edith's choice. God and they had known she had more sense than anyone else in the place *and* relatives who were worth something more than an occasional petty gift when and if they felt like it, the way it was with everyone else. Within six months of her election to prioress, Alys had brought in a niece and a cousin's daughter as novices. That had meant their dowries to the priory as well as new interest in it from their families.

So let those who opposed her remember that *she,* not *they,* had been elected—on the first vote, mind it—to be prioress; that *she* had been the priory's choice, the saint's choice, God's choice; and that because of *her,* now that her niece and cousin's girl had taken their vows last year, St. Frideswide's was back up to nine nuns. Not nearly where it should be, but it was early years yet; she had hopes of talking a great-niece out of one of her nephews before next summer, and there was little Lady Adela, Lord Warenne's daughter. The girl was a cripple, with a malformed hip and twisted leg, so what else could Lord Warenne expect to do with her except make her a nun? She was not his heir, and he had boarded her here for four years; he might as well pay her dowry over to the nunnery and be done with it. Blessed St. Frideswide knew they could use the money.

Overhead something heavy fell with a shuddering thud. Heads jerked up from prayer books and words faltered. Alys cast a dark look at her nuns and a darker look toward the northeast corner of the church. Easily audible through the boards fixed over the unfinished door hole there, a man's voice cursed, the words unclear but the intent plain.

Sister Cecely smothered a giggle. Sister Amicia caught it from her, and the contagion would have spread except that Alys turned hard, warning eyes on all of them and rose to her feet. Silence, abrupt and utter, fell.

And well it might. They ought all to be used to that sort of thing by now, and if they were not, they had better learn to be. Heads bowed rapidly under Alys' look, and although Sister Cecely's shoulders twitched, it was soundlessly. Alys nodded at Dame Perpetua. As precentor, it was her duty to set right anything that went awry during a service. Obediently, promptly, she took up the service where it had been interrupted, and the rest fell in with her, keeping place despite the mutter of men's voices that had started up beyond the someday doorway and went on in uneven counterpoint to the women's chanting.

Alys had had it out with the masons' master, Master Porter, when they first came that they were supposed to pause their work during services. He had complained as if they were paid by the hour instead of the job and she were taking the bread out of their mouths by her demand, despite they were fed at the nunnery's expense day in and day out so long as they were here. She had not heeded him, had had her way. Still, more services than not, they managed one kind of a disturbance or another. And she would swear they made more noise the rest of the time than they had to, with their battering on stone, their heaving of ropes, and shouting.

But when they were done—and Master Porter had sworn they would be by Advent and he had better see to it they were—St. Frideswide's would have a tower that would show the countryside they were there and worth the noticing.

Before she was done with it, Alys meant to have a steeple, too, and had told Master Porter to build the tower walls accordingly. That would take a time longer but she would have it, a place besides that cloister pentise to hang the priory bells—and she meant for there to be *bells*, not just the one. At least three. Five for preference. It would not be soon, she knew. Money came in with snail slowness and went out with discouraging ease, but she had plans—and the will to carry them through, God be thanked, which was more than most people had.

The smooth linen of her underdress slid comfortably across her shoulders as she shifted from one hipbone to the other. Someday she would wear silk under these black gowns of hers; and though for now she needs must settle for linen, at least it was better linen than the coarse stuff she had had to make do with in Domina Edith's day. Let the others still wear that if they wanted to, or—more to the point—if their families would not afford them better, since Alys had no intention of raising the sum allowed for clothing yearly, there being too much else the money was needed for. For herself, it was different; she managed best if she was comfortable, thank you, and so it was as much her duty to be comfortable as it was her God-given duty to lead St. Frideswide's out of the slumped heap Domina Edith had let it fall into.

Alys had long since admitted to herself, with some relief, that she was not made to be a saint. Some were and that was all very well for them—Sister Thomasine there was well on her way to sainthood, heaven bless her; anyone who knew how many hours she spent in prayer had to know how holy she was; and she was welcome to her hair shirt, too—but God had seen to Alys being made prioress and that was something different from sainthood by a long way and she knew what she meant to make of her duty now that she was.

There were others who saw it differently, she knew. The ones who were always looking to make trouble of anything she tried to do. Her glance flicked up from her prayer book, hoping to catch one of them out, whispering or some other way inattentive, but every head was bent over their books except for Sister Thomasine whose gaze was turned toward the altar just as always. She had all the offices to heart, no need for her prayer book. She lived for prayer, was here in the church on her knees whenever she had any time away from other duties and even at night when she could have been abed and sleeping, even in winter nights when it was so cold her breath showed in the low glow of the altar lamp. Domina Edith had held her back from such excesses, forbidden her to pray through the night without particular permission, but the girl was half-witted with holiness, so let her pray. Where was the harm? At least she made no trouble while she did. Nor trouble any other time, come to that. Her mind was turned to God and nowhere else. Not like some Alys could all too readily name.

But naysayers be hung, she would make St. Frideswide's into a place known for four shires around despite the lot of them. Right now weren't the granaries as full as this year's half-decent harvest would provide? None of it had needed to be sold off this time, which put paid to all the fretting some people had made over last year's necessity to do so. There was a sufficiency of apples and hedge-gathered nuts in the priory storerooms, too, and that lout of a steward had been able to buy almost all she had demanded of him in the way of spices and even rice from his Michaelmas trip to Oxford despite his complaining of the costs. The only lack that needed to be set right before winter was wine. There was hardly a half barrel left, and the way it went anymore, that would not see them through to Christmastide. But Reynold had promised to see to at least another barrel and maybe two being in store by Martinmas. And well he might, considering how much he'd helped in drinking what the priory had had.

Alys cut off the ungrateful thought. Reynold was her cousin, and the rest of the Godfreys had done more for St. Frideswide's priory than any other family in a dog's age. She was not about to begrudge him wine and the hospitality to go with it, no matter who grutched at it.

A silence among the nuns roused her to realization that she had lost her place in the prayers and that it must be her time to say something. With no notion of where they were, she offered at random, knowing it came somewhere this far along in None, *"Redime me, domine."* Redeem me, Lord. *"Et miserere mei,"* she added firmly. And pity me.

A continued silence suggested that was not what she was

expected to say here. Raking a harsh glare indiscriminately across the faces of the nuns who had dared raise their heads to look at her and the bowed heads of the rest, Alys repeated forcefully, *"Redime me, domine! Et miserere mei!"*

Of course it had to be Dame Frevisse who took it up then, out of everyone else's sheep-headed confusion. Always ready to take the lead, was that one. Her head still lowered in that feigned humility of hers, she answered Alys's insistence with, *"Redime. Pes enim meus stetit in via recta."* Redeem me. For my feet have stood in the right way.

But at least she had started them moving again. Dame Perpetua answered a little unsurely, *"Et miserere,"* and they were away again, Alys laying heavily into a final *"Redime."* Redeem me, Lord, from this nest of women who had to be led like sheep and gaggled like silly geese every step of the way she took them. She would find a way yet to approach Abbot Gilberd about having Dame Frevisse out of here, into another nunnery. She was the worst of them. If she could be rid of Dame Frevisse, the rest of them would be easy enough to manage. Or easier, anyway.

Admittedly the woman had finally learned to keep her mouth mostly shut—it seemed even Dame Frevisse could learn her lesson if the penances were hard enough and often enough—but her face still sometimes showed what she was thinking and Alys was tired of seeing it. Or of working to avoid seeing it.

The problem was that she had no wish to bring Abbot Gilberd in on any matter at all if she could avoid it. St. Frideswide's was only a priory, and so it had to be a daughter house, subservient to an abbey and not even an abbey of nuns at that, but in St. Frideswide's case, to St. Bartholomew's Abbey at Northampton. Domina Edith had made the best of it, but for Alys it rankled. If St. Frideswide's had been an abbey, its abbess would have been subject to no one in England except the Bishop of Lincoln, the Archbishop of Canterbury, and the King himself, so it was a great pity that the widow who had founded and endowed it in the last century had not had wealth or influence enough to make it one. That was a flaw that, given time enough and the chance to be rid of people like Dame Frevisse, Alys meant to correct.

The problem was that if she gave Abbot Gilberd a chance to ask questions out of the ordinary about St. Frideswide's, concerning Dame Frevisse to begin with, he was all too likely to go on to asking others; and there were those among her nuns—Dame Frevisse was not the only one, just the worst—who would take a chance like that to make trouble, when just now in particular Alys did not want trouble. Unfortunately that meant she must go on dealing with Dame Frevisse; but if the woman would not bend, then she would have to be broken and that would settle the problem just as well.

Alys realized she had lost her place in the office again, but it did not matter. Wherever they were, it had gone on long enough. It would be time for Vespers before they had finished at this rate, and she had things to do. Not bothering with whatever everyone else was saying, she raised her voice and declared loudly, *"Benedicamus domino deo gratias fidelium animae per misericordiam dei requiescant in pace amen,"* and rose to her feet.

The slower-witted among her nuns fumbled through a few more words of the psalm before joining in the uneven chorus of amens trailing after hers. Alys made an impatient sign of the cross at them, slammed her prayer book shut, and shoved out of her choir stall. There were things to be done, and the sooner they were seen to, the sooner they would be finished. That was how she saw it.

# Chapter

# 2

Frevisse came out last among the nuns from the church into the sunlight of the cloister walk. The others were scattering to their different duties, Domina Alys ahead of them all and already well away along the walk, going with her usual heavy-footed purpose as if she would tread down anyone daring to be in her way.

Drawing in a deep breath of the bright autumn air, Frevisse closed her eyes, both to shut out sight of her prioress and the better to feel the sunlight on her face. She had learned in these three years under Domina Alys' rule to take and enjoy when they came such small pleasures as a moment in the sunlight and a quiet pause among the daily troubles. There was probably no being rid of Domina Alys this side of the grave: prioresses, like priors and abbots, were elected for life. And the harvest had been bad again this year; there would be hunger among the villagers and likely in the nunnery, too, by spring. And the daily offices of prayer were increasingly badly done, increasingly uncomforting, between the builders' noise and the prioress' inattention. It seemed that day by day there was less and less peace to be had anywhere in St. Frideswide's, but for this moment, here, just now, there was sunlight and quietness; and brief though they both would be, Frevisse had learned that momentary pleasures enjoyed as fully as she could were far better than no pleasures at all. She had come to see them as God's gift given in God's way, to be accepted when nothing else seemed being given and nothing else could be understood.

Time had been when the offices with their beauty of prayers and psalms had been, day in and day out, Frevisse's greatest pleasure, a sanctuary and sure refuge from the small, unceasing troubles of every day, a time when she could let go of the world and give her mind over entirely toward eternity and God. Now, mangled as they daily were by Domina Alys' stupidity—

Frevisse cut the bitter thought short. She had gone that way too many times, never to any use. In the election for a new prioress after Domina Edith's death, too many of the nuns had separately thought to soothe then–Dame Alys' temper and ambition by giving her a single vote in the first round of voting and instead they had unwittingly given her the election. Fit retribution for their cowardice, Frevisse thought. Except that the rest of them, the few who had not bent to fear of Dame Alys, were now forced to live under Domina Alys along with the rest.

The moment of quiet ended. The few lay servants of the priory who still bothered to come to services had slipped out of the church past her and away while she stood there, and now Lady Eleanor, who always lingered a little longer for private prayers of her own, said quietly beside her, "Dame Frevisse."

Frevisse, opening her eyes, turned to her with a smile. The Rule of silence that should have confined all idle conversation in the cloister to the hour of recreation at day's end had long since gone slack under Domina Alys, and because it was difficult to keep to hand gestures when everyone else was chattering on like jays through a day, Frevisse had let it go, too, and now answered easily, "My lady. How is it with you?"

Lady Eleanor must always have been a small woman and now in her years beyond middle age she was smaller still, but rather than have dried and wrinkled and wearied with her years, she had faded gently to softness and rose, given as much to laughter as to prayers. As usual, she was smiling now, and equally as usual an insistent wisp of white hair had escaped from her careful wimple to curl against her cheek. Since coming to St. Frideswide's last spring, she made a quiet, constant effort to be what she called a "shadow nun," always dressing in simple gray gowns and plain white wimples and veils, but she admitted freely that she had no intention of ever taking a nun's vows, and she had kept her vanity of unshorn hair, as that curl gave away more often than not. She was pushing it back into her wimple as she answered Frevisse's courtesy, "Very well, thank you, my lady."

"An arthritic attack in the night," her maid Margrete muttered from behind her.

"Which has passed off and gone," Lady Eleanor responded, not turning her head. Most conversations between herself and Margrete were carried on that way, with Margrete usually the correct three paces behind her lady but joining in the talk whenever she felt it necessary and Lady Eleanor answering her without looking back. They had been together most of their lives—"Longer than I was with either of my husbands," Lady Eleanor had once said—and silence could go on between them comfortably for hours, or their conversations could be, like now, a mere sharp exchange that barely distracted Lady Eleanor from asking Frevisse lightly, "Standing here with your eyes closed praying for patience with my niece?"

Frevisse's smile twisted to wryness. "Nothing so pious, I fear. I was simply enjoying the sunlight."

"That can be piety, too, I think. Enjoying God's gifts. Better than being rude about them, even ignoring them, surely."

"Surely," Frevisse agreed. She enjoyed Lady Eleanor's directness with life and equally her kindness toward it. Had she always been so, or was it something that came with years and living? Whichever it was, it was in strong contrast to the ways of Domina Alys, her niece. That Lady Eleanor was another Godfrey had been among the reasons Frevisse had so strongly protested against her coming when her offer of a corrody had first been raised.

Accepting a set sum of money in return for keeping a lady in comfort for the rest of her life was a gamble nunneries sometimes took for the sake of having much money in hand all at once, but it was a gamble St. Frideswide's had always, with good cause, avoided until now. Too many stories from other nunneries that had succumbed to the temptation of corrodies through need or even misplaced kindness made fearfully clear how often a lady would leave behind her worldly responsibilities but bring with her into the cloister too many servants, comforts, pets, and even quantities of visiting relatives, all disrupting what was supposed to be the cloister's peace.

Besides that very immediate risk, there was the chance that the lady might live too long. A corrody was a set sum of money, paid when she first came. If her life ran out before her money did, then the nunnery had a profit; if she lived on, the nunnery faced uncompensated expenses that could eventually, disastrously, far outweigh any advantages there might have been in having her money at the beginning.

All that and the fact that Lady Eleanor was Domina Alys' father's sister had been reason enough to Frevisse's mind for refusing her. There had even been others among the nuns who not only agreed but dared to say so. The argument over it in chapter meeting had gone on more mornings than one, but anyone who dared go against Domina Alys always found she had more ways than a few to make them feel her displeasure. She did not give in to opposition, nor forget or forgive it, and at the last, driven and drawn by that reality and by Domina Alys' insistence that, "She's too old to live long enough to be a trouble to us and we *need* the money," most of the nuns had given way.

In truth, the need had indeed been real enough; was still real enough. Replacing the wooden bell pentise in the garth with one of carved stone had only seemed to enlarge Domina Alys' ambitions for St. Frideswide's. Last year she had persuaded the nuns to the bell pentise; this summer she had simply announced that she had hired men to build a tower and that Lady Eleanor's corrody would pay for it. By then, worn down by the arguments over the corrody to begin with, almost no one had dared rouse her temper by challenging her on anything else if they could help it, even so great a matter as this. Only Frevisse had dared start a question against it, and been given a week on bread and water and one hundred aves every day of that week—"That you may learn a like humility to blessed Mary's," Domina Alys had snapped—for her presumption.

That had sufficed to silence the rest of the nuns, except those who enthusiastically supported whatever their prioress chose to do. Now there was nothing for it but to hope that Domina Alys was right, that Lady Eleanor's corrody would cover the costs of stone and masons and lead for the roof when it reached that high. But that did not change the fact that the corrody should have been husbanded for the priory's use over years, not spent all at once on a thing for which there was no need at all.

The one comfort was that Lady Eleanor had proven to be far less a trouble than Frevisse had feared. When she came just after Easter, she had brought only Margrete, very few of her household furnishings, and just two fluffy, blessedly well-behaved small dogs. Against all Frevisse's expectations, she had settled gently into her place in the priory. She had even proven to be someone pleasant to talk with sometimes, so that now, with their ways lying the same way around the cloister walk, they went on together, neither of them hurried, Margrete following behind them, as Lady Eleanor said, "None went none so well, did it?"

Frevisse held herself to only "No," but knew her voice's edge gave away a great deal of what she did not say.

"The pity of it," Lady Eleanor said, "is that Alys' heart *is* in it. It's her mind that's not."

Frevisse forbore to say what she thought of Domina Alys' mind. They reached the corner of the cloister walk where they would part. Lady Eleanor's room lay farther along while Frevisse would go by way of the shadowed passageway that led to the cloister's outer door, beyond which normally no nun should go without especial permission and cause. But by St. Benedict's Rule, every Benedictine house had to provide shelter and food for travelers, receiving even the poorest as guests and seeing to their needs. Frevisse, as hosteler of St. Frideswide's, had the duty of overseeing that all of that was done, with the two guest halls that flanked the gateway to the outer yard in her charge, and she went and came from the cloister as her duties necessitated. She knew Domina Alys had made her hosteler for the sake of having her out of the cloister as much as might be, but she did not care. Better that than being cellarer and needing to deal daily and directly with Domina Alys over all the nunnery's everyday needs, the way Dame Juliana had to.

Unfortunately, through the past two years, most of the priory's guests were Godfreys, mostly come to see Domina Alys or to visit with Lady Eleanor or both, but always to enjoy the nunnery's hospitality at little or no cost to themselves except in the way of such gifts as they might choose to bring. Admittedly, some had been untowardly generous, especially Lady Eleanor's eldest son when he came at midsummer to see how his mother did, but Domina Alys too often invited whoever was visiting to spend their evenings in her parlor with her, for wine and for talk and laughter that could sometimes be heard across the cloister to the nuns' dormitory, where lately listening seemed to be too often taking the place of sleeping.

Worse, whichever nuns were currently highest in their prioress's favor were sometimes invited to share the evening's merriment, and their open delight and the tidbits of talk they gave out afterward had set up a rivalry among too many of them to stay in Domina Alys' good grace, to better their chance of being chosen. Only Dame Claire, Dame Perpetua, Sister Thomasine, and Frevisse were still excluded and were a little scorned by the others for it, though Sister Thomasine was too lost in her duties and her prayers to notice. Frevisse doubted she was more than distantly aware of even the builders' noise, let alone how Domina Alys spent her evenings or the present intrusion of her cousin Sir Reynold and his men.

Through the past half year Sir Reynold had come more and more frequently, usually with only a few men and servants and usually for no more than a few days at a time, but two weeks' end ago, with no word sent ahead, he had ridden in with half a score of his knights and squires, and their servants for good measure, and so far had given no sign of when he meant to leave. It left scant room in the guest halls for anyone else who might chance to come, even casual travelers for a single night, and stores that should have served through Christmastide at very least were being used up far too quickly.

This morning, as they sometimes did, Sir Reynold and his men had ridden out during Tierce's prayers, with laughter and shouting and the clatter of their horses' hooves on the cobbles of the yard, and though they would be back, Frevisse had taken the chance to have the disorder made by too many men living idle too many days cleared and cleaned before their return. She was going now to see if everything had been done as she had ordered, with the hope she would be back inside the cloister before they rode in. The less she had to see of Sir Reynold or any of his men, the better she was pleased.

Because there was no use in complaining, she had said nothing outside of chapter meeting of what was happening, but as she and Lady Eleanor paused together Lady Eleanor asked, "How much trouble have my nephew and his men made for you?"

Frevisse tried to answer lightly, as if there were no need to take much heed, "Enough."

Quietly smiling—she had known her nephew Sir Reynold far longer than Frevisse had had the misfortune to—Lady Eleanor said, "If I were you, I'd see to there being a sleeping potion in his ale and all his men's at supper every night. And mornings, too, come to that, until they grow so bored with being here they leave."

"It would be a comfort if we had some notion of when they were going to go," Frevisse said, and did not try to hide how much she meant it.

Lady Eleanor nodded. "I know. The only comfort I can

offer, my dear, is that nothing goes on forever." Her smile deepened, warm with sympathy as she added, "It only seems to, sometimes."

Frevisse smiled back, agreeing there was comfort in perspective—not necessarily the comfort she wanted, but comfort nonetheless.

They parted, Lady Eleanor away to her room, Frevisse along the short length of the chill, shadowed passageway to the heavy outer door. Made of two thicknesses of wood, it was kept barred at night but during the day was only shut on the latch, and though according to the Rule, someone was supposed to watch at it all the day and through the night, St. Frideswide's was too small for that to be worth the while. Someone was always near to hear if anyone came knocking, and with the inner yard and its gateway and then the outer yard with its clutter of buildings and workers to notice and question the coming of any stranger, and finally the gateway to the road all lying between the cloister door and the outer world, with the other way into the inner yard only through the busy kitchen yard and a small side gate, no one unwanted was likely to come so far as the cloister door unnoticed.

Some of Sir Reynold's servants were passing the afternoon's time at ease in the courtyard between the cloister and guest halls, stretched out on the steps up to the new guest hall or gathered around the well where the sunlight was presently warmest. Frevisse crossed to the older of the two guest halls without seeming to heed them, her head bowed enough to swing her veil forward to hide her face on either side, showing she was willing to ignore them if they would return the courtesy by ignoring her and they did.

Knowing she was hosteler only to keep her out of Domina Alys' way did not give her any leave to slack her duties; nor did it mean she had any right to draw her work out beyond necessity. She went about what needed seeing to now as quickly as care made possible, pleased to find that the guest-hall servants had managed to put more to rights than she had hoped but finding, now that she had chance to check more carefully the guest-hall stores, that even more had been eaten and drunk away than she had guessed.

When Frevisse spoke of it to Ela, head of the guesthall servants, while poking at the few remaining bundles of onions hanging from the storeroom ceiling to be sure there was no rot, Ela said, "There was talk they'd bring something back with them today, like they've done those other two times. Nothing clear, mind you, so I'll not be surprised if nothing comes of it, but that's what some of them were saying, because what we have isn't good enough for them, that's why. They're wanting better."

"If they bring it, they're welcome to it," Frevisse answered shortly.

Ela saw to guesthall matters when Frevisse was not there, and neither of them made pretense to each other of how little they wanted Sir Reynold and his men on their hands, but neither did they bother to talk of it at length. There was no need; they had worked together long enough to understand each other's mind.

The stores were the last thing Frevisse needed to see. That done, she was free to make her escape back into the cloister without having to deal with Sir Reynold, just as she had hoped. But the hope was blighted by the too familiar sound of Domina Alys' voice railing at someone at the far end of the guest hall's great hall as Frevisse came up the stairs from the kitchen. The words were unclear but the irk was plain, telling that someone had come under the prioress' displeasure, and Frevisse flinched to a stop, then drew a deep breath and went on out into the high-roofed hall where meals were shared and most of their guests and servants slept. The trestle tables had not been set up yet for supper, so except for benches, the hall stretched open to its far end and the outer door, a generous space for Domina Alys to rant in, and she was taking full advantage of it, standing over Nell, one of the kitchen servants, declaring at full pitch of ire, "And don't think I don't know what you're all at here! Helping yourselves to food and ale beyond what you're given and then my folk blamed for eating us out! Fool who you can, I know better! And don't think . . ."

Nell was taking the battering of words with bowed head and hunched shoulders, probably thinking of nothing except the likelihood that a blow would come with the words before they were over. Domina Alys had been hosteler in her time; the guest-hall servants knew as well as anybody else that she believed a hard slap would drive words into a thick head better than anything—and to Domina Alys all heads were thick but her own.

Frevisse, as afraid for Nell as Nell was and knowing the surest way to draw Domina Alys off one anger was to give her another, started up the hall toward them, saying far too loudly for respectful, "My lady, is there something I can help you with?"

As expected, Domina Alys turned on her. "Dame! Where were you when I was looking for you? I've seen what's toward here, don't think I haven't."

Frevisse made a small flick of one hand toward Nell, telling her to escape while she was forgotten. Hands knotted in her apron, shoulders still hunched, Nell slid away toward the kitchen stairs as Domina Alys closed on Frevisse, declaring, "I've seen enough to warn you here and now that your accounts had best be better than I expect them to be or you'll be answering for it from now to Lent. And where's my cousin gone to? Why's he not back yet?"

Forcing her voice to hold level, lowering her eyes for some semblance of humility, Frevisse said, "I don't know, my lady."

"Well, he ought to be back by now!"

Frevisse was saved from finding a reply by the clatter of horses and a burst of men's voices and laughter and shouting in the yard outside. Domina Alys swung toward the doorway. "And there he is!" she declared as triumphantly as if she had just proved some point on which Frevisse had been willfully troublesome.

With no other way to go, Frevisse followed her out of the hall to the head of the stairs and down to the yard, where the afternoon's sun-warmed doze had turned to a loud crowding of mounted men and a scurry of servants among shifting horses, a confusion of movement and laughing exclaims, raucous as a roost of rooks. Domina Alys stopped at the top of the stairs and, hands on her hips, glared out at it all until she found whom she wanted and yelled to him across the seethe of men and voices, "Reynold, you dullard, hereafter leave your horses in the outer yard, thank you!"

"Cousin!" Sir Reynold yelled back at her, unoffended, taking off his riding hat and tossing it toward her over the heads of the men between them. Domina Alys caught it and flung it back at him, less true, but he reached out a long arm and caught it under the face of the man beside him while she shouted, "You heard me, Reynold! The outer yard after this!"

"Ever yours to command!" Sir Reynold called back, laughing, sweeping her a bow from his saddle. He was large-built, heavy-boned, well-muscled    so like Domina Alys, except that he was tall above the average, that he could as easily have been taken for her brother as her cousin. They were matched in tempers, too, Frevisse had found; she would not care to be near at hand if they should ever turn ill-tempered against someone at the same time or, probably worse, against each other.

But just now Sir Reynold was alight with laughter that took no heed of Domina Alys' anger. He crowded his horse toward the foot of the stairs, asking, "What brings you out of your hole, Alys? Come to see the sun for a change?"

"Come to see you," she snapped. "Did you bring back something more than your appetites this time or have you slipped your word again?"

Sir Reynold threw back his head, breaking into immense laughter. "No holding coy with you, my girl! Look you." He pointed toward the yard's gateway, crowded with a dozen mounted men with heavy bags slung either side, in back and front, of their saddles. "There's enough of this and that to see us through a few days, surely, and something or two better than usual for you and yours, too, so don't be looking to quarrel with me over it."

Domina Alys, swinging her gaze around the yard to see if there were still more, drew her breath in harshly. "And *that*?" she demanded, finger out accusingly. "What is *that*?"

"What?" Sir Reynold looked around where she was pointing, his face too elaborately casual for true innocence. "Ah, that." He grinned like a boy who did not care he had been caught out at mischief. "Benet!"

Among the shift and clutter of men and horses, Frevisse had not particularly noticed anyone beyond Sir Reynold. Between them, he and Domina Alys took up most of any noticing wherever they were, and all Frevisse was truly interested in just now was returning to the cloister as simply as might be, but now she looked past him to the man whose head jerked around in answer to his call. A young man, not much beyond a boy but his face already strongly Godfrey in its bones and coloring and probably in pride and temper, too, to judge by the strong line of his dark brows, drawn together now as he turned toward his lord and Domina Alys. But Frevisse read alarm in his face, too, and well there might be, because in front of him on his saddle he was holding tight in the circle of his arm a girl who did not—to guess by the set of raw scratches scored down one side of Benet's face from brow to chin and the closely wrapped cloak that pinioned her arms to helplessness—want to be there.

Her dark hair had fallen loose from whatever had once held it; it was tumbled now around her shoulders and to her waist, obscuring her face as she twisted angrily in Benet's hold despite that she had no chance of breaking free, trapped as she was in the cloak and his tight hold. Cheerfully Sir Reynold called, "Don't let her slip! Some of the taming you're going to have to do yourself from here on."

There was laughter among the men to that, though not from Benet, as the girl threw back her head, missing his chin with the back of her skull only because he ducked away from it. Domina Alys, finally finding words, demanded at Sir Reynold, "What have you done, you fool?"

Sir Reynold answered, grinning, "There's naught wrong. Benet means to marry her."

Her hair thrown back from her face at last, the girl cried out in open fury, "Not this side of hell he won't! Help me!" She turned desperate eyes on Domina Alys and Frevisse.

"You're nuns! I won't marry him! Don't let them do this to me!"

"No one is doing anything to anyone, marriage or otherwise, until I know more about what's toward here," Domina Alys said grimly. "Dame Frevisse, have her down from there. Take her into the cloister."

Frevisse started down the stairs to obey, for once as openly angry as Domina Alys; but Sir Reynold backed his horse across her way and said over her head to Domina Alys, now above her on the stairs, "Alys, Alys, come on, my girl. It's not so bad as all that. Benet means to *marry* her. Your priest can do it ere supper, if you like. She's only merchant-get, but there's money enough in it to make it worth the while. And better that Benet have her than that fool of a Fenner her people were planning to betroth her to."

"Fool or not," the girl cried, still twisting in Benet's hold, "he has friends at court and they'll make you sorry for this!"

Without looking around, Sir Reynold said, "Benet, muzzle her."

The girl instantly twisted her head around as far as it would go, to snap her teeth at Benet before he had made any move at all against her. Around him the other men were offering suggestions, none of them helpful, some of them lewd. Benet, tight-mouthed and intent, answered nothing, kept hold of her and clear of her head. Frevisse moved sideways to go around Sir Reynold, but again he backed his horse, still blocking her way, saying over her, "Call your nun off, Alys. The girl is Benet's."

"I'm not anyone's!" the girl cried back.

"Dame," Domina Alys snapped, "I said take her into the cloister."

"Alys, don't push this," Sir Reynold warned.

"Don't you push it, Reynold," Domina Alys warned him back, fists on her hips, her face mottled red with temper in the white surround of her wimple. She had nothing to set against him but God's displeasure and her own, and Frevisse doubted that either was likely to matter much to Sir Reynold. Worse, Father Henry had come out of his chamber door beside the gateway and was taking in what was

happening. He was a burly man, almost a match in size for
Sir Reynold, but with no complications in him. Direct to the
point of simpleness in both his religion and his living,
he would side without thought with Domina Alys once he
understood what was happening here, even if it came to
blows, as it all too readily could, given the tempers there
were; and if it did, Frevisse doubted his priesthood would
protect him from Sir Reynold or his men.

As he stood trying to decide what was going on in front
of him, before Domina Alys saw him and demanded his
help, Frevisse threw up her hands and her full black sleeves
at Sir Reynold's horse's face. The animal startled backward,
tossing its head aside out of her way, and more quickly than
Sir Reynold could recover control, Frevisse ducked not only
past him but between the two riders beyond him, to Benet's
side. Grabbing hold of the girl's skirts as if laying a claim of
her own to her, she ordered, "Give her to me, Benet. Now."

Unhesitatingly, he did, shoving her from his saddle into
Frevisse's hands as if only too willing to be rid of her as Sir
Reynold shouted, "You fool! Don't let her go!" But Frevisse
noticed that he did not fully loose her until he was sure that
Frevisse safely had her. Only then did Benet let her go, but
if the girl noticed, it made no difference to her. The moment
she was on her own feet, she twisted free of Frevisse and the
cloak, flinging the cloak from her as she spun around to
snarl up at Benet, "You ever touch me again, I'll kill you!"

Raw color surged across Benet's face and Frevisse urged
the girl away from him toward the cloister door as behind
them Sir Reynold ordered, "Someone stop them both!"

Another rider swung his horse in front of them, and
Frevisse jerked the girl to a stop and her own head back to
look up at him, ready to demand he let them pass; but he
was Sir Hugh, one of the few of Sir Reynold's men she
knew by name, another Godfrey, fair-haired where most
Godfreys were dark but large-built like Sir Reynold and as
close to being his next in command as anyone was in the
rough order among the men. He sat looking down from his
horse's height at them with an easy smile that said any try
they made to pass him would only pleasure him, and

Frevisse, feeling the girl trembling with fury or fear under her hand, tightened hold on her, willing her to stand steady. Neither fear nor fury would serve any better now than Frevisse's own desperation to reach the cloister's safety before somebody's rashness made more trouble than there already was.

From the cloister doorway beyond Sir Hugh and out of Frevisse's sight, Lady Eleanor's clear voice inquired, raised to carry over man and horse and across the yard, "Pray, what's toward here? Hugh? Reynold? What are you about?"

Before they could answer, Domina Alys flung back angrily, "These fools have grabbed a girl to marry to Benet, but she doesn't want him."

"A girl?" Lady Eleanor's voice rose in sharper inquiry. "Hugh, move. I can't see anything."

Sir Hugh's head had turned from her to Domina Alys and now back again, but he did not shift his horse, and impatiently Lady Eleanor slapped its flank, repeating, "Move, I said."

Grudgingly, Sir Hugh pulled back from her way.

And Benet, before anyone else could do anything, dismounted and in a single swift movement caught up the fallen cloak and put himself between the girl and Sir Hugh, holding out the cloak to her with one hand, holding out his other toward the cloister door as a lord at the height of manners would do to make way for a lady.

"Benet, you idiot," Sir Hugh muttered. His leg tensed as if he would urge his horse forward, but Lady Eleanor, equally low, said quellingly, "Hugh," and he held where he was, while Benet—as if he more than half expected to have his words shoved back down his throat—said stiffly, with a slight bow, his eyes on the girl's face, "My lady, this way, if it please you."

The girl would have drawn back from him, but Frevisse wasted no time on hesitation or revulsion, simply pushed her toward Lady Eleanor and the cloister door. Sir Hugh spat out a word that she chose not to hear. Behind them Sir Reynold swore, "You're a fool, Benet!" and louder with rising anger, "There's no use to this, you women! She can go in, but she's not coming out again except to marry him! Be sure of it!" while Benet said low and in a rush, as they passed him, "Joice, this isn't what I meant to happen. This isn't how I meant for it to be."

The girl turned a fierce and disbelieving stare on him. "But it *is* this way, isn't it?" she hissed. "And you can't *unmake* it, can you?" And as he recoiled from the force of her anger, she snatched the cloak from him and swept on past Lady Eleanor into the cloister, followed by Frevisse who gave a grateful look at Lady Eleanor, who nodded acknowledgment and followed them both, shutting the door behind them, against Benet and all the rest, with something more than necessary force, leaving Domina Alys to whatever else she might want to say to Sir Reynold.

# Chapter
## 3

As THEY CAME out of the passageway into the cloister walk,
Frevisse overtook the girl, laying a hand on her shoulder
again to turn her around, wanting to ask the questions for
which there had been no time in the yard, but the questions
fled as she saw Joice had gone ash white and was beginning
to shudder the whole length of her body, her eyes dark and
large with all the fear she must have been hiding behind her
fury until now it was safe to give way to it; and instead of
questions, Frevisse took the cloak from her and swung it
around her shoulders without a word. Joice gathered it close
to her, huddling into it with an unsteady attempt at a grateful
smile. Cut in a full circle, made of close-woven, Kendal-
green wool and lined with lambs' fleece, it reached from her
chin almost to her feet. Her gown was equally fine, Frevisse
had noted—of light wool dyed darkly red and falling in
deep folds from the close-fitted, high-waisted bodice to the
floor, its high-standing collar shaped to her delicate throat
and the wide sleeves gathered to cuffs at her wrists. Such
quantity and quality of cloth in cloak and gown meant
wealth went with her, bearing out Sir Reynold's contention
that she was worth the risk of carrying her off.

But none of that was any ward against the fear-cold shaking her now, and Lady Eleanor said, "My room, I think. And warmed wine. Spiced warmed wine. For all of us. You, too, Dame Frevisse."

She said it briskly, but Frevisse saw with an edge of alarm that the soft rose of her cheeks was paled to white and she was trembling a little herself. Her show of determination against Sir Hugh and the rest must have cost her more than Frevisse had realized, and quickly Frevisse agreed, "Yes, that would do well," and took Joice by one elbow to lead and support her toward Lady Eleanor's room. Neither Lady Eleanor nor the girl was overly tall and both were delicately boned; for Frevisse, fine-boned but tall for a woman, Joice was an easy matter, and she would have reached to help Lady Eleanor, too, except the older woman had gathered herself and was firmly leading the way for them, showing no apparent need nor desire for anyone's help.

Her room, like Domina Alys', was on the first floor in the cloister's west range but there was no connecting way between them, so although the stairs up to Domina Alys' rooms were close at hand, they had to go further along the cloister walk to the other stairs. Dame Juliana, going toward the infirmary with an armload of clean, folded linens, stopped, staring at Joice, a stranger where so few strangers came. Her curiosity would have gone to outright questions, but reading Frevisse's look aright, she held her tongue and hurried on, intent now on being rid of linens so she could go to someone to tell what she had seen.

More usefully, Margrete appeared at the head of the stairs as they started up and, having taken them all in with a single quick look, was already turning back as Lady Eleanor ordered, "Warmed wine with spices, please, Margrete. Quickly," so that by the time they reached the room, she was busy at the aumbry along the near wall, pouring wine into a brass pan, the cinnamon and other spices ready to hand.

Like most of the nunnery's rooms, Lady Eleanor's had no fireplace, but the coal glowing in a brazier in one corner gave heat enough for warming it. Her own wine and her own coal were among the few luxuries Lady Eleanor had brought with her when she came, but a room to herself was by itself more luxury than any of the nuns except their prioress had. Even the small cell each of them slept in, partitioned off from each other in the dormitory by thin wooden walls, was not supposed to be thought of as a nun's own. Lady Eleanor's room, shared only with Margrete, took up the full width of the range and was long enough that her wide bed with its canopy and curtains set at one end of it left ample room at the other for the aumbry, two chests with her clothing and other belongings, two chairs, a low stool, and the square, tall-legged table with shelf underneath where Lady Eleanor kept her few books. A painted tapestry brightened one of the white-plastered walls, and at this hour of the autumn afternoon the westering sunlight through the window spread across the dark polished wooden floor and golden matting of woven rushes.

Lady Eleanor's two dogs, ankle-high pieces of white fluff, hurtled out from under the foot of the bed in a scrabble of nails and eagerness to see who had come, but Lady Eleanor countered them with a sharp word, stopping them where they were. "Not now," she added, and disconsolately they removed themselves back under the bed. To Frevisse and Joice she said, "The chair by the brazier would do best, I think. Let me move it nearer."

She did, and Frevisse sat Joice down in it while Lady Eleanor tucked the cloak more closely around her, murmuring, "You'll be fine now, dear. Just sit and be still until the wine is ready."

"And you should sit, too," Frevisse said, drawing the other chair close to the first. "Here."

Lady Eleanor looked momentarily surprised, then smiled and did as Frevisse bid, before leaning toward Joice to ask, "Is it better with you now?"

Stiffly upright in her chair, her hands gripping its curved arms, the girl shook her head. "No, it isn't better and it's not likely to ever be 'better' again, is it? Not after this!" She let loose of the chair to make fists and pound them on the arms. "I could kill them for doing this to me! Benet and all the rest! I could kill them!"

Margrete coming to set the pan to heat over the coals cast her a look of question more than alarm, and Lady Eleanor took Joice's nearest fist, gentling it between her hands as she asked, "You haven't been . . . harmed, have you?"

Joice snatched her hand away, striking the chair arm again. "Not that way. They grabbed me and flung me onto Benet's saddle, that's all they did, but do you think Sir Lewis will marry me after this? Do you think anyone will marry me after this?" Her face and voice and body were all rigid with rage. "Not without my father having to pay twice the dowry he meant to and my taking less marriage settlement than I should have had! That's what they've done to me!" Her voice dropped to brooding bitterness. "And likely anyone who has me will make me listen every day of my life afterward to how good he was to take me even at that."

Not if he knew what was good for him, Frevisse thought. Slight of build and delicate of face though Joice was, there was nothing slight or delicate about her temper.

With the fury that seemed to have driven out her brief facing of fear, Joice sprang to her feet, throwing the cloak back onto the chair behind her. "And all that supposes I'm ever able to leave here to make any kind of marriage at all! I heard what Sir Reynold said. He won't let me leave. I'm worth too much. He'll try to take me himself if he has to, I'll warrant!"

Lady Eleanor began a soft denial of that. Ignoring it, Joice spun around, pointing at Frevisse. "And don't think I'll ever become a nun, because I won't!"

Frevisse held back from saying aloud her sharp-edged thought that a less likely possibility for a novice she had rarely seen.

Lady Eleanor, as if oblivious to the girl's fury, said thoughtfully, "You could possibly change your mind and marry Benet, you know. He's an uncomplicated boy and there's property to be had with him when he inherits."

"All I want from Benet is his death!"

"Ah," Lady Eleanor said. "But if you married him first,

my dear, you could then be a widow, and that's frequently a very pleasant thing to be."

Joice stared at her, shocked to silence by outrage, until, like Frevisse, she must have seen the small smile crooking at the corners of Lady Eleanor's mouth and—apparently as much to Joice's own surprise as Frevisse's—the girl began to laugh. "I hadn't thought of that!" she said around the laughter, and then broke down in tears that seemed to take her as much by surprise as the laughter had done so that, hiding her face in her hands, she sank back down into the chair, sobbing helplessly.

Lady Eleanor exchanged a look with Frevisse who nodded in return, agreeing with her that the crying was for the best. This girl had been through fear and courage and cold shock and rage, almost all together and far too rapidly; her tears would exhaust her and then the wine would quiet her and she would be able to rest, even sleep, and after that be better able to deal with whatever came next.

Margrete had taken the pan from the brazier back to the aumbry and was pouring the wine into goblets. Frevisse crossed to the window that overlooked the yard. Whatever came next would have much to do with how things had gone—or were going—between Domina Alys and Sir Reynold, and from here she could see them, Sir Reynold dismounted now, standing on the guest-hall steps in gesturing talk with Domina Alys who looked to be returning as good as whatever he was giving her, with Sir Hugh and Benet, both dismounted now, standing close below them. The rest of the men had all dismounted, too, and were drifted away or standing about at discreet distances from the steps in talk of their own but undoubtedly listening, while servants led off the last of the horses to the stable. There was nothing to be told from all that except that neither Domina Alys nor Sir Reynold seemed in a rage at each other now, and Frevisse found herself wary at the thought that they must be coming to some manner of agreement. Given Domina Alys' willingness to indulge her relatives, she might even be coming around to Sir Reynold's view of matters, ready to take his side against the girl. But then again, she rarely changed her mind on any matter, so mayhap she had brought him around to her way of seeing it and so to peace between them.

Margrete served the wine. The rich savor of mixed spices wafting from it was warming in itself as Lady Eleanor laid a kind hand on Joice's shoulder and urged, "Drink now. While it's warm. You'll be the better for it."

Drawing a deep, shaken breath, Joice raised her head. The worst of the crying had passed and she wiped her eyes with the edge of one sleeve, took the goblet Margrete held out to her with an unsteady smile, and said, "Thank you."

She drank a little while Margrete brought Lady Eleanor and Frevisse their goblets, and then leaned back in her chair, nursing the goblet's warmth between her hands and against her breast. Even with her face marred by the crying, she had a simple loveliness that made clear how easily young Benet could have been drawn to her, low birth or not; and because of its simplicity, it was a loveliness likely to last through the years, not fade with youth, although just now, with her hair still fallen loose and the tears and anger at least momentarily gone from her face, she looked even younger than she was, as if she were a small, exhausted child in need of her supper and bed. And with a child's simplicity she said, "I'm sorry for the crying. I won't do it again."

"Unless you need to," Lady Eleanor answered. "Tears are as good for easing the heart as warmed, spiced wine is for easing the mind, and you may want the comfort these next few days. Cry if you need it."

Joice smiled a little unsteadily and looked down into her goblet as if the remaining wine might have answers for her. "It would help," she said, "if I at least knew that my people knew where I was, that they knew what had happened to me."

"What did happen?" Frevisse asked.

Joice looked briefly bewildered at the question. Exhaustion was beginning to overtake her, making her thoughts hard to draw together, but she said, when she had had chance to think about how to say it, "I was coming home from the market. It's market day in Banbury and I'd gone to the market, of course, and was coming home."

"You live in Banbury, then."

"No. In Northampton. My father is Nicholas Southgate, a draper there. I'm in Banbury these few months because my aunt is ill and her children small and I'm seeing to her household."

"How did Benet know to find you in Banbury?" Frevisse said.

"He saw me there a week ago, at last market. We were both surprised. I didn't even remember him until he spoke to me and then like a fool I told him why I was there and for how long."

"But how does he know you at all?" Frevisse asked.

"My father has partners in London and goes there a few times a year. Last spring Sir Lewis Fenner was going to be in London with his cousin Lord Fenner, so Father took me with him so Sir Lewis could have chance to see what he was bargaining for."

Lady Eleanor and Frevisse exchanged looks. Between the Fenners and the Godfreys there was a long-ongoing quarrel, entangled for years now in legalities and angers, over some piece of land. So Joice Southgate was more than simply someone young Benet wanted—she was a prize snatched from a Fenner. For Frevisse, that explained Sir Reynold's interest in the matter, let be that the girl was wealthy in the bargain; and unfortunately for both reasons he would be loath to give her up, easily or otherwise.

"We went other places, too, my father and I. He had some very fine brocades and Italian silks to show around to ladies he thought best likely to be interested—and he took me with him so I could see what sort of life he's going to marry me into. One of the places was a Lady Joanne Godfrey—"

"Sir Reynold's mother," Lady Eleanor said, and added with a careful eye on Joice, "My sister."

Joice snapped her head around to face her. "You're one of them?" Accusation, wariness, and regret were all in the question together.

Lady Eleanor smiled at her. "It's why Sir Reynold

listened to me in the yard. It's why he may listen to me better than he does anyone else as this goes on."

Impulsively, Joice reached out to clasp her wrist. "Thank you."

Lady Eleanor patted her hand. "It's only right. Simply because he's of my family doesn't mean I have to back him in his greater stupidities. So young Benet saw you in London last spring. And any other time?"

"No, and it was only for a little while then. He came and talked to me while Father was showing the cloth to Lady Joanne. I hardly noticed him. It was already expected I'd be betrothed to Sir Lewis, so what would be the point in my noticing anyone? I never thought of him again until we met in Banbury market last week."

"But he thought of you," Lady Eleanor said. "Thought very well of you, apparently."

"To my grief," Joice said bitterly. "He had them grab me up from the street as I was going home! I didn't even know they were there until suddenly there were horsemen all around me and one of them flung me onto Benet's saddle, and when I tried to fight him, he wrapped me into my cloak so I couldn't even move and—and—" She gestured helplessly. "I'm here and nobody knows what happened to me or where I am."

"But people saw what happened to you in Banbury," Frevisse said. A town was always full with people on a market day; mounted men snatching a resisting girl would not have gone unnoticed. "And it won't be secret long where you are. Even if Sir Reynold and his men went unrecognized in Banbury, word will be out that there's been a girl stolen and people will have seen them riding this way with you. Nor there's no way to stop our own servants here that go back to the village every night from talking about you. By suppertime the whole village will know you're here and the rest of the countryside will have it tomorrow this time."

"Then my father will come for me!" Joice said gladly. "He'll ransom me if he has to. Or Sir Lewis, for honor's sake, will force them to give me up. He has men enough to make them do it!"

"Has your betrothal been made?" Lady Eleanor asked quickly.

Betrothal vows were as binding as those of marriage. If Joice were actually betrothed to Sir Lewis, any marriage forced on her otherwise, to Benet or anyone else, would be worthless.

Knowing that as well as Frevisse and Lady Eleanor did, Joice was abruptly close to tears again. "No. They're still drawing up the agreement. It isn't signed yet. He won't come. What he wants is my dowry. If I look like being too much trouble—and this is very much trouble—he'll simply drop it altogether. And it would have been a good marriage for me! He's cousin to Lord Fenner and has lands in three counties!"

"But if your dowry is very great," Lady Eleanor said gently, "you may still be worth the trouble to him."

"So what it comes down to," Joice said bitterly, "is whether my dowry makes me worth fighting over or not. Whether I'm worth what it might cost to have me out of here."

"Yes," Lady Eleanor said simply.

Joice's eyes widened with another thought. "It might even come to Father agreeing I marry this Benet if everything else is too costly and the marriage is good enough. You said he had lands to inherit. If Sir Lewis fails me, this is something Father could agree to."

"Yes," Lady Eleanor said again and left it at that, for Joice to think on. Joice did, staring at the wall in front of her in full-eyed shock.

Frevisse finished her wine and handed the goblet aside to Margrete. Very regrettably, this was not a matter that would be sorted out in a day. For now it would have to be enough that Joice was under the nunnery's protection—and perhaps more importantly, in Lady Eleanor's. "I have to go," she said. "It's nearly time for Vespers."

Lady Eleanor nodded, understanding, and began a polite reply, but Joice rose quickly to her feet, recovered enough to hold out a hand that Frevisse, in surprise, took as the girl said in a rush, "Thank you for helping me there in the yard. I'm sorry for what I said about my never being a nun. It was rude of me. But," she added firmly, "I never will be, come what may."

For which they could all very likely be much grateful, Frevisse did not say, and left.

# Chapter

## 4

VESPERS WAS A welter of inattention and whispering, betraying how many of the nuns knew at least something about what had happened this afternoon. With more on her own mind than prayers, Alys made no attempt to hold them. Arguing had given an edge to her appetite and the sooner they were to supper and done with it the better, not least because she was supposed to see Reynold afterward. The matter of this girl was not settled between them, not by a long way, but they had both judged it best to finish their arguing somewhere besides in the yard for everyone to hear.

Her nuns seemed to have heard enough about it as it was. Their minds were no more on the office than hers was, and the final "amen" was as much a relief as a conclusion. Released by it, Alys surged to her feet and out of the choir, headed for the refectory with the others crowding at her heels, but she turned at the door into the cloister to glare over her shoulder, warning them back and to less talk. She did not mean to listen to their chatter all through supper, either. Magpies and crows, the lot of them. Sister Thomasine was the only holy one in the lot. And if Dame Frevisse and Dame Claire thought she had not noticed them back there behind the others, their heads together, talking her down, they were wrong.

She knew what they were saying, too, and ill thanks to Reynold for it. What had he been thinking of, snatching that girl and then bringing her here?

For that matter, what had the girl been thinking of, to let herself be carried off like that?

Nor was there any use in pretending that it would be enough, when her people came for her, to show, even on Aunt Eleanor's witness, that no harm had come to her. They would want more recompense than words, and if they wanted it from both Reynold and St. Frideswide's, then she would have the priory's share out of Reynold's hide.

More problems. More expenses.

She took her place at the head of the long refectory table and bleakly watched her nuns, still jay-jabbering among themselves, ease into their places along benches down both sides. The dull ache that seemed to be always at the back of her skull of late had a noticeable throb to it now, and not wanting their voices keeping it company through supper, she impatiently whacked her spoon on the tabletop, startling them to silence.

According to the Rule, they were supposed to be read aloud to at meals, something holy, to better their souls when they might otherwise be too concentrated on their bodies, with each of them taking a week's turn at it, turn and turn around. No one much listed anymore. They had all heard the priory's few books too many times already, could have recited them without looking if they put their minds to it, probably, but tonight, for a change, they could actually pay heed and keep their mouths for chewing instead of talking.

"Dame Perpetua," she said. "Read." Making it both an order to Dame Perpetua and a warning to the rest.

Sister Cecely, already leaning toward Sister Emma, mouth open to speak, jerked upright in her place, startled. The others cast warning glances at each other and held silent, even Dame Perpetua, until Alys jerked a hand at her to get on with it. Nervously, with an uneasy glance at the silent faces turned her way, Dame Perpetua did, taking up the Life of St. Katherine where she had left off at dinner's end, with yet another of the emperor's threats against her life if she did not marry him. Alys, satisfied, rang the small bell at her place to tell the serving women to bring in the meal.

The first of them to come, apparently disconcerted by the sound of only Dame Perpetua's voice, hesitated uncertainly on the threshold. Alys gestured sharply to set her in motion again and the rest followed quickly enough, some setting the bowls of white pottage and the last third of each nun's daily bread loaf at their places, others pouring warmed ale into the waiting goblets.

As they began to eat, Dame Perpetua reached the saint's defiance of the emperor's last offer to let her live. " 'No! Do not delay my dying further, king, but command it speedily! It is not appalling to see a thing fall that will rise a thousand times fairer, ascend from sorrow to everlasting laughter, from grief to every joy, from death to undying life!' "

Mopping a piece of bread into the pottage, Alys nodded in full agreement. St. Katherine had been a woman able to show men up for the fools they were and refuse their stupidities to their faces. The end had been what could be expected—they had killed her to stop her because nothing else would. But that was how martyrs were made, and by St. Katherine's blessed bones, it was a better way to go than giving in to them and all their kind—the folly-ridden cousins and pushing abbots and bullying master masons.

Alys' head gave a deeper throb. In her rage at Reynold she had managed to forget that Master Porter, the master mason, had been at her again this afternoon about when his men would have their money, but he would not stay forgot, unfortunately.

Or stay unpaid. Unfortunately.

She had set his ears back flat against his head right enough this time, demanding back at him what use had he and his men for money out here at the priory, away from everywhere, anyway? Pay them now and they would likely be off to Banbury and into trouble. Let them finish what they had started and then they would have their money in hand and be off to wherever they wanted and welcome riddance to them, but she'd have the work done first, by blessed St. Frideswide she would! And if he did not think so, let him remember she had her cousin and his men to change his mind for him.

He had backed off right enough then, and well for him that he had, but she doubted he would stay backed off, and most certainly he would not if she lost Reynold.

For that reason and several more she could not afford to lose Reynold, but he was making it difficult, with his half-kept promises and now this girl. What she truly needed was more money. With money enough, every problem would give way, from Master Porter right down to her silly women. The trouble was that there was not more money.

And even if there had been, she had no true wish to be rid of Reynold.

Grimly she chewed her way through the rest of the meal. While St. Katherine went to her joyful martyrdom, a bowl of apples, still crisp from the harvest, was passed down the table; and while a soldier was severing her holy neck, Alys watched Sister Cecely take open pleasure in peeling her apple in one long strip. Since waste was unallowed, she always ate the peel afterward, so why did she bother? But at least she ate it, unlike Sister Thomasine, who, when she bothered to come to meals at all, left half of whatever she was given to be handed off as alms to whoever showed up at the priory gate for it. That was piety but one that Alys understood no better than she did Sister Cecely's apple peeling. Food was for eating, and how did it help if one went hungry when one of them had no need to? But that was how it was with saints. Pious but impractical, every one of them, and where were they then?

"'And so the blessed maiden Katherine went crowned to Christ,'" Dame Perpetua read reverently, "'in the month of November, on the twenty-fifth day, a Friday, near the hour our Lord gave up his life on the cross for her and for us all. Amen.'"

That was the familiar end. Dame Perpetua fell silent, then sighed, closed the book, and rose from her place with it clasped to her breast, to curtsy to Alys and then go away to the kitchen for her own meal. Alys, having contained impatience that long, rose to her own feet, the rest of the nuns with her. She ran them through grace, then stood eyeing them unfavorably, knowing what they wanted.

There was an hour's recreation now, between supper and the day's last prayers at Compline, and they were all eager to be off to make the most of it, to crowd around the fire in the warming room and let their tongues run away from their wits over everything they thought they knew about this afternoon, with Dame Frevisse to lead them on.

Briefly, bitterly, Alys considered ordering them to silence for the evening—or forbidding them their fire. That would curb their ways a little, give them something else to think on.

But suddenly they were not worth the bother. What she really wanted, besides to be rid of her throbbing head, was to not be looking at their foolish faces anymore and that was easily managed.

"Tell Dame Perpetua she's to lead you in prayers at Compline," she said curtly, and ignoring everything but the need to hide how much her head was hurting, left them with stiff dignity.

Outside, in the almost dark of the cloister walk, she let her shoulders slump and increased her stride so that she was well away toward her rooms before they came out of the refectory behind her, heading the other way for the warming room, already in low-voiced, eager talk.

Alys paused at the foot of her stairs, listening but not able to make out the words across the darkening cloister. She supposed she did not need to. They would be on about her and none of it to the good, likely.

Discouraged by the thought, she climbed the stairs to her rooms with heavy-legged weariness and the relief of escape.

She had not known when she became prioress how greatly she would come to depend on her rooms. The other women—just as she had all her years after coming to the nunnery, until she became prioress—slept in the dormitory across the cloister, each in her own cell, closed in by thin wooden walls and a curtain for a door, with a bed and not much else, but the prioress had two rooms for herself— bedroom and parlor all her own—and even a fireplace, the only one in the cloister except for those in the kitchen and the warming room. It gave her somewhere all of her own, somewhere away from all the endless demands and needs and envies turned on her for being prioress.

Envy. That was the sin that drove Dame Claire and Dame Frevisse on and on against her. They had both wanted to be prioress, had been counting on it being one of them when Domina Edith died, and could not forgive that the election had gone against them, that God had chosen her instead.

That was the thing she clung to at the end of days like this one. God had chosen her.

Standing in her darkened doorway, peering into the parlor's gloom, where there should have been at least lamplight and, better yet, a fire on the hearth and wine set out, she demanded, "Katerin!"

A scrabbling near the fireplace showed Katerin was there. Alys took a step into the room.

"Katerin, where's my fire?"

"Nearly," Katerin piped a little desperately from the darkness. "Nearly." The scrabbling went on, steel struck flint, and there were sparks and then small flames in dry tinder on the hearth, with Katerin's earnest face leaning over them, red-cast in the dark as she blew gently on the flames, urging them alive, with a hand poised to the side with more tinder for when they were strong enough.

Alys had stayed where she was but now went forward to stand beside her, near the warmth that would soon reach out as the fire grew. Katerin glanced up with a pleased smile. Alys nodded back reassuringly. Katerin's brain had been burned out by a fever when she was a child; she had spent much of her nearly thirty years following her mother around the village like a toddling infant, until, when the woman came to die, she begged, by way of Father Henry, the nuns to take Katerin into the priory.

"She's cleanly kept and good at simple tasks. She'll earn her keep," Father Henry had said on Katerin's behalf. "And it would be a mercy to her mother to know what's going to become of her."

For no good reason that Alys remembered now, except maybe to spite the distaste some of her nuns had shown at the thought of having a half-wit among them, she had agreed. As it had turned out, although Katerin had little to work with in the way of wits, what little she had was given over entirely to trying to please. Finding that if only an order was simple enough for Katerin to grasp, she never questioned or hesitated over it, Alys had very shortly made her entirely into her own servant. The only troubles were that an order had to be very simple, and that if Katerin felt she had failed or someone was angry at her, she panicked into complete incompetence. On the whole, it was easiest not to panic her by showing any anger, so Alys said nothing about her being late with the fire, only nodded to show it was all right and waited until Katerin had nursed the fire past kindling into flames licking along logs before saying, "That's a good fire, Katerin. Very good."

Katerin stood up, wiping her hands on her apron, smiling widely, and made a curtsy with much of the gladness a puppy would have shown for being patted.

"There's something else I want you to do for me," Alys said. Katerin bobbed her head eagerly, to show she was ready. She rarely spoke unless she had to, but she was always ready to do whatever was asked of her, if only she could understand it.

"I need you to go to Father Henry and Sir Reynold," Alys said with careful slowness, giving time for the names to take hold in Katerin's head. "You remember Sir Reynold?"

Katerin nodded willingly. It was a chancy thing what would stay in her mind and what slip away, but she always remembered Father Henry and Reynold seemed to stay more often than not.

"I want you to go to them and tell them I'm ready for them to come here. To come here now. You understand?"

Katerin's nodding increased in eagerness to show she did. Alys found she was nodding along with her, and stopped herself before saying, still carefully, "Go on, then. Go find Father Henry and Sir Reynold. Tell them to come here."

Katerin curtsied, smiling with gladness for something else to do, and scurried away. Alys, with a sigh for her aching head and weary legs, sank into the tall-backed chair beside the hearth leaned her head back and shut her eyes.

Because there was occasionally need for the prioress to entertain guests apart or see to business better not dealt with in chapter meetings, her parlor was more richly furnished than anywhere else in the priory, with not only the fireplace and chair but another chair besides, almost as good, and a table covered by a richly woven Spanish cloth, and brightly embroidered cushions on the seat below the long window overlooking the guest halls' yard.

And when the evening was done, there was her bedroom. Domina Edith had kept it sparsely furnished, with a plain prie-dieu and a straw-mattressed bed. Alys had been rid of the prie-dieu her first day as prioress, moving in her own that had been kept cramped in her cell until then. Elaborately carved to pleasure the eyes, thickly cushioned to ease the knees, it was to her mind much more the kind of prie-dieu a prioress should have. And the straw mattress had been replaced by a feather one as soon as might be, too.

Alys opened her eyes, not aware until then that she had closed them. This was not the time for being tired. The flames had good hold on the kindling now, feeding along its slender lengths and up into the larger wood above. Watching them, her elbow on the chair's arm and her chin leaned into her hand, Alys tried to decide how she should handle Reynold and found she was thinking instead of Domina Edith, sitting here through all those years she had been prioress, watching other fires through other evenings, just as Domina Geretrude had done before her and Domina Hawise before that, back to the priory's founding; all of them probably in this same chair, just as Alys now was and just as the prioresses who came after her would do.

Alys had had that thought before, other evenings, sitting here, and mostly took a kind of comfort from it that she never troubled to look at too closely. Looking too closely at things tended to lead to muddled thinking, she had found, and she did not need her thinking muddled. What she needed was a way to deal with Reynold tonight, and find more money for her priory soon.

They had always understood each other, she and Reynold; had always seen things straight on and from the same angle, with none of this wrongheaded fumbling about that most people called thinking. Most people could not think at all, needed their thinking done for them—or undone for them after they had made a mess of it—but it had never been like that for her or Reynold. They thought their way through to what they wanted and then went after it.

So why wasn't he seeing how impossible a thing he was expecting of her about this girl?

And he wasn't charming her into changing her mind. He always thought he could manage that whenever they disagreed, but this wasn't a thing she could be charmed into and that was something she would have to have into his head before they had finished tonight.

The difficulty lay in doing it without losing him. She could not afford to lose him. She had told him the second or third time he had come to visit her this summer how much in need of him St. Frideswide's was.

"Other places have patrons to benefact them. Why shouldn't St. Frideswide's?" she had said. "It's for the good of the givers' souls, and the better they give, the better for their souls."

Reynold had laughed. "And next you'll tell me that my soul needs all the bettering I can buy it."

"You know about that better than I do," she had answered austerely and he had laughed at her again, but he was the only person in the world who could laugh at her without rousing her anger and she had simply pressed on. "But yes, for the good of your soul, among other things, it wouldn't harm you to help us."

He could afford it. He had been a younger son without much to inherit, but he had found an heiress to marry and through her had come into property enough that he could lord it over the dozen or so knights and squires he liked for company. Alys, being a third daughter in a large family, had not had his chances, but she had won the gamble she had made in choosing St. Frideswide's instead of marriage—she was prioress. But that was not going to be the end of it. There was more she wanted and she needed help to see her ambitions through to the end. Reynold's help.

"But there won't be an end to your ambitions," Reynold had pointed out. "A tower now. A tiled floor later. A fountain for the garden after that. I know how it goes."

She had not thought of a fountain until then, but all she had said was, "And is that so much when set against your soul safe in heaven instead of sent to hell?"

He had made her talk a great deal more, teasing her along, but come around to admitting she was right, that he needed heaven's favor as much as she needed his help.

Not that it had come to much so far. So far he and his men had cost her more than he had brought in, and now he had saddled her with the problem of this girl; but at least he had brought food in today, too, as he had promised. He had done it last week, too, and once before that. It was a beginning. All she had to do was be patient at him.

She heard his laughter from below and Father Henry saying something and Katerin's quick footfalls on the stairs as she hurried ahead to open the parlor door. Alys straightened in her chair. She would have preferred to deal with Reynold alone, but for decency's sake Father Henry and Katerin would have to be here. By rights so should at least one of her nuns, but Dame Frevisse was undoubtedly telling them enough of what had happened in the yard this afternoon to keep their tattling tongues busy without one of them here to gather more for them.

Katerin came in smiling and stood aside to hold the door open. She did not need to but it was a skill she was proud to have and Alys let her. Reynold followed her, concentrating on carrying a fat, green-glazed pitcher with a linen towel laid over it.

"Spiced wine, cousin mine," he said cheerfully. "To take the chill off both the evening and your humor." He set it down on the table, crossed to her, and took her hand to kiss.

Trying to be gracious in return—you caught more flies with honey than vinegar—Alys let him and found as he stepped back with a grin, freeing her hand, that he had left a small leather purse in it.

"To show I'm sorry I've upset things for you," he said.

She could feel the coins through the leather. A lot of them and goodly sized. Not gold surely?

"Only some of them," Reynold said, as sure of her mind as if she had asked it aloud. "But some is better than none!" He swung away to the table. With Father Henry safely in, Katerin had left the door and was hurrying to fetch three of the priory's six silver goblets from the carved aumbry against the far wall. She reached the table with them as Reynold did and he rewarded her with a smile that she returned, round-eyed and gazing up at him in a way that told Alys that even an idiot could go more idiot for a man's smile. Why did women do that? Pleasurable it might be to have a man smile on you, but it was hardly worth giving up your wits for, though women did—even when they had no wits to give, like Katerin.

Reynold poured the wine with the same deft-wristed skill he had shown as a squire serving at her father's table, raising and lowering the pitcher so the wine fell in long curves, ruby-glinting in the firelight. The goblets filled, he set down the pitcher, and taking up two of them, turned to Alys, asking as he held one out to her, "Will you drink with me, cousin? Despite you're angry with me?"

She knew what he was doing—trying to buy her off with gold and charm. It would not work, she knew him too well. But that did not mean she would turn down the coins or good wine either, and she held out her hand, saying grudgingly, to show she was not giving ground, "I'll drink with you."

"There's my girl!" said Reynold. "Angry but not unforgiving." He came to hand her a goblet, and she took it, saying at Father Henry, "Take yours and go sit at the window, Father. Katerin, you stand by the door." They were here for propriety's sake, but they did not need to be near enough to hear what passed between her and Reynold. Father Henry understood as much and went where he was told. Katerin had no thought about it at all and obeyed as simply. Reynold pulled up the other chair to hers and the fire but did not sit, instead raised his goblet to her and declared, "To us, whatever comes of it!"

That was none so bad a wish and Alys drank to it, only to find when she lowered the goblet that he was looking down at her with a semblance of solemnity but a dimple showing beside his mouth, betraying him the way it always had when they were young and he was trying to deny a mischief.

"So, I'm forgiven?" he asked.

"Not yet nor by a long way," Alys snapped. "Sit down." Her head still ached. She refused to think about it, but that did not mean she wanted to crane her head back looking at him.

He sat and they eyed each other, their wine-warmed goblets between their hands, until Reynold leaned back in his chair with a deep sigh she did not believe came from as near the heart as he made it sound, and said, "So, what can we agree on about this girl?"

"Probably very little," Alys returned without hesitation.

"It could be simple, if you'll just let it be."

"Simple for whom?" She did not wait for his answer but gave him her own. "She's made clear she doesn't want Benet, and beyond that she's asked the priory's protection. I can't give her over to you or him."

Reynold leaned forward earnestly. "Alys, be reasonable. If you keep her, there's going to be trouble when her people and the Fenners find she's here."

"And that's the real way of it, isn't it? It's not helping Benet to a bride you're interested in, so much as doing down the Fenners." But that was something she could understand and, more than understand, agree with. The Fenners had given the Godfreys trouble more than once over the years. Lord Fenner still held Godfrey property he had seized ten years ago, and neither force of arms nor law had been able to pry him loose from it. "It isn't what you've done but that you've caught me in the middle." She set her goblet down on the chair's wide arm with exasperated force. "You shouldn't have brought her here!"

"But I *have* brought her here." Reynold spread his hands, appealing to her to see it his way. "Now let's take the simple way out of it. If she's fully married to Benet past redress before they find her here, there won't be any trouble worth mentioning, from the Fenners or her family."

"But she doesn't want to marry Benet and I've given her the priory's protection," Alys repeated with what she meant for him to understand was dangerous quietness.

He did not. "The priory's protection is yours to give or take as you choose, and what's her wanting or not wanting Benet have to do with anything? She's rich, Benet wants her, and if she's married to him, no Fenner can have her. Give her over to Benet tonight—let your priest even marry them first, if you want—and I warrant you that come the morning, she'll be thanking you for it."

Alys' face probably showed him he had taken the wrong way there because even as she started to open her mouth to answer him, ready to bludgeon such a quantity of stupidity out of his head—with words or otherwise—he rapidly shifted ground, leaned forward, and put his free hand on her knee, his voice dropping into warmth and urging. "Alys, let's not quarrel over it. That won't help anything. But what else is there to do? Because I've already sworn that she's not coming out of here until she's married to him."

"Let him court her."

"Court her?" Reynold echoed. He drew slightly back with surprise. "Court her?"

The way *you* do every woman that crosses your path, even so slight-brained a thing as Katerin, Alys thought but did not say it. "Court her," she repeated firmly, enjoying his surprise.

Reynold made a short, disbelieving laugh. "Why? Why waste the time? Why not simply let him have her and be done with it?"

"Because I say so."

They had neither of them ever lacked a temper and Alys could see Reynold's rousing now, his face darkening with it as he said warningly, "Alys, I can have that girl out of here anytime I choose and there's no way you can stop me, say what you want to."

He could, and would care nothing for the consequences. Not her threats of God's wrath, of fines, penance, episcopal displeasure, even excommunication if she forced him to turn the matter violent enough—and by St. Frideswide's blessed veil she would before he had the girl that way. Alys had her temper, too, and was only holding it back because she was remembering one thing more than Reynold was. She laid her hand over his knee and squeezed it with what might have been affection but was hard enough to be a warning, too and said, "You could," she agreed, "but you won't." And before he could ask why not, she answered, "Because Aunt Eleanor has taken her in charge, and whatever you might do against me or God, I doubt you'll do anything against Aunt Eleanor."

Reynold stopped, his mouth half-open, staring at her. They sat still long enough, in silence deep enough, for a log to pop and roll a little on the fire and Father Henry to grow nervous and clear his throat and Katerin to shuffle a little in the restless way she had when she did not understand what was happening.

Then a smile ticked at the corners of Reynold's mouth. He tried to hold it in check, but it grew, forcing both his dimples into view, and he gave way to it, grinning openly. "You have me there, my lady. Of all things in the world, I don't think I would care to go against Aunt Eleanor." He pulled free his hand and sat back in the chair, still smiling but less widely, with a light frown of thinking between his eyes. More to himself than not, he said, "I wonder what she's playing at?"

Before Alys could think of an answer, Reynold rose with abrupt grace, turning toward the table and the wine. "All right, then. Benet will come courting. Just don't be blaming me if her folk and the Fenners come ranting to your gate and nothing has been accomplished. Now, about this mason of yours you've been complaining of. Is he still giving you trouble?"

# Chapter

# 5

THE MORNING MASS, like the offices and breakfast before it, was subdued under Domina Alys' heavy eye, no one caring to chance her humor by unwary move or word. She had not come to Matins and Lauds at midnight but at dawn had carried through at a headlong pace that had warned Father Henry to be no less brisk about the Mass. In the few years since Domina Alys had become prioress, he had managed to efface himself from the priory almost entirely, spending most of his time in the village except for his necessary duties in St. Frideswide's. This morning he managed the Mass at a pace just short of unseemly, and afterward, while he retreated to the sacristy to divest himself of his vestments, the nuns left the church to go along the cloister walk to the warming room for chapter meeting.

Frevisse walked in huddled haste with them, everyone with chins tucked into their wimples and their hands pushed up their opposite sleeves to hold on to what warmth they had left after the cold time in the church. Domina Alys had not yet given permission for the heavier woolen winter gowns to be put on, and though the day was shining with early light, the sky clear except for little feather wisps of sun-gilded cloud directly overhead—the only sky that could be seen from inside the cloister—the sun was still below the roof ridge and the cloister walk still shivering cold in shadow. Wealthier nunneries had a separate room for the daily chapter meetings, some of them most beautifully made, but at St. Frideswide's the warming room sufficed, lacking elegance but with a fireplace that on cold mornings such as this one was much to be preferred over chill beauty.

So she was as bitterly disappointed, if not so loud about it as some, to find no fire there as they crowded through the door. Sister Amicia turned on Dame Juliana, who, as cellaress, would have to tell the servants of their failure. "Go tell them now!" she cried.

Dame Juliana shook her head miserably. "I can't. I had to tell them not to light a fire here this morning. Domina Alys said so."

"Why?" Sister Johane exclaimed. "It's not fair!"

"Hush," Dame Perpetua hissed from near the door. Domina Alys always came in to chapter meeting last and expected to find them standing silently, heads respectfully bowed, waiting for her. Dame Perpetua's warning was that she was nearly there, and in quick silence they spread out among the low stools, to wait for leave to sit.

Sister Thomasine, as she did even when there was a fire, had already slipped to the farthest place and was standing with her head bowed, hands folded, no sign that her thin body felt the morning's chill at all. Frevisse wondered if it were a sin to envy her that. For herself, wary of what Domina Alys' humor might be today, not wanting to be noticed if she could help it, she tried for a place in the midst of the other women, neither too forward nor too back, but found Dame Claire, Dame Perpetua, and Dame Juliana all had the same desire. There was a momentary shifting of skirts and a scraping of stools, then sympathizing glances at each other as they realized they were at matched purposes and settled wherever they were.

The four younger nuns, lacking their wariness, were crowded to the stools nearest Domina Alys' chair. Last night during recreation they had talked into the paving stones everything they knew or guessed about what had happened yesterday afternoon and been annoyed at Frevisse when she refused to embroider on the bare facts that she told them once and not again: a girl had been seized by Sir Reynold's men in Banbury, had been rescued here by Domina Alys, and was now in Lady Eleanor's keeping. Chapter meetings were for dealing with the nunnery's daily business and they were looking forward to asking questions at length about this particular business.

Frevisse doubted it was going to be that easy. Domina Alys' face was set this morning with a heavy-jawed stubbornness that did not bode well. Neither did her refusing them a fire. Admittedly, there were supposed to be no fires, except in the kitchen, from spring until Allhallows and they were barely to St. Crispin's, so the warming-room fire had been an indulgence on Domina Alys' part, one that she was within her rights to cancel if she chose. But shivering slightly, Frevisse thought that it was bitterly unfair they should lose it because Domina Alys was displeased over something that was none of their fault.

And, she promptly added with wry humor at herself, it was bitterly unfair for her to resent Domina Alys not keeping within the rules for some things and then being annoyed when she did if it led to discomfort. Diverted by how easily her own virtue could slide when she was faced with a cold room when she had hoped for a warm one, Frevisse made her curtsy with the rest as Domina Alys entered and then stood with her eyes down and hands folded in front of her, wishing she were as quiet in her mind as she hoped she outwardly seemed.

Domina Alys went to stand beside her chair, resting one hand on its high back as she looked them over with a darkly critical eye but saying nothing until Father Henry hurried in. As he took his place beside her, she declared, *"In nomine Patris, et Filii, et Spiritus Sancti.* Amen," and proceeded to pray—or order—the Holy Spirit to guide and bless what they would do here. Then Father Henry read the chapter of St. Benedict's Rule designated for the day, first in his uncertain Latin, then again in English, and made his brief commentary on the reading, to the effect that they should obey the holy St. Benedict's Rule. With Father Henry the obvious was always his strongest point. He was deeply sincere but never profound, and Frevisse, having managed after a long effort to accept that, barely listened to him anymore, thereby saving herself much aggravation.

He finished, blessed them, and departed, and Sister Emma and Sister Amicia thrust up their hands. Domina Alys' gaze flicked back and forth between them and then she chose to nod at Sister Amicia, who, eager as arrow from bow, sprang to her feet exclaiming, "About that girl Sir Reynold brought yesterday, was she really—"

Domina Alys snapped, "That's not something for discussion now. Sit down."

Sister Amicia stood staring, mouth open on her unfinished question.

"Sit!" Domina Alys ordered.

Sister Amicia sat, and Domina Alys turned a daunting stare on the rest of them. This was the time for accusations and confessions of faults to be made among the nuns, and disciplines and penances given, but today no one seemed inclined to rouse Domina Alys by either confession of their own faults or accusations against anyone else. There was only an uneasy shifting and silence under Domina Alys' gaze while she waited for someone to begin; and when it was clear she would not go on with chapter until something had been said, Dame Perpetua ventured to suggest uncertainly that Sister Cecely might have been a little abrupt in answering her yesterday over a matter of a book that had not been put back where it should have been.

Domina Alys set her glare on Sister Cecely. "Were you abrupt to Dame Perpetua?" she demanded.

"I—I—I might have been," Sister Cecely admitted. "Yes." She tried to sound more certain about it. "Yes, I think I was."

"Fifty paternosters on your knees sometime today before Compline," Domina Alys said. "And mind your tongue better after this. And you," she added at Dame Perpetua.

"Don't be so careful over what's said to you and not meant or you'll be doing penance, too."

Having established that she was not about to let anyone be innocent of anything, she looked at Dame Juliana and asked, "What have you to say?" to show she was ready to go on to the obedientiaries' reports. As cellarer, Dame Juliana was supposed to see that the nunnery had all it needed of food and other necessities, and because St. Frideswide's was small, she served as kitchener as well, with the kitchen and the daily preparing of meals under her supervision. The nunnery's needs not only from day to day but for the months ahead was her responsibility. Frevisse suspected that Domina Alys had appointed her to those duties, first, because of Dame Juliana's unwillingness to impart ill news and then because she was unlikely ever to presume to challenge what Domina Alys chose to tell her about the nunnery's accounts.

Unfortunately for Dame Juliana, that did not mean she was easy in her mind over any of it, and of late her formerly serene brow had begun to show the creases of concentration and worry. Now, at Domina Alys' demand, she unconsciously drew a breath, let it out as a deep sigh, and stood up to answer. "There's word . . . it's being said . . . I've heard . . . that Yorkshire had a drier year than we did and . . ."

"From who?" Domina Alys demanded.

"It's being said . . . among the servants. It's talked of . . . in the village."

"And what's it to us?"

Dame Juliana blinked, gathered her words, and said in a rush, "There may be wheat for sale there. They're saying that, too."

"I thought," Domina Alys said warningly, "that you'd told me we have enough to see us through the year."

"I did. We did," Dame Juliana quickly agreed. "But . . . but . . ."

"But now we don't?" Domina Alys' lowering voice warned that this was not the answer she wanted to hear.

Somewhat desperately Dame Juliana said, "We've used more . . . our need has been . . . greater than we expected." Because of Sir Reynold and his men, she refrained from adding. Hands clasped to her breast as if in prayer, she forced out, "If we could send someone to Yorkshire . . . to see about buying wheat there . . . it would be . . ."

"Useless," Dame Alys said with a darkening look. "Where's the money for it supposed to come from, for one thing? Not just for buying the wheat, supposing there is any, but for paying to have it brought here. Do we have funds I don't know of?"

Dame Juliana did not even try to answer that. She had already dared more than Frevisse would have cared to, and for the second time in hardly a month. Near Michaelmas, when it had still seemed the nunnery would have enough grain for the year but it was plain the village would not, she had hesitantly suggested the nuns might lessen their daily ration of bread, to make their stores last longer so that later they would be able to give to the village. Domina Alys had unhesitantly pointed out, "All that will do is mean we go hungry with them. Where's the point of that? Our first duty is God's worship and we can't do it if we're ill from hunger. God looks after his own. He made villeins better suited to beans than to wheat bread anyway, and if they haven't enough, they'll learn to work the harder next year."

She had made it clear she did not want to hear of the matter again, or anything like it. So it was all unexpected that now she smiled instead of going into rage. "But it doesn't matter whether there's wheat in Yorkshire or not. I've promise from Sir Reynold to see that we have wheat enough and anything else we might lack before he leaves."

Frevisse bit back the urge to ask when he purposed to leave and where he would find this sufficiency of food he promised. Everywhere they knew of close to hand had had poor harvests, Yorkshire was a long way off, even if the harvest had been better there, and she had seen no sign that Sir Reynold was well provided with money. So how was he going to keep this promise? And what would happen to them if he failed at it?

No one asked. Dame Juliana, staring at the floor, sat down without another word.

The other obedientiaries made brief reports of how matters went with each of their offices, with nothing to disturb their prioress, except from Dame Perpetua as sacristan. With the all-important order and propriety of the church and holy services in her care, she was compelled to make yet another protest against the masons' noise during the offices, little good though she thought it would do.

"They've been told!" Domina Alys answered. "There's nothing more to be done about it. Don't bother me with it again!"

Goaded by frustration, Dame Perpetua forgot herself so far as to cry out, "But if we only knew how much longer it was going to be!"

Domina Alys slapped her hands down angrily on her knees. "As long as it takes, Dame! The work is three-quarters done. It can't be that much longer! Now sit down or you'll spend the day on your knees with paternosters enough to take your mind off anything else!"

Dame Perpetua sat.

Frevisse, as hosteler, was last to be called on. Eyes down, she stood up and said, "The guest halls are presently full and no one is expected to depart today. There is presently food and drink enough for them. There are no complaints to be made against anyone or about anything."

She stopped, forbearing to add that if any travelers came now, asking the priory's hospitality, there would be no place to put them, thanks to all the Godfreys presently there, and that as things were going, by Christmas there would be nothing to feed them either, whether there was room for them by then or not.

Domina Alys gave her a sharp nod. "Good. Sit." She looked around at all of them. "Is there aught else?"

Her tone indicated there had best not be. Sister Amicia and Sister Emma squirmed a little, Sister Cecely exchanged a glance with Sister Johane, but no one said anything.

"Good. Then we'll see to the matter of this girl."

Heads came up alertly among the nuns, and not merely the four youngest. Domina Alys gave no sign of noticing it.

"Dame Frevisse, you dealt with her yesterday. Who is she? What have you learned about her?"

"She's Joice Southgate. Her father is a draper of Northampton."

"What was she doing in Banbury, then?" Domina Alys demanded.

Not waiting to be carried off to marry a Godfrey, Frevisse held back from answering as curtly; but Domina Alys had wanted no answer, was demanding, "Is his father as rich as Sir Reynold says?"

"I gather so. She says he's in partnership with someone in London."

Domina Alys nodded satisfaction with that. "She's content enough in Lady Eleanor's keeping?"

"When I left her yesterday, yes," Frevisse said.

"She's not going to make trouble?"

Frevisse forbore from asking, In what way? Joice's refusal to marry Benet was trouble in itself and she certainly meant to go on making it. But that was something else Domina Alys did not want to hear, so Frevisse merely said, "She's content to be in Lady Eleanor's keeping. She understands she should not try to leave."

"Best she keeps that understanding, too," Domina Alys said. "Now, all of you heed me on this. Young Benet Godfrey is going to be coming and going in and out of the cloister this next day or two or so."

Heads lifted again, with alarm or wariness or open interest. Several mouths opened, but Domina Alys cut off anything that might have been said with, "There's no discussion of this. I don't want to hear a thing about it."

"Oh! But . . ." Sister Cecely began.

Domina Alys turned on her fiercely. "I said I wanted to hear nothing! Two hundred aves lying on your face before the altar and you'll fast until you've finished with them, however long it takes you."

Sister Cecely visibly paled and shrank inside her habit. There would be no question of shirking her other duties because of the punishment. The aves would have to be fitted

into what little free time there was in a day, and she might
go hungry until tomorrow because of them.

Domina Alys raked the rest of them with an angry stare.
"Anyone else?"

Sister Amicia's open mouth snapped shut. Sister Emma
pressed her hands to her own mouth to be sure no word
escaped her. When no one else made any move at all, not
even so much as a shake of a head, Domina Alys drew a
deep breath and said, "Then I'll say this once and that's all
I'd better have to say it. Young Benet will be coming in to
see this Joice Southgate, in hopes he can persuade her to
marry him. He'll see her in Lady Eleanor's room, with Lady
Eleanor to watch. He'll come and go as seems best to him
and Lady Eleanor, and you're none of you to take note of
him or be in his way or find reason to speak to him or about
this to anyone, even among yourselves. Do you all understand that?"

No one dared raise any question or objection or even look
at one another. They did not have to see the tears running
silently down Sister Cecely's cheeks to be reminded what
the wrong word could cost them. Slowly, first Dame
Juliana's head and then one by one the rest made their nods
of agreement. Satisfied, Domina Alys raised her hand to
bless them before dismissing them, only to be interrupted by
a scratching at the door.

"What?" she demanded, and Katerin, set daily to watch
the cloister's outer door—and sweep the cloister walk while
she did—should anyone come while all the nuns were shut
away in chapter meeting, put her head hesitantly in and said
in her uncertain way, "Master Naylor. He's asking to speak
to you."

"Now?" Domina Alys did not try to hide her displeasure.

Katerin nodded, watching Domina Alys' face like a dog
eager to be told which way to go. Domina Alys flicked a
dismissing hand at her. "Tell him to wait. I'm almost done
here."

Katerin shifted uneasily from foot to foot. "He wants to
come in now. To chapter. He says."

"Does he?" Domina Alys' displeasure visibly deepened.

Roger Naylor was the priory's steward, charged with overseeing the priory's properties and the worldly matters necessary to sustain its spiritual life. He had done well enough with Domina Edith, each of them granting the other's particular and separate skills so that they had worked together in equal respect toward the same end, St. Frideswide's well-being.

He and Domina Alys had come to lack that shared respect, neither of them wanting to hear what the other had to say, so that his meetings with her had become infrequent and, Frevisse gathered, unsatisfactory. She could not remember when he had last asked to be heard in chapter meeting and doubted Domina Alys would allow it. Too much of what she suspected their prioress was trying to keep from them might come out if he did.

To her surprise, Domina Alys said impatiently, "Bid him come, then. Let's be done with him."

Nor did she have time to change her mind and dismiss them before he came. He must have been waiting barely beyond the door, because Katherin hardly disappeared before she was back with him, standing aside to let him enter, making a quick curtsy to Domina Alys and shutting the door behind her as she retreated. Master Naylor crossed to Domina Alys and bowed, first to her and then to the rest of them before looking her full in the face.

He was never a man much given to smiling, but today he looked more grim than usual. Although stewards were proverbially said to be greed-ridden, Frevisse had always found him a fair-minded man, careful of both St. Frideswide's well-being and of the people under him. Now her unease roused toward alarm as he straightened from his bow and said abruptly, "Good day, my lady. Could you give me some guess as to how long your cousin and his men are going to be here?"

"As long as need be," Domina Alys returned as abruptly. "Beyond that it's none of your concern, Master Naylor."

"It is if their score and more of horses are eating up the priory's hay at a rate that will leave us beggared of it before

Lent and some of the cattle having to be slaughtered because of it while our own horses starve."

"God will provide," Domina Alys snapped.

"God helps those who help themselves," Master Naylor returned curtly.

Frevisse could not stop her own indrawn gasp at his discourtesy, and she was not alone. A ripple of alarm passed among all the women while Domina Alys stared at him, momentarily wordless, before she surged to her feet and thrust her face toward his own as she spat back, "You'd best remember, Master Naylor, that you're here to do what I tell you to do and keep your mouth closed unless I tell you to open it! My cousin and his men and what they do is my concern, not yours!"

"Then you had best be more concerned about them than you are!" he answered.

There were more gasps among the women, and Domina Alys, in fury beyond words, swung a hand up and back for a blow at his head. Master Naylor, not flinching, flung up his arm to block it and they froze in mutual glare and rage.

No one dared stir either, in fear of what would happen if they did, until Domina Alys pulled her mouth into an angry, ugly smile and let drop her hand. "You've overstepped your duty, Master Naylor. Be out of St. Frideswide's and nowhere on my lands by midday today or I'll loose my cousin on you. Nor don't come begging back for me to recommend you elsewhere because I'll tell them exactly what you are and see you ruined. You're finished here and everywhere. Go!"

He was breathing hard, his face rigid, his anger cold in his eyes, but he gave no more response to her order and threat than to turn without a bow and leave, jerking the door open and not bothering to close it after him, so that they heard his footsteps going away along the cloister, going and then gone, and no one moving in the long-held silence until finally Domina Alys heaved a deep breath and said, grimly pleased, "Good. That needed doing. I've wanted to be rid of him."

Maybe too shocked to realize she was saying it aloud, Dame Juliana quavered, "But now we need a steward."

It was true enough, although not the best of times to say it. There was no way any of them could deal with all the worldly matters of St. Frideswide's outside the cloister while seeing to the duties they already had and all the hours of prayer, too, even if any of them had had the competence for it.

Domina Alys waved the problem aside. "Sir Reynold will recommend me someone who'll serve us better than Naylor ever did. Someone who'll know his place, for one thing." The blessing she should have given them for the day forgotten, she gestured them away. "Now go on about your duties, all of you. This has gone on long enough."

Frevisse stood up as readily as the others, no more willing than they were to remind Domina Alys of what she had left out and with an urgent need to reach Master Naylor. It was against her vows to send word to anyone outside the nunnery without her prioress' knowledge and permission, and until now she had been able to tell herself that matters in St. Frideswide's were not so ill that she should break them, even if she had been sure of a safe way to send a message to Abbot Gilberd at St. Bartholomew's; and without a safe way, she was afraid of what would surely happen to her if she tried and failed and Domina Alys found her out.

But matters had changed, were worsening, with no likelihood of being better, and Master Naylor was leaving. He was no longer bound to the priory by any duty or loyalty, and if she could manage to see him before he left, say even half a dozen words to him, tell him . . .

"Dame Frevisse," Domina Alys said.

Frevisse's heart lurched heavily up toward her throat and she stopped the single pace she had taken forward. Quickly, in hopes her face had not shown something she wanted hidden, she bowed her head and said, "My lady?"

"Before you go to the guest halls, tell Lady Eleanor and that girl that Benet is coming to talk with her this morning. Tell her she's to see him and why. Make it clear to her. We want to have this over with."

"Yes, my lady." Frevisse kept her voice unshaded and her frustration in check. The delay would not matter. Master Naylor would not be away upon the instant; he had wife and children to slow his going. She had time.

She also had a chance, with the other nuns crowding out the door, to be alone, briefly, with Domina Alys, not something she generally wanted, but she took the chance this time to say, "She'll want to know if word's been sent yet to her people that she's here and safe. Has it?"

A moment too late and too tersely, as if in haste to be past a lie, Domina Alys answered, "It's being seen to. Now go on."

Frevisse doubted that was an outright lie. An outright lie was a thing Domina Alys could not help but admit, even to herself, was a sin. What it was, probably, was a forestalling of the truth, a going around it. Word was going to be sent—sometime. It would be "seen to" but had not been yet—and would not be for as long as Domina Alys could possibly delay it.

# Chapter

## 6

JOICE HAD HAD the night now to think on what had happened to her and on what might happen to her and on her own helplessness, and she listened to Domina Alys' message silently, standing very still and straight, her fine-boned face as white and frozen as it had been flushed and alive with anger yesterday. When Frevisse had finished, she went on standing still a moment, then turned her head to Lady Eleanor across the room, sitting behind her embroidery frame where the light through the window fell most strongly, and asked, "Do I have to?"

Gently, Lady Eleanor said, "It would probably be best."

"For whom?" Joice asked sharply. She might have quieted but she was not quiescent.

"For you. It will buy you time."

"Time?" Joice exclaimed with vast indignation.

Lady Eleanor's mouth twitched with the smallest of smiles but her head was turned toward her embroidery, so that only Frevisse saw it, which was as well. Joice would not have understood, was too young yet to have learned that time, well used, could be more than an impediment between her and her desires, it could be an ally. There was much to be said for not being that young anymore, and Lady Eleanor looked at her with a sympathy that Frevisse understood, to say gently, "So long as Benet and Sir Reynold think you're about to be won over with words, they're unlikely to turn to force to persuade you."

Joice flinched and stiffened, then swung around to Frevisse. "Who thought of this?"

"Domina Alys gave the order in chapter meeting just now. That's all I know of it."

"But who thought of it?" Joice insisted. "Is she trying to help me or is there something else they have in mind?"

"It might have been Benet who thought of it," Lady Eleanor suggested quietly. "It sounds more his way than what happened yesterday. Yesterday was more Sir Reynold's doing than Benet's, I'm sure."

Joice's face tightened with anger. "All I know of Benet is that he agreed to it. More than that about him I don't need to know. I don't want to see him or hear him or have him near me!"

"But for your own sake, it might be best for you to at least listen to him," Lady Eleanor insisted, still gently.

Joice paced away from them the little distance the room allowed for pacing. Lady Eleanor's small dogs were curled together at the foot of the bed, an occasional twitch of a furry ear and a bright gleam of eyes under their shaggy fringe of creamy fur betraying they were watching every move made in the room. When Joice came near, they raised their heads and she stopped her pacing to scoop one of them up. Her back to Frevisse and Lady Eleanor, she cuddled it to her, her face against its furry back.

"We won't leave you alone with him. Margrete and I will be here all the while he is. Nothing will happen," Lady Eleanor assured her.

Joice faced them again. The dog tried to lick her chin with a quick flick of pink tongue past its own black nose, but she avoided it while asking Frevisse, "Is word gone to my people about my being here? Do they know where I am?"

"I don't know." It was a careful answer, meant neither to

curb nor raise her hopes, and it was fully true. Frevisse only suspected, she did not know what had been done.

Joice was not interested in careful. "I need to know how much time I have to play for!" Still holding the dog close to her, she came toward Frevisse, her desperation showing. "And even when my uncle knows, he won't come here himself. He'll go to Father. Or send word to him. It will be Father who comes. But that means not until tomorrow at the very best and probably not until the day after that!"

Frevisse thought even that was optimistic but did not say so. Joice needed what hope she could make for herself.

"You can deal with Benet that long," Lady Eleanor said encouragingly.

"I don't want to deal with Benet at all!" Joice cried and swung away from them both, past Lady Eleanor to the window. She stood there, her back to them, her chin sunk in the dog's ruff, and they waited while she worked through the thing, finally raising her head and turning around to say defiantly, "He can come, but I won't listen to him."

Lady Eleanor smiled and held out a hand. "You only need to look as if you are. That's a useful thing to be able to do with any man, no matter how you feel about him."

With a bravery that was very essentially her, Joice smiled back and put her hand into Lady Eleanor's. "As long as that's all I need do," she said firmly.

"That's all," Lady Eleanor assured her.

Relieved that she would not have to take a refusal to Domina Alys, glad that Joice had seemingly found a friend as well as a protector in Lady Eleanor, Frevisse excused herself, curtsied to Lady Eleanor, and left, certain that between them, Lady Eleanor and Joice would manage Benet well enough.

She went out of the cloister without other trouble. At this hour it was usual for her to go out to the guest halls, so no one remarked her going; but once into the courtyard, she crossed not to either of the halls but to the wide-arched gateway to the outer yard.

As she went she tried to assess where she might most quickly find Master Naylor. The outer yard was crowded from the walls inward with the stables, byres, workshops, and people needed for the nunnery's life, and she knew Master Naylor's dwelling was somewhere near the outer gate, across the yard. He might well be there even now. Breaking word of his dismissal to his wife and quieting her afterward would have taken time, and there was the need to see to the hurried gathering up of such belongings as they could manage to take with them in the little while he had been given to be away. There were three half-grown children, too, but those and the gathering of things he might leave to his wife while he saw to horse and cart to carry them away. So he might be at the stable now, and the stable was close to hand beyond the gateway. It would be worth her while to go there first, because if he was there—please God he would be—it would save her having to go farther astray from where she ought to be and lessen the likelihood that Domina Alys would come to hear of it.

Except, inevitably, Domina Alys would hear of it, because Frevisse herself would have to tell her tomorrow in chapter meeting.

Frevisse had not thought that far ahead until now, but what she was doing was a willfully committed fault and under obedience she would have to confess it. She shrank a little, inwardly, at the thought and could not stop the one that came treacherously after it: why should she confess it? If Domina Alys saw fit to treat all rules—even the Rule itself—as things to be ignored or shifted as suited her own purpose, why shouldn't she do the same?

She had the answer even as she asked the question. The Rule and the lesser rules that hedged it about were what bound St. Frideswide's into a whole instead of leaving it disparate pieces. If everyone came to think themselves free to go when and how and whatever way they chose away from the Rule or even the rules, and to declare themselves free of the consequences, there would be no whole in St. Frideswide's. Its gathered strength would be broken and gone, the heart of their life here dead; and without heart, the body would be pointless. There was no use saying hers was a small fault, done for a greater good. It was not the size but the fault that mattered. She would not lie by silence or wait cowardwise to see if she was discovered. Tomorrow in chapter she would confess it and by her own choice take the consequence.

So, she thought wryly, she had better make the most of her fault while she had the chance.

There seemed far more men and some women—mostly priory servants but some of Sir Reynold's, too, clustered in small groups around the outer yard and buildings—than there should have been this early in the day when surely there were tasks enough they could have been doing. Talk dropped away as she was seen, a nun unexpectedly there. Some began to fade away from whomever they had been talking with, disappearing into doorways or around corners. Others tried to shift into looking as if they were in the midst of going somewhere. Frevisse, seeming not to notice, closed on the nearest clot, three men with buckets and a pitchfork, before they could find somewhere else to be. Trapped, they threw disconcerted glances at each other and bent in quick, awkward bows. Simply glad to find someone to question so readily, Frevisse ignored their guilty unease and asked, "Where's Master Naylor?"

They traded more uncertain glances before one of them made bold to say, bobbing his head to show he meant nothing disrespectful, "Gone, my lady."

"Gone?" she said more sharply than she meant to. "Gone where?"

The man flapped a hand toward the outer gateway. "Gone. Left. Like he was told to. Gone."

He couldn't be, Frevisse wanted to say. He couldn't be gone that quickly. "His wife and children?" she asked with feigned quiet. "Did he leave them behind, then?"

"Oh, nay," another of the men said. "He sent them away nigh to a month ago. Just after Michaelmas."

"Michaelmas?" Frevisse repeated blankly. Almost a month ago at September's end? No word of Master Naylor sending his family away had come into the cloister. But why should it? If he did not choose to mention it, no one else was likely to; it would not have seemed that great a matter.

"Gone to relatives somewhere," the third man put in, seeming to decide it was safe to be helpful. "For a visit, like. Only it looks to be for longer now."

"So he's gone?" Frevisse repeated, not willing yet to believe it.

"Oh, aye." The third man's confidence was growing. "He came out from in there"—he nodded back toward the cloister—"looking like whey, only I couldn't tell if 'twere from anger or what, he didn't say above a dozen words beyond ordering his horse saddled and he didn't stop for naught then, just threw his pack behind the saddle and was out of here." He sounded faintly envious of so easy an escape.

"His pack?" Frevisse said. "He had his pack ready to go?"

"Aye." The second man took her up quickly on that, understanding, as she did, what it meant. "It was waiting just inside his house door. He didn't even have to go in, just swing down, pick it up, sling it behind the saddle, mount, and be off. We saw him, didn't we?"

The other men nodded, agreeing. "Aye, that's true."

"Makes you wonder," the first one said.

It made Frevisse more than wonder. Master Naylor had sent his family away almost a month ago, and he had been ready to leave before ever he came into chapter this morning.

He had known what was going to come of his confronting and defying Domina Alys and he had made ready for it.

He had more than made ready for it. He had caused it.

Thinking of what he had said and how he had said it, she was sure of that. Which left her with the question of why.

"Who do you think will be taking his place, my lady?" the third man made bold to ask.

"I don't know." Just now it was enough that Master Naylor was gone beyond her reach and she had put herself in peril of Domina Alys' wrath to no gain at all. "There's been no time to think on it," she said vaguely, then gathered her mind back to what was to hand, raised her voice, and said, "But for this morning anyway, you all must know what needs doing and you'd best be doing it, whether Master Naylor is here or not."

It was more order than hint. The three men backed off from her with hasty bows, the few others who still lingered within hearing suddenly seemed to remember where else they should be, and Frevisse, to follow her own advice, turned back to the guest halls and her morning's duties.

# Chapter

# 7

THE MORNING WENT on with an outward calm that did not
match the disquiet of Frevisse's thoughts. Near time for
Sext, as she passed along the east side of the cloister walk
with a book Dame Perpetua had asked her to fetch from the
book chest in the storeroom above the sacristy, she glimpsed
Benet following Margrete along the cloister's other side,
toward the stairs to Lady Eleanor's chamber. She could not
clearly see his face, but he walked more like someone being
led where he did not want to go than like a hopeful lover.

She wondered what he thought of the choices being made
for him and waited until he and Margrete were gone before
she went on around to the small room that Dame Perpetua
used as her schoolroom and was not surprised to be met at
the door by Lady Adela's bright face looking up at her
eagerly and not, Frevisse suspected, because of the book she
carried.

As the priory's precentress as well as sacristan, Dame
Perpetua was charged with tutoring their novices, when they
had any, and any children boarded with them, which
presently was only one, little Lady Adela, Lord Warenne's
daughter. She had been in St. Frideswide's four years now,

was ten years old—or was she eleven?—and aside from reasonably regular payments toward her keep, there was no sign her father had thought about her at all since sending her there. He had sons and another daughter, and so little Lady Adela, perhaps unmarriageable because of a malformed hip, was not a vital matter to him. There was an occasional murmured hope by Dame Perpetua and others that he would decide she should become a nun, but Frevisse had never seen any great turn toward devotion in Lady Adela despite her years in St. Frideswide's. Not that that would matter— except to Lady Adela—if her father decided on nunhood for her, but assuredly just now a prayerful life was the farthest thing from the child's mind as she asked eagerly, leaning out the door to look along the walk the way Benet had gone, "Is that who carried off Mistress Joice? Is that him?"

"Is that he?" Frevisse corrected without thought.

Lady Adela did not care. "It was, wasn't it?" she insisted.

"It was," Frevisse agreed.

"Lady Adela," Dame Perpetua said from behind her, "you were told to stay in here. The young man is no concern of yours. Of ours."

"I'm in," Lady Adela protested. "Most of me."

Most of her except her head and shoulders and almost down to her waist as she craned out the doorway, still looking along the empty walk in the clear hope of another glimpse of Benet.

"Lady Adela," Dame Perpetua repeated.

"He's gone," Frevisse said firmly.

Lady Adela sighed and regretfully straightened back into the room.

Frevisse followed her in. Dame Perpetua was beginning to find it difficult to keep the child sufficiently occupied. Lady Adela's reading and conversation in both English and French were as good as almost anyone in St. Frideswide's. Dame Perpetua had reached the end of what she could teach her of mathematics. Dame Claire's lessons on herbs and healing were only occasional. She could not be kept at needlework or spinning all day, every day, or be left out to play in the garden. Dame Perpetua had turned to Latin.

She had already given the child the rudiments of it, sufficient for her to find her way through the breviary and prayers. Now she had decided to go further and asked Frevisse to bring her the priory's one collection of Latin works, a volume of extracts from the most profound of the church fathers. Frevisse had sometimes labored at that particular book over the years and she felt a momentary sympathy for Lady Adela as she laid the fat, dull-bound book on the table in front of her. Then, seeing the set look of loathing on Lady Adela's face as she looked at the book, she thought that possibly her sympathy should go to Dame Perpetua because the girl's narrow-eyed look did not bode well for her dealings with St. Augustine and the other church fathers, or anyone who tried to force them on her. Lady Adela was a sweetly featured, rose-and-cream-fair child who rarely gave overt trouble. She was mostly biddable but only, Frevisse had discovered in the past, to a point, and it seemed that Dame Perpetua might have reached that point.

Happily oblivious, Dame Perpetua directed, "Say thank you to Dame Frevisse."

"Thank you, Dame Frevisse," Lady Adela obligingly echoed but her eyes strayed to the door, betraying what interested her more as she said wistfully, "I wouldn't mind being carried off by him."

"Yes, you would," Dame Perpetua corrected her.

Frevisse left them to it.

During Sext she nearly managed to escape the troubled turning of her thoughts, losing herself in the lovely complexity of the prayers and psalms that even Domina Alys seemed almost concentrating on for once; but as they neared the end there was a wild shout of men's voices from above and then the thunderous crash of stone falling inside the tower and shattering as it hit bottom close behind the boarded doorway.

With screams and exclaims, all of the nuns except Sister Thomasine sprang to their feet. Sister Emma began to sob and Domina Alys slammed her prayer book shut. "That's it for them! I'm not paying them to smash my stone to bits. Sit down!" she directed as she lunged out of her own choir stall and toward the boarded doorway. With both fists she pounded on its reverberating wood and yelled upward, "You come down and meet me in the orchard, Master Porter, and I mean now! Don't think you'll hide by perching up there on your undone, worthless, miserable tower like some broody-minded bird! You come down *now*! To the orchard!"

Without so much as a glance back at her nuns, she stormed down the church toward the shortest way around into the orchard. Overhead men's shouting still mixed with curses but without the desperate yelling there would have been if anyone had been hurt. In the choir, no one had sat down at her command. Sister Emma's sobbing was straggling away to silence, but Sister Amicia and Sister Cecely were tentatively beginning to giggle.

Sister Thomasine, unmoving until then, stood up and in her clear, light voice took up the office where it had been broken off. *"Domine, exaudi orationem meam."* Lord, hear my prayer.

She should have been answered then by the nuns across the choir from her with the next line of the prayer. Instead Sister Emma hiccuped on a final sob and began to giggle, too.

Frevisse, staring across at Sister Amicia and Sister Cecely and belatedly following Sister Thomasine's lead, declared forcibly, *"Et clamor meus ad te veniat."* And let my cry come to you.

Sister Thomasine promptly answered; and unevenly Dame Claire, Dame Perpetua, Dame Juliana, and even, at the last, Sister Johane joined in, carrying the office through the short way to its end, over the other nuns' now smothered but unstoppable laughter. They had reached, ". . . *per miseri-cordiam Dei requiescant in pace.* Amen"—through the mercy of God rest in peace—when shouting that was unmistakably Domina Alys' and certainly Master Porter's erupted from somewhere near outside. Mercifully, the words were incomprehensible, but Sister Emma, Sister Amicia, and Sister Cecely lost their little remaining control over their laughter. It pealed out despite their hands over their mouths, and hastily Dame Juliana, exercising her duty in the prioress' absence, closed the office, exclaiming rapidly, *"Et ne nos inducas in tentationem."* And do not lead us into temptation.

Dame Claire, Dame Perpetua, Frevisse, Sister Thomasine, and Sister Johane followed hurriedly with, *"Sed libera nos a malo"*—But free us from evil—and crossed themselves in an uneven flurry.

Outside, Domina Alys and Master Porter's voices rose into a greater height of rage. Sister Emma, Sister Amicia, and Sister Cecely, giving up completely to their laughter, collapsed into their seats. Frevisse and the others escaped the choir and then the church with more haste than grace, stood briefly together in the cloister walk looking at each other with nothing to be said, and then went their ways.

Frevisse, with a curiosity she admitted to, went to learn how it had fared between Joice and Benet but realized as she paused outside the open door to Lady Eleanor's room that he was still there, saying earnestly, ". . . three manors. They're none of them large, but all of them are good. You'd have one for your dower. . . ."

Wooing her with properties, Frevisse guessed. Something he should have tried first, instead of yesterday's stupidity.

She scratched lightly on the door frame and Margrete came to let her in as Lady Eleanor, Joice, and Benet all turned to look at who had come. Lady Eleanor was seated in one of the chairs, her embroidery frame in front of her and turned a little toward the window, away from the room in a polite pretense of leaving Joice and Benet alone, while Joice was seated in the other chair, across the room from her, with Benet standing uncomfortably in front of her. She might be willing to listen to him but she was not going to make it easy for him.

Seeing him there, quite obviously scrubbed and neatened, Frevisse thought what a pity it was he had not troubled to let Joice see him this way before: a not uncomely young man with a very real longing to win her liking.

"Should I come back later?" she asked.

"No!" Joice sprang to her feet before Lady Eleanor could say anything. "Please stay. Sit here!"

"Thank you but no," Frevisse declined graciously. It was not her place to come between them and Domina Alys' purpose. "I'll keep Lady Eleanor company instead. Pray, go on," she urged.

Neither of them much looked as if they wanted to go on, but she passed them to join Lady Eleanor beside the window and they had no choice. Warily they faced each other again, trying to find another thread of conversation to follow.

Lady Eleanor, watching them circumspectly from the corner of her eyes, smiled. "She isn't making it easy for him."

"Nor for herself," Frevisse said. Equally trying to seem she was not watching them, she sat down on the window seat.

"If she did, he'd likely be suspicious. He's not a fool, is young Benet." Lady Eleanor's smile deepened. "Only foolish. And weren't we all when we were young, one way or another?"

"Too true," Frevisse agreed. To her surprise she found she was wishing Benet well, however his present foolishness turned out. "If nothing else, he's learning now that more than liking goes into love. Unfortunately, it's at Joice's cost."

"Unfortunately for both of them," Lady Eleanor said mildly.

With a smile and nod of agreement, Frevisse turned a little away, toward the window, to stop watching them. In the yard below, a goodly number of Sir Reynold's men were idling on guest-hall steps and around the well. She looked to be sure there were no priory servants idling among them, then looked more intently at the group beside the well, half rising to her feet to see them better. The whorled glass of the small panes blurred what she saw, but someone was there who did not seem to be either one of Sir Reynold's men or anyone of the priory. As she looked, there was a burst of laughter and scattered clapping among the men around him, and he rose to his feet and bowed with a wide sweep of his arm, acknowledging them. Frevisse stood completely up.

"Is something wrong?" Lady Eleanor asked.

"No. Only there's someone new come down there. I should go see he's been taken care of."

Joice looked around at her sharply. Frevisse made a small, refusing shake of her head, telling her it had nothing to do with her.

"I'll come with you," Benet said.

She nearly told him she was forbidden to have aught to do with him, that even being seen with him could cause her trouble, but his voice had an edge to it she could not read and she held back, waiting by the door while he made his farewells to Joice and Lady Eleanor, then going out ahead of him and halfway down the stairs, as private as they were going to be, before she stopped and turned to ask him, "Is there something I should know?"

He had the solid Godfrey build but not the thrusting arrogance that was so usually a part of Godfrey blood, and no longer hiding his urgency, he said, "It didn't go well with her."

"Could you expect it to, this first time?"

"Not after yesterday, no."

Mindful it was not his success she should be concerned for but to win time for Joice, she asked encouragingly, "But you'll go on trying?"

"As long as may be," Benet said fervently. "As long as she'll let me. To keep her safe, if nothing else."

Frevisse tensed. "Safe?"

"I couldn't tell her, it would frighten her too much, but it's Sir Reynold. He doesn't mean for any Fenner to have her. He says her dowry is for the Godfreys. If I can't bring her to marry me and I don't . . ."—he flushed red from his collar up to his dark hair but forced out anyway—"and I don't take her, I'm afraid he'll force someone else on her."

"He's told you that?"

"Not the last part, but it's there behind what else he's said. You have to make sure she goes on seeing me, no matter how much she hates me. It's the only way I have to keep her safe."

He was right: Joice should not be told that while she was protecting herself from him, he was protecting her from Sir Reynold. She was already holding too close to one fear to need another added to it. But at the same time Frevisse realized she could not tell him that Joice was deliberately using him with no intention of ever giving way to his suit. Better he go on believing he had some hope.

"I'll do all that I may," Frevisse said, then added for her own sake, "but Domina Alys has forbidden any of us to notice you coming and going through the cloister. I'll be in trouble for speaking to you now, so after this, if there's aught you think I ought to know, tell Ela in the guest hall, and I'll send word to you the same way."

"Ela," Benet repeated. "Ela. I'll remember."

"Good. Now go, please."

He made her a bow and left her, loping away down the stairs and out of sight along the cloister walk, an overgrown boy who was going to be in worse trouble than he probably deserved if he went on with the company he presently kept. She waited until she heard the outer door close behind him with a muted thud before she followed him. Though it hardly mattered if they had been noticed or not. Tomorrow in chapter she would have to confess, along with other disobedience, that she had spoken to him. It was only a small comfort that her other confession would put her so far in trouble that this one was hardly likely to make matters much worse.

And in the meanwhile there was the matter of the man she had seen beside the well.

When she came out into the yard, the men who had been gathered around him were drifting off toward the guest halls but he was still seated on the top step of the well curb, head bent over the lute he held as he made some adjustment to its strings. Frevisse stopped a ways away from him and asked, "Joliffe?"

He looked up. Merriment and recognition danced into his

eyes, and snatching off his cap, he stood up to sweep her an excessively deep bow. "Dame Frevisse!"

He had been part of a company of players the only time they had ever met—five years ago? six?—so slender and fair-faced then that he had played the woman in whatever plays they did, though there had been nothing womanly about him when he dropped the roles and was himself. Or as much of himself as he had ever shown to her. He could slip from one seeming to another more easily than most folk changed clothing, with the only constant thing about him the easy air of mockery behind almost everything he said and did.

"The others. Where are they?" Frevisse asked as he straightened from his bow. "Are they here?"

They had been a small band of players, come on hard times but closely bound to each other, so that in all the years since they had been so briefly at St. Frideswide's, sheltering through a bitter Christmastide, she had never thought of Joliffe as anywhere but with them.

Joliffe struck a momentary pose of heart-stricken grief. "No, alas. Never no more."

Hearing the familiar warm edge of Joliffe's mockery there, Frevisse did rise to alarm, only asked shortly, "Then where?"

Joliffe raised his head and said simply, all flourish gone, "Rose decided a few years past that Piers should have something more than what a player's life would give him, so she and Evan have settled down to run an inn in Oxford for a man they know while Piers is supposed to be learning to be a pewterer."

Remembering the little rogue of a boy who had fretted at being kept to one place for too many days together, Frevisse said, "He must hate that."

"With a passion, but he comforts himself with the hope that he can turn the skill to forgery someday."

So Piers was still himself. "And Thomas?" He had been the oldest of them and their leader. How had he taken Rose's decision to quit and take Ellis and Piers with her, effectively finishing what little there had been of their band?

But Joliffe said cheerfully enough, "I think he was relieved to have the choice of going on or quitting taken away from him. He's set up as a grammar teacher in some grocer's charity day school for poor boys, and as he says, he now has an audience who can't escape him."

"And no matter what they think of the performance, he's paid anyway," Frevisse said.

Joliffe laughed. "You have it to the core. Besides the fact he has the added pleasure of being free to grumble to his heart's content that he was torn from the life he was meant to live by a mean-spirited woman's weakness."

"And when he does, Rose tells me what she thinks of that."

"In clear and unmistakable terms."

"And you?"

Joliffe stepped back and spread his arms as if to invite applause. "As you see."

He was dressed in doublet and hosen that must have been gaudy once but were muted now by weather and much wear. His high leather boots were rubbed and darkened with long use; he was slightly in need of a shave. The years had edged in on him; he would not pass in a play as a fair-faced maiden anymore, and though he was as slender as he had been, it was with a man's lean strength now instead of a boy's.

Frevisse eyed him, decided he still showed no more than what he wanted to be seen, and said, "It doesn't tell me much except that whatever you're doing, it keeps you clothed and fed."

"Clothed and fed and sometimes with a penny in my purse. What more can a wandering minstrel ask?"

"I shouldn't care to guess or even ask." She matched his mockery and laughter with her own. "But for the sake of knowing something of the guests within our walls, I have to ask what it is that brings you here. Besides your feet."

Joliffe, his mouth already opening to reply, stopped, then protested, "I wasn't going to say that."

"Then you were going to say it was for the pleasure of seeing me again."

"What better reason could I give than that?"

"The true one."

"What if I say I've taken to minstrelsy and my wanderings have happened to bring me this way?"

"That is a thing I'm willing to believe."

He swept her another bow. "Your ladyship is most gracious."

"My ladyship is also bound to find how it is with others of our guests. If you'll pardon me?"

"Of everything and anything, my lady," he declared, hand over his heart. "And hope you'll do as much for me should chance arise."

"That," she said dryly, "is probably another matter," and went on her way.

# Chapter

## 8

THERE WAS AN unexpected quiet to the rest of the morning and the early afternoon. Domina Alys, come back from quarreling with Master Porter, went to her chamber, gave order for the steward's accounts to be brought to her and, when they had, closed herself in with them, sending word by Katerin that Dame Perpetua should see to the offices when they came. She did not come down to dinner either but had Katerin fetch it to her, and Katerin afterward would answer no questions of how she was except with a shake of the head that told no one anything.

The day had moved into the drowsy warmth of afternoon when Frevisse went out to the guest halls again, to see how things went and if all was well in hand for supper. As she crossed the yard she had the regretful thought that it was a pity these bright, dry days had waited for October instead of blessing them at harvest. They would have made no difference then. Now they were hardly better than illusion, their brief warmth gone as soon as the day began to fade, the cold returning with the sunset shadows that in these shortening days came ever earlier.

In the guest halls there was nothing beyond the expected.

In answer to Frevisse's asking, Ela answered, "It's as well as may be. Bad when they're here, good when they go, worse when they come back." With small hope, she asked in her turn, "Be there any sign of it ending?"

Frevisse gave no false comfort. "For all that's been said about their leaving, they could be here for the winter."

"Then they'll be starving with the rest of us by Martinmas."

It was too slight an exaggeration for Frevisse to contradict.

She was taking her discouragement back across the yard and the lengthening shadows when she was loudly hailed, "Hai! Nun!" and she jerked around, offended, to see Joliffe coming toward her from the gateway to the outer yard. She had wondered where he was when she had not seen him in the guest halls or yard. Now she wondered how angry he meant to make her, hailing her thus; but even as she wondered it she knew that whatever else Joliffe was, he was never casually ill-mannered. If he was rude, there was a purpose to it, so she kept her immediate frown but not her anger at him as she answered with rudeness equal his own, "What is it?"

Fists on his hips, irritation in his voice pitched to carry well beyond her to the hand count of men and servants scattered around the yard, he stopped in front of her and said, "The way you keep your guests here. Where am I supposed to sleep and is supper going to be as scant as dinner was?"

His arrogance was easy to respond to in kind. Her own voice sharp with apparent impatience and almost as loud as his, Frevisse answered, "If you don't like what we offer, you're welcome to be on your way."

"You don't offer much at all, leave by whether I like it or not!"

"The Rule requires us to give. Your liking it or not is never mentioned. And if you mean to go on speaking to me, you will do it in a lesser voice!" He might be able to keep this up, but she could not.

He dropped back a pace from her, one hand flying to his

breast as if he had taken a blow. Then he bowed. "At your behest, my lady."

"And courteously," Frevisse added for good measure.

As if a little curbed, he stood with slightly bent head and said low-voiced, for only her to hear, "How long have all these men, horses, servants been here?"

"Two weeks and looking to be longer," Frevisse answered. "Why?"

"Not for choice, surely?"

"Our prioress likes their company," she said bitterly. "The rest of us aren't asked."

"And they're all Godfreys?"

"Godfreys or their followers."

"Can the priory afford them?"

"We can hardly afford ourselves, the way this year has gone."

"So how do you manage them?" Joliffe asked.

"Sir Reynold has brought in something toward their keep and I gather he's promised more, but we've not seen it yet. Why so great an interest?"

"An idle brain invites the devil."

"And curiosity has killed more than cats."

Joliffe smiled warmly and leaned toward her. "I'm trying to convey the impression that I'm charming you. Could you look slightly more charmed?"

"This is as charmed as I become."

"I feared as much. What about this girl?"

"Why are we feigning an argument?"

"Because anyone friendly with you is unlikely to be friended by the Godfreys and it's the Godfreys who are likely to pay me something, not you. What about the girl? She's not here willingly, I take it?"

"No." It was difficult to force questions on him when he was shoving them at her, and now mention of Joice diverted her to a sudden hope. Holding out an eager hand toward him, she asked, "Joliffe, could you take word to her people in Banbury that she's here? And to our abbot in Northampton of what Domina Alys is letting happen with us? If you could . . ."

He seized her hand in an apparently ardent grip, as if she had bestowed a favor on him. "Gladly but not soon."

Frevisse pulled her hand free. "Stop that!"

Joliffe bent his head with a tremulous sigh but went on evenly, "I've already said to people I'd stay two nights and maybe more." He lifted his head enough to look at her with what she supposed he meant to be a melting gaze. The laughter behind it spoiled the effect. "It's not often a minstrel can find so great an audience in a country priory. All the Godfreys, a herd of masons, and I'm bid tonight to play for your prioress." He came a step nearer to her, playing his part out for anyone who was watching. "If I go too soon, there might be suspicions I don't want to risk rousing."

Frevisse had opened her mouth to ask, "What suspicions?" when a rabble of noise from the gateway distracted them both to look around to where a clot of Sir Reynold's servants were shoving at what Frevisse first took to be a heap of dirty clothing on the cobbles, until it scrambled onto hands and feet and tried to scuttle away from them, almost succeeding but only because they let him before someone kicked his legs from under him and he went heavily down again.

"Ah," Joliffe said. "One of the few things we've been lacking. A scabrous beggar or a madman."

Frevisse supposed it was the latter; even beggars were in better condition than that poor creature looked to be. Mostly the mad were poor, harmless creatures, kept and cared for, if not by their relatives, then by the church out of charity. But there were always those who were not kept, either deliberately turned out or else wandering off, making their way—usually a brief way for the most witless ones—by chance and happenstance through a world that could be cruel or kind as fortune and people's humors took them. Some of them were hardly worse than vague, like strayed dogs in need of feeding and an occasional friendly pat to keep them going. Others lived with their bodies in this world but their minds in places strange and often horrible. Frevisse had encountered enough of both kinds in her childhood on the road with her parents to want nothing to do with any of them, ever. They frightened her, all of them, the greatly mad and the lesser, because madness was a black reft in the reason of God's world, an all-too-clear reminder of how near hell was to mankind's soul.

Unfortunately, what she wanted had nothing to do with her duty in the matter, and she and Joliffe moved in the same moment toward the men and their sport. Whomever they had, madman or not, he was in St. Frideswide's now, and if they thought they had some right to be tormenting him, she knew she had a greater one to stop them.

How she would do it was the problem. The half dozen or so men were well into it now. The open-handed blows at his head, so poorly shielded by his tangled arms, and the kicks at his undefended backside as they tried to make him run again so they could pull him down, would shortly turn more vicious. He was a new game to be played and they were bored enough not to give him up easily, to her or anyone.

Joliffe, laughing, shoved in among them, some of their blows and kicks finding him instead of the madman as he fended them off, exclaiming, "Here now! What are you doing to my servant?"

The men fell back. "Your servant?" one of them protested. Another pointed disbelievingly at the dirty, crouching thing at their feet. "That?"

"My servant," Joliffe insisted, and laid a proprietary hand on the madman's filthy head. "I pay him good wages for the privilege of beating him. Why should you do it for free?"

"That's not your servant," someone scoffed.

"It is!" Joliffe sounded immensely offended anyone could doubt it. "I sent him on ahead of me to ready my lodgings."

"But you were here first!"

"Ah." Joliffe held up an admonitory hand. "Do you expect things to make sense between a madman and a fool?"

"Not when it's so hard to tell one from the other," Frevisse said, cold-voiced with apparently offended authority. "Are you all quite finished cluttering up this gateway?"

Her fear just then was not for the madman but for Joliffe. He had come between the men and their game and they could as easily turn on him as not. Some of them looked already near to doing it, preferring their own kind of jest to his, and what she would do then she did not know.

Behind her, curious, Benet asked, "So why *are* they cluttering your gateway?"

"For this!" Joliffe made a dramatic gesture toward the huddled madman.

"For that?" Benet came nearer to take a closer look, first at the madman, then, apparently deeply puzzled, around at the men. "No, I don't think they'd be cluttering a gateway for that. I think they were just going by and it was in their way."

"Oh!" Joliffe swept off his cap and bowed while spinning around on one foot, making apology to them all. "I'm sorry. I mistook your purposes. I'm sorry *she* mistook your purposes." He pointed at Frevisse as if the whole thing, if they really thought about it, were probably her fault.

"Then since that's straightened out, we'll be going and leave that"—Benet nodded dismissively at the madman— "to you." He dropped an arm across the shoulders of the man nearest him and strolled away, taking the man with him, the others following, some a little confusedly as if not sure what had happened to their sport, others sauntering to show they'd finished there anyway and did not care, others grumbling below their breath and with an unfriendly glance or two, until Joliffe called after them, "How, if for more apology, I sing you a song at supper tonight? About the madman and the nun!"

That brought laughter and a shout that they would see he kept his promise.

Watching them scatter across the yard, some of them crowding around Benet, poking at him friendly-wise and him jabbing good-humoredly back at them, Joliffe said quietly, "He did that very well. Clever boy."

"That clever boy is the reason we have a stolen girl on our hands," Frevisse said. "But yes, out of the lot of them, he's probably the best."

"So he's the thwarted lover, is he?" Joliffe said with interest. "Any hope for him?"

"Not at present. Joice would rather see him hanged. A song about a madman and a nun? You have one like that?"

Joliffe shrugged. "Not until I've changed a word here and there in 'The Priest and the Nun.' Probably you'd best not hear it when I have, though," he added thoughtfully.

"I suspect I probably shouldn't even before you do. Now, what about him?"

They looked down at the madman, crouched on his heels with his arms wrapped around his legs and his face buried against his knees, rocking a little and making no sound. He wore a dirt-thickened shirt, filthy leggings, and rough-wrapped cloth for shoes, and smelled most particularly of pig manure.

"Fellow," said Joliffe and touched his shoulder.

The man flinched violently, lost balance, and sprawled sideways onto the cobbles, then scrambled back into his huddled heap, but now an eye gleamed out from the tangle of hair, shifting uneasily from Joliffe to Frevisse to Joliffe to Frevisse again.

Partly because of the smell of him and partly not to frighten him, Frevisse made no move to come closer but asked, because food seemed the most likely way to reach him, "Are you hungry?" She patted her stomach to help the thought go through to him. "Are you hungry? Food?"

The man made no answer except to shift his eye to Joliffe again. Joliffe knelt down and said very gently, "We're not going to hurt you. Are you hungry? Do you want food?"

The man's eye was wary but not wildly afraid now, and Joliffe said without changing his voice or position, "I think two of us are too many for him. Maybe you should leave him to me."

Frevisse drew back a willing step. "Take him around to the kitchen. Not inside but to the kitchen yard. I'll go through the cloister and tell someone to bring out food for him and a cloak or doublet, whatever is to hand in the alms clothing."

"Better that than anywhere around the guest halls," Joliffe agreed. "I'll see him fed, then put him out the back gate, maybe find someone to take him to the village. Away from here for certain."

"It would probably be better for you if you were away, too," Frevisse said.

"And leave behind what I'm likely to make here? No thank you. But when I've seen him on his way, I think I'll spend my time until supper trying my luck with your masons, safely on the other side of that wall." He jerked his head toward the wall that closed off the far end of the yard and the priory buildings from the orchard beyond the church, where the masons had set up their lodge for stoneworking and now were mostly living, since the crowding of the guest halls by Sir Reynold's men. It crossed Frevisse's mind that Joliffe had learned a great deal of how things were in the few hours he had been here; but the quick movement of his head had made the madman cringe and begin to shiver. "You'd best go," Joliffe said. "It will make this simpler for me, and she went."

# Chapter

## 9

ALYS LEANED HER head against the high, carved back of her chair, her eyes closed, her fingertips pressed to the sides of her forehead where the pain seemed trying to break through her skull. "Are they finished yet?"

Reynold answered without turning from the window, "Your nun is coming back toward the cloister. The minstrel is leading the madman off somewhere."

"Good." Everything hurt the worse when she moved in one of these headaches; she had been afraid she would be needed in the yard. "Why does everything have to be trouble? Why can't it all be simple?"

"Because no one lets it be." Reynold turned from the window and crossed to the table. "So there's no use your worrying on everything the way you do."

Her head gave a throb of greater pain. "I have to worry on everything. Nothing is done if I don't worry on it." He was pouring some of the wine he had brought; she could hear him and said without opening her eyes, "I don't need wine. My head hurts enough as it is."

"I'm not giving you the bottle, only a gobletful. You try

too hard, my girl. That's what makes your head to ache. This will ease you."

Alys opened her eyes to find him standing beside her, smiling down and holding out the goblet.

"Drink," he urged. "It'll help."

She took the goblet blindly, shutting her eyes against the unexpected bite of tears, not wanting Reynold to see how near she was to crying because of his kindness. When was the last time anyone had bothered to be kind to her simply for kindness' sake? She could not remember. All they ever seemed to want was for her to give and give and give so they could take and take and take. And she gave! God knew she gave. She was all but giving her sanity, come to that. Today, for the nunnery's need, she had worked over those crab-handed accounts until she was sick with this headache as well as sick with being unable to make the foul things give her the answers she wanted.

"They fight me on everything," she whispered, more to herself than Reynold. "They all fight me." Her nuns, her erstwhile steward, the master Mason, even those miserable accounts that went on lying, went on saying there was not enough money when there *had* to be. That was why she had sent Katerin to fetch Reynold to her. He was the only hope and help she had, and her nuns grudged her even him. She knew they did and talked about her behind her back. They grudged her everything. So she had sent Katerin for him while they were at dinner so they would not know he was here. And she had only Katerin companioning them so there would be no tattletales of what they said; and she meant to have him leave while they were closed away at Vespers. That would serve them as they deserved.

She pressed her eyes desperately tighter. Tears were no good. They were a weakness and she could not afford weakness, not with everything she wanted to do, hoped to do, for St. Frideswide's. She had no time for weakness, her own or anyone else's. Reynold was the same. He understood demands, not tears, and to show she was not weak, she said fiercely, eyes still closed, "I want my tower done. That will do more for me and my headaches than wine will."

Reynold had gone back to the table to pour wine for himself. Not looking full around, he answered over his shoulder, laughing a little, "Wine is just to help see you through. Don't worry over your tower, girl. You'll have it."

"Not according to Master Porter." She had the urge to cry under control now, out of her way, and she took a deep draught of the wine, savored it before swallowing, then said resentfully, "I had to fight with him again today."

"As if all the priory didn't hear you." Reynold sat opposite her in the other chair with his own wine and leaned forward to nudge her hand. "Drink. It won't do you any good in the goblet."

She drank. Ale was what they mostly had in St. Frideswide's, wine only with Communion or when someone thought to give it as a gift. That was another of the things she meant to change when she had made St. Frideswide's into what it ought to be. There would be wine every feast day then. Good wine. Bordeaux wine. Wine like this.

But that solved no present problems, and she reached her free hand out to grasp Reynold's wrist to make him hear her. "You have to make Master Porter finish my tower. He'll listen to you where he won't listen to me."

"He'll finish it or he won't leave here," Reynold said simply. "I've told you that."

"Have you told *him*?" Alys demanded.

Reynold turned his hand over in her hold to grasp hers in return, warmly smiling while he did and lightly laughing at her. "He'll hear reason better if he's not in a foaming fury. I keep waiting for a day when you haven't driven him into a rage before I try to talk to him. So far you haven't given me one."

There was no one else but Reynold she would let laugh at her, but she pulled free her hand and slapped at his arm anyway. "You just tell him, that's all. You make promises, but so far I've seen small return on them."

Reynold leaned back in his chair, unoffended. "Little? Isn't there food and wine here that wasn't here two days ago?"

"And a girl who wasn't here two days ago either."

Reynold snorted dismissively. "That will all come right. Benet says it went well this morning. She's coming around. Prickly but persuadable. Drink. It's not a sin."

Alys drank. It was easeful to be able to obey sometimes, instead of always having to be the one who thought things through and gave the orders. Reynold was in the right of it; she gave herself these headaches by trying too hard. Her elbow propped on the chair's arm, she rested her chin on her free hand and stared down into the goblet, thinking about the possibility that the pain was a little less. She prayed it was and prayed to St. Pancras to take it from her completely. A throb between her eyes was the only answer. She cringed, closed her eyes, and leaned her head back against the chair again.

"Hasn't your infirmarian anything to kill that for you?" Reynold asked.

Her eyes still shut, hardly moving her mouth for fear of jarring the pain to worse, she answered, "Dame Claire is one of the ones who thought to be prioress instead of me. I'm not giving her the satisfaction of knowing I'm in pain." No weakness in front of any of her nuns: that was how to keep control.

"Then I'd find me a different infirmarian."

"It keeps her out of my way and that's what I want."

"Find a different way to keep her out of your way."

As if she had not thought of that. "The only other office that would do for that is hosteler, and that's keeping Dame Frevisse out of my way."

Reynold made a disgusted sound. "That one. She sours the whole hall when she comes in. Never a friendly look, never a smile. Long-faced as a dying dog. Don't you have a kennel you could put her in?"

"I wish I did," Alys said bitterly. Then, despite the pain, she smiled. "But I've finally caught her out at something." There had been one other good thing today, besides Reynold.

"Have you?" Reynold roused to a mild interest. "What?"

"She was seen talking with Benet in the cloister this morning. . . ."

"Oh, a great offense," Reynold mocked.

Alys barked a laugh back at him, ignoring the pain it cost her. "After I'd forbidden anyone to notice him when he was here." But leave it to Sister Amicia to be watching out to see him and then tell what she saw. "So tomorrow in chapter meeting Dame Frevisse is in my hand, to punish as I choose."

"And you'll surely choose to give her something she'll remember," Reynold said.

"Oh yes." Alys nodded with grim satisfaction. "Now she's given me the chance, I mean to give her something to remember."

# Chapter

# 10

FREVISSE HAD A brief thought that she might escape into the church for the while before Vespers to pray, to gather her thoughts, simply to be quiet once she had left the necessary orders for the madman's food and alms clothing with someone in the kitchen; but in the cloister walk as she turned kitchenward, Lady Adela, limping down the steps from Lady Eleanor's room, waved to her and whispered loudly, "Dame Frevisse!" Unhappily certain this was the end of any hope of escaping to the church, Frevisse went to meet her.

"Joice needs to see you," Lady Adela said eagerly. "That was a lunatic in the yard, wasn't it? That you and Benet and the other man were saving from Sir Reynold's men? We saw you from the window. Is he horribly mad?"

"Only quietly mad. And, no, you may not go see him." Frevisse answered what she knew Lady Adela was going to ask next. For someone so quiet with Dame Perpetua, Lady Adela had words enough otherwise. "I'm going to see to having him fed now and then he'll be sent on his way. Tell Mistress Joice I'll be with her shortly."

Lady Adela started to go, then paused and looked back at

her, frowning. "I wouldn't hate Latin if it wasn't all church things," she said reproachfully, turned away with offended dignity, and limped away up the stairs, dragging her lame leg more than necessary.

Knowing she had been rebuked but not certain how, Frevisse went on to the kitchen, where there was no trouble about giving the first kitchen servant she happened on the needful orders. That done, she turned reluctantly back toward Lady Eleanor's chamber and, as she went up the stairs, looked at her reluctance, trying to find the reason for it. Much of it had to come because of her worry over what would happen in tomorrow's chapter meeting. Knowing what she had to do was not the same as actually facing whatever humiliation Domina Alys would delight in giving her. The rest of her reluctance . . .

Joice met her at the open door in a swirl of scarlet skirts, grabbing her desperately by the hands and exclaiming without other greeting, "I can't go on seeing him! How long do I have to do this? I can't!"

. . . was because she had nothing to tell Joice that Joice wanted to hear, nothing that would be of any comfort to her.

"Joice." Lady Eleanor spoke mildly from across the room, where she stood with Margrete by the window. "There's no need for this."

"And no use either," Frevisse said. She pushed the girl back into the room. This was not something the whole nunnery needed to hear. "Lady Adela, close the door."

Lady Adela, hovering bright-eyed near the bed with one of Lady Eleanor's dogs in her arms—the other was curled where Lady Eleanor's skirts spread on the floor around her feet—limped eagerly to obey.

"Hasn't anyone come yet?" Joice begged, still clinging to Frevisse's hands. "No word from anyone at all?"

"There hasn't been time. It's too soon."

"Joice, child," Lady Eleanor said, still patiently, "this isn't going to help."

"Nothing's going to help!" Joice cried.

Frevisse pulled free of Joice's hand, seized her by the shoulders, and forced her down onto a stool, then leaned over her, still gripping her by the shoulders, and ordered, "Tell me what's happened."

Joice tried to leap back to her feet. Frevisse forced her back down. "Tell me! I can't help if I don't know!"

"Your prioress!" Joice all but spat the word. Fragile with fear an instant before, she was suddenly fiercely angry. "Your miserable, treacherous prioress!"

Better pleased to have her angry rather than wild with fear, Frevisse drew a steadying breath and said evenly, "What's she done?"

Her hands in fists, beating at her skirts with rage, Joice exclaimed, "She's ordered me to spend the evening with her! With her and Benet and Sir Reynold!"

Frevisse looked around to Lady Eleanor who answered calmly, "Katerin came a while ago to tell us. I'll be there, too. And Hugh."

And Joliffe. Frevisse remembered he had said he was summoned to play for Domina Alys this evening. She took hold of Joice's hands, forcing them still and Joice to look at her. "It's nothing," she said, matching Lady Eleanor's calm. "There's a minstrel come today. That's what's put it in Domina Alys' head. You only have to go and play out the game you're already playing. Surely you can do that through one evening."

"You can talk with Benet, surely," Lady Eleanor said. "You've done it easily enough this morning and again this afternoon."

"Not easily!"

"But more easily than you could face what might happen to you if you don't!" Frevisse said back at her.

Joice, mouth open for more angry words, stopped, disconcerted into thinking; and when she had, she drew a deep, unsteady breath and said softly, "Your prioress wants me to marry him, doesn't she? And I'm safe here only so long as she keeps me safe, aren't I?"

She was, but admitting to it would be of small use just now, and Frevisse said evenly, believing it, "She won't let you be forced to anything."

"I'm being forced to be there tonight!"

"She's giving you more chance to come around to Benet of your own will," Lady Eleanor said gently. "That's all this is. That's all she's trying to do."

The trouble was that Domina Alys' ways of trying were never subtle, and neither was Joice's temper. If they came openly up against each, with Domina Alys' only answer to anger being more anger . . .

Frevisse did not want to think of it.

From where she stood beside the window, looking down into the yard, Margrete said, "Sir Hugh is coming into the cloister."

"To here or Alys?" Lady Eleanor said. "Adela, see."

Lady Adela quickly set the dog on the bed and went out to the head of the stairs as Joice rose sharply to her feet, declaring, "I don't want to see anyone!"

"If he's coming here, you have small choice," Lady Eleanor said evenly. "Adela?"

Lady Adela limped excitedly back into the room, shutting the door. "He's gone past Domina Alys' stairs. Sister Johane is bringing him here!"

Joice started another protest. Frevisse did not wait for it but took her by the arm across to the bed and sat her down on its edge, ordering her, "Stop playing the fool and play with the dog. Lady Adela, come, too. Lady Eleanor, is he likely to be coming to see Mistress Joice?"

"No," Lady Eleanor said mildly. She had not stirred. "He's likely coming to see me. Margrete."

Margrete had already crossed to the door and at her lady's word opened it to Sir Hugh just as he reached it, Sister Johane apparently left at the foot of the stairs. Smiling at him, Margrete stood aside, curtsying to him as he entered. At Frevisse's prod, Joice rose, the dog in her arms, to join Frevisse in curtsy to him, too, while Lady Adela merely bent her head toward him, as a lord's daughter needing to do no more. Sir Hugh returned their courtesies with a bow of his own and, "My ladies," before turning to Lady Eleanor with another bow. The dog that had been curled on her skirts came scampering to sniff at his boots, and Sir Hugh scooped him up, saying, "Furry rat," as the dog writhed around happily in his hold, trying to lick at his chin, then letting himself be stroked down into the crook of Sir Hugh's arm as if it were a thing they were both used to. Sir Hugh turned back to Frevisse.

"Before anything else, my lady," he said, "my apology for what happened in the yard with the madman. The men were in the wrong of it."

Inwardly surprised that he either knew of it or cared, Frevisse answered back with outward graciousness, "Worse might have come of it than did. Thank you."

"He took no harm?"

"Fright was the worst of it, I think. He's being fed and then he'll be seen away from here."

"That's likely for the best."

"Yes."

Sir Hugh bent his head to her, and to Joice and Lady Adela for good measure, and with the dog now nestled contentedly into the crook of his elbow, crossed to Lady Eleanor with, "And how is it with you, my lady mother?"

Joice, the other dog clutched to her as tightly as she had held to good manners while Sir Hugh was facing her, gasped and looked disbelievingly at Frevisse. "His mother? Lady Eleanor is his mother?" she whispered.

Frevisse's surprise was as great, though she was trying to hide it better. Lady Eleanor had never mentioned that Sir Hugh was her son. But then—the realization startled her—she was not even sure how many children Lady Eleanor had, let be the names of any of them. There were sons and at least one daughter, but that was all she was sure of. How had she talked with Lady Eleanor so often and not learned more than that? By never asking questions, she realized. Because it had not interested her. What sort of friendship had she been giving Lady Eleanor, not to care about what must matter very much to her?

It was equally disconcerting to have Lady Adela say easily, "He's the third son. There's Sir Geoffrey, who inherited, and then John, who's in Abingdon Abbey. Sir Hugh has just the one manor and it's small and he hasn't managed any marriage yet, but now that he has Lady

Eleanor's dower manor, too, because she's here, she hopes
he'll be able to marry after all."

"How do you know all this?" Frevisse asked.

Lady Adela gave her a slightly cross look, as if wondering how she could be so stupid. "Lady Eleanor tells me."

"When?"

"When we talk." Lady Adela said it with an impatient
undertone that told she was rapidly losing faith in Frevisse's
ability to grasp the obvious.

And it was obvious. Or should have been. She knew that
Lady Eleanor and Lady Adela kept company when Dame
Perpetua was done with the girl. "It will be good for both of
us," Lady Eleanor had said when she first came. Dame
Perpetua had been pleased because it meant Lady Adela
would not be so much alone or in the company of only
servants. Beyond that, Frevisse had given the matter no
particular thought. No more thought than it seemed she had
spent on Lady Eleanor, to know so little about her.

Lady Adela, busy with either trying to take out a tangle in
the white plumed tail of the dog Joice still held or else to put
one in, was going on, "There are two daughters, too.
Katherine and Elizabeth." She looked up at Frevisse. "Lady
Eleanor says she never talks to you about them because it
seems unkind to talk much about children to someone who
won't ever have any of her own."

That was an aspect of it so far from Frevisse's mind that
she had no answer for it at all except a startled stare. It was
Joice who said abruptly, following another thought altogether, "If that's how it is, she may not be so much trying to
protect me from Benet as hoping to bring me around to
marrying Sir Hugh!"

Lady Adela brightened at that. "Then I could marry
Benet!"

"You'd want to?" Joice asked disbelievingly.

Lady Adela nodded. "He's almost handsome. And I think
he's brave. And . . ."

"Then you can have him," Joice said fiercely.

The bell began to ring to Vespers. Frevisse stood up in
haste, more grateful than graceful, then paused to lay a hand

on Joice's arm and say quietly but forcefully when the girl looked up at her, "It doesn't matter who wants what for you. Keep going at what you've started. Play it out. It's your safest way."

Joice hesitated, verging on rebellion before finally her chin came up and she said in defiance of seemingly everyone, "I'll even go tonight as if I wanted to and let them think they're winning."

Margrete was still at the door and opened it as Frevisse moved to leave. Frevisse nodded thanks as she went out, but from beyond it, in the moment of Margrete shutting it after her, looked back at Lady Eleanor and Sir Hugh across the room. Deep in talk with one another, they had not noticed her going. They were leaned toward each other, small outward resemblance between them and yet a familiarity in her hand on his knee, his nod to whatever she was saying, the way their eyes held, that Frevisse hoped would have told her something more about who they were to each other if she had seen them together like this before.

Or did she see it now only because she knew?

The door closed and she turned to answer the bell's calling, but the thought of her own willed ignorance went with her, shaming and discomfiting her. She had chosen, when she chose to be a nun, the enclosed life that was meant to go with her vows, but the enclosure was supposed to be of the body, not of the mind or heart. What else of things around her had she not bothered to notice, to know?

# Chapter

# 11

THE NUNS AWOKE to shivering cold at dawn, their breath in white clouds about them as they hurriedly slipped their outer gowns on over the underdresses they had worn to bed, arranged wimples around their faces, and pinned veils into place with stiff and uncooperative fingers by what little light there was from the lamp kept burning through the night at the head of the stairs.

"She *has* to give us leave to change to our winter gowns," Sister Amicia wailed from her sleeping cell. "We'll all freeze before Allhallows if she doesn't!"

Frevisse wondered if Sister Amicia would ever grasp, once and for all, that when they had elected Domina Alys prioress, they had given her the right not to *have* to do anything she did not want to do where the priory was concerned.

Hurried along by the chill, they were all dressed, even Sister Emma, and already going down the stairs in huddled haste, when the bell began to ring to Prime. The lamp threw their shadows past them, tangling the darkness as they went down the stairs, but their feet were too used to the way to be confused. In the cloister, dawn had only just begun to come, a softening at the edges of the dark. They passed along it in a whisper of skirts and soft-soled shoes and entered the deeper shadows of the church, where the altar light beyond the choir was the only brightness as they spread out to their places in the stalls.

They rustled and coughed and settled as Dame Perpetua lighted the rushlights set along the choir stalls' railing with the small taper she had brought from the lamp by the dorter stairs and carried shielded behind her hand from the draft of her walking until now. As the soft golden light bloomed around them Frevisse found her place in her prayer book for Prime's familiar beginning. She hardly needed the words in front of her anymore, the complex weave of prayers and daily changing psalms through the circle of the Church's seasons had become so much a part of her, but the feel of the book was familiar and therefore comforting.

Now all they lacked was their prioress, but they were becoming used to her being late, both at midnight's prayers and Prime, and Frevisse huddled down over her prayer book, trying to will her body to warmth and quietness instead of shivering while they waited. She wondered how it had gone with Joice last night. And despite her resolve not to think of it until it happened, she wondered how it would go with herself this morning.

She was afraid.

She faced that. She had done what would be seen as wrong and she was very certainly going to suffer for it. Whatever good she had meant by what she had done, she would have to endure the bad that was going to come from it. And not only endure but not let anger and defiance corrode her while she did.

*Firmum est cor meum, Deus, firmum est cor meum.* Firm is my heart, God, firm is my heart. *Cantabo . . . Excitabo auroram . . .* I will sing . . . I will rouse the dawn. . . .

She loved the courage of Prime's prayers. They promised that there had been days before this one and that there would be days after it, and if there was ill, there was also good, and that though the two were inextricably conjoined in this day, in every day, in all of life, it was not the good or ill that mattered but the firm heart that could turn to God and sing.

Today was only this one day. It was not all of her life. She would endure it. *Firmum est cor meum, Deus. Firmus est cor meum.*

A slump and thump and complaining murmur from Sister Cecely told she had not held firm against the pull of sleep. Someone laughed softly. Sister Cecely whispered, "It's not fair, our being here in the cold and dark when she isn't." Dame Juliana whispered back, "Hush," and there was quiet again.

Beyond the east window, the darkness was easing into the gray of gathering day as, with a rush and thrust of shadows and heavy footfalls, Domina Alys appeared from the darkness and mounted to the prioress' stall, sat down, slapped her prayer book open, squinted at the page as if her eyes were not so awake as the rest of her, and said loudly, *"Laus tibi, Domine."* Praise to you, Lord.

She sounded more as if she were ordering him to take it than humbly offering it and set a brisk pace afterward, but for once she passed over nothing and slurred very little, and because it was too early, too little light, for the masons to be at work, there were no interruptions. They reached the end with its closing prayer for the souls of the faithful departed. Domina Alys slapped her prayer book shut, rose to her feet, and led the way out of the church.

It was dawn light now and they could see as they crowded shivering at her heels that a heavy rime of frost lay along the stone of the low wall between the cloister walk and the garth, and that in the garth every leaf, petal, stem, the paths, and bare earth were crusted white, with Katerin's footprints to the bell showing black where she had come and gone. It was the last small corner of summer ended, but Dame Juliana was the only one who paused to look and mourn a little over the year's last-dead flowers. The rest of the nuns were too eager to be out of the cold.

The day had grown to full light in the short while it took to break their fast with warmed cider and bread. Frevisse was willing to draw out time then, but Father Henry set a cold-hastened pace through Mass, and then there was nothing left between her and chapter meeting but the brief walk from church to warming room. There the others crowded close to the fire, excepting Sister Thomasine, who went, as always, aside to the farthest stool and stood there with bowed heads and hands tucked in opposite sleeves, waiting. Frevisse hesitated and then went to stand by the stool nearest her in like pose if not in like quiet of mind. Sister Thomasine brought humility to everything she did, and in the corner of her mind not taut with apprehension of what was coming, Frevisse knew that if she were able to accept whatever punishment and penance Domina Alys chose to lay on her with humility anything near to Sister Thomasine's, then the humiliation of it would not be able to touch her.

Domina Alys entered and took her place. Reluctantly leaving the fire, so did the other women. Father Henry came, made his familiar, dogged attack on the Latin and the lesson, and left. Now there was no more time to be ready, no more waiting to be lived through, as Domina Alys asked, according to form, "Are there any faults to be confessed or revealed here today?"

Frevisse, her eyes kept to the floor until then, raised her head to reply—and found Domina Alys looking at her, waiting with open satisfaction and anticipation.

It was the sight of the satisfaction that brought Frevisse to her feet, humiliation and fear forgotten. Confession was to be made with eyes humbly lowered, and Frevisse forced hers down when she was standing, but it was through a seethe of anger—all of this was happening because of Domina Alys and she dared sit there being pleased about it—that she forced out, "I sinned against your word yesterday by speaking to the man Benet in the cloister."

An excited stir and rustle passed among the nuns. Frevisse raised her eyes to see Domina Alys nodding in satisfaction. So that was what she had been waiting to hear, or else to accuse her of if she had held silent. That meant she did not know the rest, and defiantly, with a satisfaction of her own, Frevisse went on, "More than that, yesterday morning I went alone, without permission and in neglect of my duties, to the outer yard to speak with Master Naylor."

Domina Alys' face gave away that she had not known that, and with rousing anger she leaned forward in her chair to demand, "What business did you have with Master Naylor after I'd dismissed him, Dame? What did you have to say to him?"

"I thought it wrong for him to go without so much as a word of well-wishing from any of us after all the years he's served us. I wanted to bid him farewell. I—"

Domina Alys, her face beginning to suffuse to its familiar red, thrust up out of her chair. "*That* was not for *you* to decide or do, Dame. *Did* you wish him well?"

"I never spoke to him. He was already gone."

"Less a fool than you, it seems. And now you're hoping for mercy, I suppose."

"Not from you," Frevisse returned, contempt answering contempt.

"That's to the good at least," Domina Alys snapped back, moving aside from her chair to reach behind it and bring out a white birch rod. "Because you're not going to have it. Kneel, Dame."

Around her, Frevisse heard the gasps and startled shifting of alarm among the other nuns, but she was suddenly in a great stillness far apart from everyone around her.

Penance by prayers, penance by fasting, penance by vigils—made rigorous or light as the prioress determined was necessary for burdening the body while the soul sought cleansing—that was what followed confession in chapter, that was what had always been the way in St. Frideswide's. Never whipping.

Whipping was allowed by the Rule but only for the worst of offenses, or when nothing else had worked to turn someone from their sin. Even taken together, Frevisse's offenses were not that grave, and Domina Alys had planned this when she only knew of one. It was not penance she intended. It was humiliation and the end of Frevisse ever daring to challenge her again.

Frevisse saw that in her fierce, pleased smile, and as she

saw it, all the possibility of humiliation fell away from her. Whatever was done to her was going to be done not out of justice but out of Domina Alys' hatred. A hatred Frevisse had not come even close to guessing at until now. A hatred that, in that moment, she was very near to giving her in return.

It scalded up in her, a sickening roil of black desire to hurt as she was going to be hurt, to humiliate the way she was meant to be humiliated, to savage mind and heart and body, even her own, if it meant she could do as much to Domina Alys.

Beside her, Sister Thomasine, seated unmoving until then, reached out a hand and laid it on her arm.

It was the most light of touches, hardly felt through the layers of cloth, but a sickening sense of the black ugliness she was opening her heart and mind to, a clear sight of the corrosion she was asking for her soul wrenched through Frevisse. And deliberately, cold with seeing hatred's possibilities inside herself, colder with how near she had come to them, she turned her back on Domina Alys, knelt, and leaned forward over the stool on which she had been sitting, lowered her head until her forehead pressed against the wood, and gripped two of its legs to steady herself against what would be coming, submitting not to Domina Alys but to her own guilt in being so near so deep a sin.

When it was over and Domina Alys stepped back, not breathing hard despite the strength she had put into it, Frevisse straightened, careful of the pain across her back, rose slowly to her feet, turned, and sat down without a sound or betraying expression. Head raised, her hands up either sleeve to hide her fingers gripped into her forearms in compensatory pain, she stared steadily at nothing across the room while Domina Alys, seated in her chair again, the white birch rod laid across her lap and satisfaction plain in her voice, said, "That was for a beginning. You'll also fast on water and no meat from now to Martinmas, and after that have ale again but still no meat until St. Thomas day, and you will, at the end of chapter meetings and when we leave the refectory after meals and the church after offices, go out first and lie down beside the door until we've passed you, giving what judgment on you we please. That you will do from now until I say otherwise."

Judging by the pleasure in Domina Alys' tight-lipped smile at her, the saying otherwise would be a very long while coming, but Frevisse bowed her head and said, choking only a little on the words, "Yes, my lady."

Finally done with her, for the moment, Domina Alys took up the chapter meeting where it had broken off. With the white birch rod still laid across her lap and satisfaction strong in her voice, she asked if there were any other confessions or any accusations to be made this morning. When silence met the question, she nodded and went forward to the obedientiaries' reports. They were given with almost whispered carefulness, in few words and rapidly. Even when Domina Alys at the end of the cellarer's report informed Dame Juliana that the warmer winter gowns should be given out today after Tierce, there was no stir of response from anyone, even Sister Amicia.

Frevisse, waiting to be called on in her turn, sat motionless, concentrating on wearing down the pain. It had been only twenty strokes, done with only a birch rod and through the layers of her clothing; there would be only swollen welts, no torn flesh or blood. She tried to concentrate on that, on how little it was compared with what it could have been; but Domina Alys had laid the strokes across one another, not side by side, and the deep, crisscrossing pattern of the pain was almost stronger than Frevisse's will against it. When time came for her report, she stood up, wary of moving too much, said carefully what needed to be said—that there were supplies enough for now but the guest halls were presently overburdened with guests beyond the ordinary—and was about to sit down when Domina Alys ordered, "Stay up, Dame."

Frevisse stayed, her gaze fixed to the far wall, while Domina Alys said past her to the others, "Since Dame Frevisse has proven untrustworthy in her duties, her place as hosteler is now Sister Amicia's."

Sister Amicia gave a small squeak of excitement, and for once Domina Alys did not subdue her with even a look. Instead she said at Frevisse, "You have these two days, Dame, to show her what she needs to know. You will leave the cloister to do that, but for no other reason and always with her. When the two days are done, you will not leave the cloister again for any reason at all without I say so."

Frevisse drew her gaze aside from the wall to fix it on Domina Alys' face, her own face and voice utterly expressionless as she answered, "Yes, my lady."

# Chapter

# 12

DOMINA ALYS PRONOUNCED the blessing that closed the chapter meeting—"*Dies et actus nostros in sua pace disponat Dominus omnipotens*. Amen." The almighty Lord order our day and deeds in his peace—without seeming to hear how ill it accorded with the day so far. Frevisse heard but with no urge to laughter. With Domina Alys' gaze on her, she bowed her head at last, crossed the room in front of everyone else, and went out into the cloister walk where golden light from the risen sun was flowing over the roof's ridge into the garth. But the warming room was on the cloister's east side and the walk there was still in shadow, the stones still cold with frost as, with the pain across her back reminding her to make no sudden movement, she eased down to lie with her face to them. The cold went through her clothing into her flesh, and she tried to curb the prideful hope that the other nuns as they filed past her knew her shivering was from the cold, naught else.

She had lain like this before, and so had others of them for one reason or another, but only as a single punishment, not punishment added to punishment, done only once and then ended. She was going to face this eleven times a day from now until Domina Alys tired of it, and she doubted that would be soon.

Striking the offender with a foot in passing was permitted, and Domina Alys, coming first, did so, kicking solidly into her hip, but the blow was sidewise and with only a soft shoe, so there was more intent than hurt in it. No one else touched her. Most of them passed as quickly as they could and as wide from her as might be.

And it would be like that from now on, Frevisse thought bitterly. Maybe no one but Domina Alys would strike at her, but neither would anyone approach her, now or any other time through the days to come. They would avoid her out of fear of Domina Alys' displeasure turning on them as fiercely as it had turned on her, leaving her almost as isolated as if locked away into a room.

As sick with that thought as from the whipping, she gathered her will to face the pain of rising to her feet again. But as she started to rise hands took her under each elbow, helping her. Startled into sudden movement and then wincing from the pain of it, she looked to find Sister Thomasine holding her on one side, Dame Claire on the other. Carefully they helped her to her feet and made sure she was steady before they let her go. Then Sister Thomasine simply—the way that she did everything: prayers and duties and dangerous kindnesses, Frevisse thought—bent her head, tucked her hands into her sleeves, and went away.

Dame Claire, with an expression of rigorous disapproval on her face but not, Frevisse hoped, for her, said, "You'd best come to the infirmary now. I have an ointment that will help your back."

Frevisse shook her head. "I have to see to the guest halls." She looked around. Sister Amicia was standing at the corner of the cloister, nervously shifting from foot to foot, waiting for her.

"They'll keep," Dame Claire said briskly, taking her by the arm again. "You need to have your back seen to."

Frevisse pulled free of her hold. Her precariously begun acceptance of her pain and of what she still had to face was already unbalanced by Dame Claire and Sister Thomasine's unexpected kindness. More kindness might undo her completely, and that she could not afford. If once she gave way, if once she began to bend out of the pride that was keeping her upright and moving, she might collapse into her misery, might break as completely as Domina Alys wanted her to, and so she said, abruptly and ungraciously, "No. Not now. I have to go," and turned her back on Dame Claire's protest, refusing to hear it. She passed Sister Amicia without speaking or looking at her but knew she turned and followed her as behind them Dame Claire said quietly, "When you're ready, then."

The pain in her back and the effort to hide it made it difficult to concentrate on telling Sister Amicia even the simplest things she would need to know and deal with as hosteler. Frevisse had small hope that good would come of Domina Alys' choice. Sister Amicia had never shown strong inclination toward anything but talk and finding reasons to leave the priory on visits to her family. While Domina Edith was prioress, she'd had small indulgence in either, but things had bettered for her under Domina Alys. Silence in the priory no longer burdened her and she had managed to go home twice a year the past two years—and been late by a day or more in returning to St. Frideswide's each time.

Frevisse also saw, with a weary premonition of trouble, how often sister Amicia followed with her eyes, though careful not to turn her head, men as they passed by.

She also noticed how often some men managed to return that notice.

What surprised her was that Sister Amicia seemed actually to hear what she was being told. Once she even asked a sensible question, about how count of the linens was kept. Ela, who at Frevisse's request had been explaining the linen press to her in the unemotioned monotone Ela saved for people with whom she did not want to deal, fixed her with a considering look, answered her, and went on with slightly less constraint.

It was better when after their breakfast Sir Reynold and his men, dressed and armed for riding, left, taking their noise and insolence with them to the outer yard and presumably away. With fewer men around, mostly servants who knew better than to be in Frevisse's way, Sister Amicia's concentration was marginally better, but by then Frevisse was near the end of what she could endure for now. She only barely managed to keep on until the bell began for Tierce, and when she heard it, stopped in mid-sentence a detailing of when and how the hall rushes were changed, to say, "Enough. We'll do more after Sext," hoping that by then she might have found a way to cope with her back's aching and the rest of the day.

As they crossed the yard back to the cloister, Benet overtook them, went past them to reach the door ahead of them and hold it open with a smile. In her surprise at seeing him and with bitter remembrance that there was no injunction against speaking to him outside the cloister, Frevisse said, "You didn't go with Sir Reynold, then."

Benet smiled, rueful. "He thought I might profit more by staying here and seeing Mistress Joice again. It went so well last night, you see." He was reddening. "With Joice."

Bound up in her own worry, Frevisse had hardly thought of Joice since yesterday, but it seemed the girl must have carried the evening through. With a pang for Benet, she brought herself to ask, "You have hope, then?"

Benet's expression mixed a number of things, none of them very clear except, at the end, uncertainty. "I don't know," he said lamely.

Sister Amicia, more than willing to stand there talking than go in to Tierce, chimed in, "At least Lady Adela favors you. She talks about you to everyone."

Visibly embarrassed, Benet said, "I know. Joice told me."

"And Lady Adela is telling everyone else," Sister Amicia assured him cheerfully.

"We'll be late," said Frevisse, partly out of pity for Benet but mostly because what interested her most just now was the coming chance to sit down in the shelter of her choir stall; and she went on into the cloister, Sister Amicia following her, leaving Benet to go his own way.

\*     \*     \*

Neither her choir stall nor Tierce's prayers were the refuge she had hoped for. The pain had subsided into a pervasive ache, deep and ready to rouse to pain again if she moved incautiously. That and awareness of the other nuns' constant looks and sidelong glances toward her through much of the office kept her from losing herself in the prayers and psalms as she had hoped to do. And when, at the end, she went to lie down outside the door, she found her back had stiffened enough there was no way to lie down either gracefully or without pain, nor an easy way to rise when everyone had gone past her. Domina Alys was again the only one to strike her, and again Sister Thomasine was there at the end to help her up, but Dame Claire was not. Illogically angry at her for going on and at Sister Thomasine for waiting, angry, too, at her body for its treachery in stiffening and, more logically at Domina Alys for everything, Frevisse accepted Sister Thomasine's help because she had to and managed to say, when it was done, "Thank you."

Sister Thomasine, starting away after the others, paused to look back shyly around the edge of her veil. "You're welcome," she whispered.

"But you'd best not do it again or she may turn on you next."

Sister Thomasine lifted her head, surprise on her pale face where her overfasting showed in the shadows under her hollowed cheeks. "Oh no," she said as if disbelieving Frevisse could say so strange a thing. "She won't do anything to me." Her shy smile swiftly came and went, and before Frevisse could think of any answer to such certainty, she had lowered her head and was gone after the others.

Frevisse should have gone, too. Dame Juliana was giving out the heavier woolen winter gowns now, something Frevisse would have been eager for this time yesterday. But now, today, even more than being warmer, she wanted to be alone, if only for a little while. There were a few places for that in the cloister. To go to any of them would have looked as if she were hiding. And she would have been. Hiding was exactly what she wanted. But she would not give Domina

Alys the satisfaction of knowing it or the chance to have her hunted out if it were guessed what she was doing, so instead she turned back to the surest refuge, into the church.

It was where she always went by preference when she had the chance or need, usually to her choir stall or else to kneel at the altar in prayer. Today, when she had shut the door between her and the cloister, she simply stayed where she was, leaning against the heavy wood, not even bothering to take her hand from the handle, her eyes thankfully closed now that finally she had no need to move or seem any particular way for anybody. She was alone, with time to gather her strength—not her thoughts, she was tired of trying to think; and not her courage, she was nearly out of that— just her strength to face the rest of the day.

She had been standing there, she did not know how long, sunk as near to mindless as she could come, when Joliffe said close behind her, "Dame Frevisse," concerned.

She had not heard him come, but she was past having strength to be startled. And it had been illogical to hope no one beyond the nuns would come to know what had been done to her. Word had surely gone by way of servants out of the cloister to everywhere in the priory by now; but that did not mean she had to deal with questions, curiosity, sympathy, or anything else that might be offered. Most particularly it did not mean she had to deal with Joliffe, and she said, not moving, not even opening her eyes, "Go away."

"Now, that's unfriendly." He sounded aggrieved and mocking together. "How do you know I haven't come like Sir Orfeo, daring dangers to rescue his lady?"

"I'm not in need of rescuing. And as I recall, he failed."

"Only according to Boethius."

"'Only according to Boethius'?" Frevisse turned around. "*Only* Boethius?" A man held, these hundreds of years past, to be an authority on anything he had chosen to write about?

Joliffe shrugged away her indignation. "He was a philosopher. He only talked to make a point and the points he could make were the only ones he talked about. No, I believe the other way the story is told, that Sir Orfeo won Heurodis free of Faerye. It's much the better story."

"What has 'better' to do with truth?"

"What has truth to do with a good story?"

"And since when," Frevisse said, abruptly changing direction, "did I ever think Sir Orfeo and Heurodis were real, for me to be arguing about them so earnestly?"

"I don't know," said Joliffe lightly.

Frevisse looked at him consideringly and, finding at least the ache in her mind had lessened, said, "Thank you."

Simply, with no trace of his familiar mockery, Joliffe answered, "You're welcome." And then, "Tell me what she did."

Frevisse moved her head slightly side to side, refusing. She did not want to say the words, did not want even the feel of them ugly in her mind. If she could bury the thought of what had been done to her deep enough, it would somehow take the pain away with it. That was not logical, but the pain seemed to leave little room for logic; all she could do was refuse him an answer.

"Say it," Joliffe insisted.

Frevisse turned away from him. Too quickly. The pain caught her to rigid stillness and she had to stand, breathing in short gasps between her teeth, while it subsided. When it had, she turned carefully back to him and said curtly, resenting both him and her own cowardice, "Along with the other punishments of humiliation and losing my place as hosteler, she whipped me."

She was daring him to pity her, ready to be angry if he did; but his level, unreadable look told her nothing, and she added with bitter-edged lightness, "But after all she only used a birch rod on me and it was only twenty strokes, so I suppose I should be grateful for the mercy."

"Only it doesn't feel like mercy, does it?" Joliffe asked, level-voiced.

"No. It feels like pain!"

But as she said it, unable to stop the anger and a surge of too many other feelings, something in Joliffe's face stopped her, held her quiet before she said in a voice that matched his own, "It's been done to you, too, hasn't it?"

Joliffe's eyes widened in openly mocking surprise. "To

me? A wandering player now turned minstrel? Someone no more than half a step off the devil's tail to most people's way of thinking?" He raised his hands at her ignorance. "Why, I've found there are people who seem to feel an absolute obligation to it."

He was laughing at himself and inviting her to laugh with him, but Frevisse no more believed his laughter than she believed his surprise, and did not want to join in it. "What do you do?" she asked.

He shrugged the question away. "Avoid it when I can."

"And when you can't?"

"Like everything else. Endure it. The way you were enduring trying to teach that cow-eyed nun in the guest hall just now."

It was a deft, firm-handed change of topic, and Frevisse let him make it. "St. Frideswide's new hosteler, yes," she said. "I've lost my office, among other things, for my sins."

"A sorry thing, your fall from grace. They were talking of you last night. Your prioress and her cousins in the parlor. At least there was mention of a nun who was forever giving trouble, and I assumed it was you."

"Thank you."

"You're welcome."

"How was it with the girl?" If he could change subjects, so could she.

Joliffe frowned slightly. "My fear would be she'll break just when she most needs her wits about her."

That was Frevisse's thought, too, and she had no answer to it.

"But she kept close in talk with that young Benet last night," Joliffe said. "Is she possibly warming to him?"

"It would help if she did," Frevisse said, and would have said more but behind her the door opened and Dame Perpetua entered, followed by Lady Adela, come to ready things for Sext. She stopped short at sight of Joliffe, a man and someone she did not know; but the nave of the church was open to the priory's guests and Dame Frevisse was still somewhat hosteler, so after her first surprise, she bowed her head to him slightly and went on.

Lady Adela stayed where she was and announced firmly, "You're the minstrel."

Joliffe swept her a low bow, one hand on his heart, the other flung wide as if in surrender to her. "You have it in a word, my lady."

Lady Adela laughed and most improperly dropped a curtsy back to him, so deep he might have been an earl. "I've seen you from Lady Eleanor's window, but they wouldn't let me come to listen to you last night."

"A lady fair in durance vile," said Joliffe. "Shall I sing your plight abroad so your knight may find and rescue you?"

"I don't have a knight," she said regretfully.

"Then I'll sing your beauties everywhere and find you one."

"Lady Adela," Dame Perpetua called.

Lady Adela's brightness disappeared. With the solemness she mostly wore, as if life required a great deal of concentration, she leaned a little toward Joliffe to say, as if Frevisse were not there, "You don't have to find a knight. Just tell Benet Godfrey."

"He'll do?" Joliffe asked as solemnly. He might have been as eleven-years-old as she was.

Lady Adela nodded. Laughter glimmered in her again. "And he's already here, too."

"Lady Adela," Dame Perpetua insisted from the choir.

Lady Adela heaved a sigh seemingly from her toes, called dutifully, "Yes," and went.

Joliffe turned back to Frevisse. "Are they thinking to make a nun of that one?"

"Some are. I'm not."

"Sensible of you." Joliffe made her a bow, far less elaborate than what he had lavished on Lady Adela. "I'll go now."

Frevisse put out a hand, not touching him but stopping him before he turned away. "Thank you for . . ." Drawing her mind aside from her hurting? For making her say what she had not wanted to say? For not overtly pitying her? ". . . For Boethius."

The slightest of smiles curved his mouth. Quietly, devoid of mockery, devoid of everything but understanding, he said, "I know how it bruises the mind along with the body. Both need tending when it happens."

Frevisse nodded, understanding with him. He bowed again and she bent her head to him, and did not watch him go but turned toward the choir, ready to pray now; and after Sext she would go to Dame Claire and let her see to her back and then bespeak a winter gown from Dame Juliana before taking Sister Amicia back to the guest halls.

The west door groaned on its hinges with Joliffe going out—why hadn't she heard him coming in?—and she wished too late that she had thought to ask him if he knew where Sir Reynold and his men had been bound for today.

# Chapter

## 13

FREVISSE DREW HER body's ache slowly up from the cloister walk outside the refectory, letting herself be glad of Sister Thomasine's help. Dame Claire's ointment had eased the hurting and some of the stiffness but not sufficiently that lying down and standing up again were any pleasure. Only twice more today, she thought, nodding her thanks at Sister Thomasine who nodded back and left her. After Vespers and again for Compline. Then there would finally be the relief of going to bed, temporary though it would be and doubtful how easily she would lie. Dame Claire had said she would give her something to help her sleep, but Frevisse was unwilling to risk failing Matins and Laud at midnight, though she anticipated no pleasure in rising for them, or again tomorrow morning, when she had had time truly to stiffen.

She turned her mind away from all that. Those troubles were for later. Just now there was the rest of today to be gone through. She looked toward Sister Amicia waiting nearby and asked, "You're ready to go out again?"

Sister Amicia came forward. "Oh yes." She hesitated,

then said worriedly, "I'm not sure I'm remembering all you've told me."

Frevisse doubted it, too, but Sister Amicia was nonetheless proving better at grasping matters than she had hoped and she said encouragingly, "When the time comes you need it, you'll remember more than you think you do, and what you don't remember, Ela will know and help you with."

Sister Amicia brightened. "Yes. She likes me, I think."

That was more than Frevisse thought, but she was saved from even a noncommittal answer by Lady Eleanor and Joice coming toward her along the walk, Margrete behind them. So far today, since Sext, Frevisse had managed to keep from having to talk to anyone except in the way of her duties, but sympathy was not something she could avoid forever, so she gave in with what she hoped passed as graciously to Lady Eleanor's gentle questioning of how she was, smiled with what conviction she could manage, and answered, "Well enough. Better. And you?"

"Well, thank you. Nothing beyond the ordinary."

Margrete muttered something behind her.

Lady Eleanor, without looking back, said, "That's eased."

"For now," Margrete said in a carrying murmur that Lady Eleanor chose to ignore.

Tactfully, Frevisse did, too, asking Joice instead, "And with you? Did it go well last night?"

There was need to be circumspect, with Sister Amicia there to hear everything and too likely to talk of it later. Joice said, "It was pleasant," almost as if she meant it, but to Frevisse she seemed drawn, tense, and Frevisse wondered how much longer she would be able to keep up this game of pretense.

In an excited whisper Sister Amicia said, looking past Lady Eleanor, "Oh, here's your Benet again!"

Joice stiffened with scorn-edged anger and snapped, "He's not *my* Benet."

But he was there nonetheless, coming into the cloister walk from the outer door. He saw them, his eyes going first to Joice, then to Frevisse, and he hesitated with distressed uncertainty at sight of her. So he had heard, too. To make it easier for him, Frevisse bent her head courteously to Lady Eleanor and said clearly enough for him to hear both what she said and that she said it without anger, "We'll leave you, then. There are things we have to see to in the guest halls."

"Of course," Lady Eleanor responded, matching her courtesy.

"But . . ." Sister Amicia protested.

Frevisse took hold of her sleeve and turned her away. They would go the long way around the walk to the door, leaving Benet to come the short way to Joice and Lady Eleanor.

"But . . ." Sister Amicia tried again, pulling back.

"What happened the last time I talked with Benet in the cloister?" Frevisse asked.

Sister Amicia gulped and went without arguing.

Little was left to show her in the new guest hall. They finished with time enough before Vespers to begin on the older one, but Sister Amicia as they left the new guest hall was wondering aloud not about her duties but why Mistress Joice would want to resist Benet, he was so handsome.

Wondering how Sister Amicia could resist ever having a useful thought in her head, Frevisse did not answer. In fairness—she was just able to be fair but doubted she could keep it up much longer—her irritation was not so much from what Sister Amicia chose to chatter on about but from the day's exhaustion closing in on her rapidly now. She was convincing herself that it would probably be better not to go on to the old guest hall today but save it for tomorrow, when Sister Amicia asked, "What are they doing?"

Hoping it was nothing that would need her, Frevisse asked, "Who?"

"There." Sister Amicia pointed across the yard at the well where a hand count of Sir Reynold's servants were clotted, intent on something in their midst.

"It's no concern of ours," Frevisse said and kept on her way, only to come to a stop between one step and the next and turn toward them after all. She was tired; her mind was moving too slowly and it had taken that long for her to realize that the dirty heap among the men's feet was the madman she had thought long gone since yesterday.

"Oh no," she said.

"What is it?" Sister Amicia asked, somewhere between apprehension and eagerness.

Frevisse went toward the well without answering. Some of the men she recognized from yesterday; others were new to the sport; but all of them were too intent on their game to notice her approach. They had the madman crowded up against the well, hunched down among them, with no way for him to escape even if he had had the wits for it. A few were set down on their heels, prodding at him with daggers that were still sheathed but probably would not stay that way, while the rest were contenting themselves with gibing words and an occasionally shoe to whatever part of him they could easily reach. Frevisse knew how little time it would take for all of that to turn ugly and what would happen when it did. Her father had carried the scar across his shoulders the rest of his life from the time he interfered to save a beggar some men had taken against for no reason except they had nothing better to do. He had managed out of it alive when they turned on him as well, but the parish had had to bury the beggar.

The men here were turning uglier even as Frevisse approached. Someone's boot dug into the madman's haunch hard enough to shift him, and when he tried to scuttle a little sideways he was shoved back, hard enough to knock him over. Above the men's laughter Frevisse ordered, "That's enough now."

A few of them looked at her over their shoulders. Most of them ignored her, and one of the men had unsheathed his dagger now and was flicking the point of it too near the madman's face as he struggled to his knees. The madman threw up an arm to protect himself, and another man put a foot against his ribs and shoved him over. Others joined in, rolling him off the well's top step and down the rest onto the cobbles. Angrily Frevisse started forward, intent on coming between them and the man. Sister Amicia squeaked, "You

can't!" and caught her by the arm while the men, probably
enjoying it more now they had women to watch them being
brave, kept the madman down with kicks and jabs and at
least one more dagger unsheathed. Frevisse pulled loose
from Sister Amicia, ignoring the pain it cost across her back,
and thrust in among them, ordering in open anger now,
"That's enough!," grabbing the nearest of them by the arm
and pulling him around.

He started to swear something at her despite she was a
nun, but above the dark snarl of sound from the other men
still set on the madman, Joliffe asked cheerfully, "Isn't it
late in the day for a hunt?"

They all looked, Frevisse with them, to find him balanced
on the well curb above them, crouched down on his heels
and leaned forward on his toes to see better what they were
doing. He sniffed audibly. "Though I can't deny that the
spoor is still lying strong." He leaned farther, staring with
exaggerated curiosity at the hunched madman among their
legs. "What is it you're hunting anyway? Boar? Hedgehog?" He seemed to overbalance into falling, changed it
with a twist of his body to a light-footed spring to the foot
of the steps, so that the men drew back, grinning. He
sauntered in among them, bent over the madman for a closer
look and said, "No, not boar or hedgehog. Wrong pelt." He
straightened to look around at the men incredulously.
"You're not wanting it for its pelt, are you?"

Most of the men laughed and one made a rude comment
on what they wanted "it" for. Joliffe shook his head in mock
seriousness. "I doubt I can recommend that," he said. "Not
when we don't even know what it is. Dame Frevisse, is this
a common sort of animal around here? Do you know what
it is?"

Following wherever he was taking this, Frevisse came
forward. The men drew back and apart to let her through,
and since it seemed to her the farther they were from the
madman the better, she copied Joliffe's pretense of studying
him while half circling at an overly fastidiousness distance
so that, unwittingly, the men drew back more. Slowly, as if
deeply considering the madman still crouched at Joliffe's

feet, she said, "It does bear some resemblance to something I know. I might . . ." She drew her consideration out, copying her aunt whose indecisions on even the most minor matters had made uncomfortable suspenses for everyone around her. In her aunt's case it had come from a natural incoherency of thought; for Frevisse it was a play for time until Joliffe let her know what he had in mind. He had better have something in mind. She was watching him more closely than she was looking at the madman, and when she was most between him and the men and they least likely to see, he flickered his fingers at her in a horn sign—middle fingers and thumb bent down, the outer two fingers pointed out.

Frevisse recoiled violently, letting her voice scale up in pretended shock. "It isn't! It can't be!" She made the sign of the cross widely in the air between her and the madman. "Blessed St. Anthony against the demons! It's . . . it's . . ."

Joliffe joined in her overplayed horror. "It is!" His sign of the cross was wilder and wider than hers. "You have it!" He struck a pose of shock and dismay. "It's a failed fiend!"

The men were laughing, enjoying the show. Joliffe grabbed the madman under one arm and wrenched him to his feet, exclaiming at Frevisse as if her stupidity stood between them all and salvation, "Don't you see? That explains the stench of hell about it!" He looked around frantically and pointed at the church door. "What it needs is the odor of sanctity!"

Too rapidly for anyone to stop him, he dragged the madman up and along the well steps, outflanking the nearest men, heading for the church's wide west door, close across the yard.

"Wait on!" one of the men called out in surprise. "Where are you going with him?"

Frevisse, following Joliffe with her skirts grabbed up to let her move more quickly, swung around, her hands raised in prayer, between him and the men to exclaim in pious, ringing tones, "We've been in the presence of hell! Pray!

Pray for your souls! St. Anthony, who faced the demons in
the desert, guard us here. St. Amable, who . . ."

The men jostled each other in a confused change of
direction, less interested in their souls than in their escaping
prey; and even though Frevisse slowed them a little, forcing
them to go around her, they would have had Joliffe before
he reached the church and sanctuary, except the madman
somehow managed to break into a run with him, not
fumbling, pulling back, or falling. They reached the door
with time for Joliffe to thrust it open, shove the madman in
and himself after him, and on the safe side of the threshold
lean back out to exclaim cheerfully, "It's all right! I'll see to
him from here!," before drawing back inside and slamming
the door shut for the first of the men to run hard up against
it.

The heavy thud of the bar dropping across it inside told
how thoroughly he had it fast against their fists and angry
yells, leaving Frevisse free to retreat the other way, toward
the cloister, catching Sister Amicia by the arm as she went
with, "We'd best go in, too. Come."

Sister Amicia came, and inside, when Frevisse turned to
bring the rarely used bar there down across the door, was
enough recovered to ask, a little shrill with excitement and
fear, "They wouldn't dare try to come in here, would they?"

The men's pounding yells on the church doors were
muffled but not faint, and Frevisse was about to say that she
did not want to find out the hard way what they would dare,
when behind them in the passageway Domina Alys demanded, "What are you doing? What's toward out there?"

Frevisse and Sister Amicia swung around to face her,
dropping into curtsies, Frevisse answering while they did,
"It's some of your cousin's men. They've hunted a madman
into the church and want him out again for sport."

"They're beating my church door down because they
want sport?" Domina Alys started forward in heavy-treading
fury. "I'll show them sport!"

Frevisse swung around to jerk the door open ahead of her
while Sister Amicia shrank back against the wall, but
Domina Alys as she stalked past them ordered, "Sister

Amicia, come. It you're hosteler, you have to learn how to handle fools and dolts like this!"

Sister Amicia gapcd, then looked to Frevisse, asking help. Frevisse shook her head with none to give, and forced to it, Sister Amicia momentarily shut her eyes, then followed Domina Alys, leaving Frevisse surprised by her for the first time—both that she went and that she did it silently.

Given no other orders herself, Frevisse went the other way, toward the church's cloister door, reaching it as Dame Juliana, Sister Emma, and Sister Cecely came from somewhere else in the cloister, drawn by men's pounding and yells. To their alarmed questions, Frevisse said quickly, "It's only some of Sir Reynold's men making trouble. Domina Alys has gone out to them. She'll—"

The pounding and yells cut off.

Frevisse smiled with more assurance than she felt. "There. You see? It's done. She's taken care of it."

Sister Cecely looked a little regretful and Sister Emma started to protest, but Dame Juliana said, "Good. We can all go back to our work," and firmly shepherded them away despite Sister Emma beginning to protest that, too.

# Chapter

## ◣ 14 ◢

FROM INSIDE THE church, Domina Alys' general fury, if not her actual words, was audible beyond the west door, and Frevisse for once wished her joy of her rage.

Joliffe was partway down the nave, the madman slumped to the floor beside him and Dame Perpetua confronting them both indignantly, with Lady Adela close behind her, intent on missing nothing, and Sister Thomasine, drawn from her prayers, rising from her knees below the altar. Apparently in answer to a challenge Dame Perpetua had made him, Joliffe was saying, "He needs sanctuary. I'm asking it for him."

Dame Perpetua returned stiffly, sounding set on letting them come no further, "He has to ask sanctuary for himself. If he wants it, he has to ask for it."

Joliffe started to answer her, stopped, and bent to take hold of the madman's chin instead, forcing his head up. What the man had briefly shown of wits when he ran was gone now. He was back to being only a dirty heap, his hands clutched to his head, not resisting or, probably, comprehending as Joliffe demanded into his face, "Do you claim sanctuary?" The madman's eyes did not even focus on him, and when Joliffe let him go, his head dropped and bobbled loosely; but Joliffe turned back to Dame Perpetua with, "You see? He nodded. He's asking."

"He never asked anything!" Dame Perpetua protested. "You did that."

"He can't ask," Frevisse said as she joined them. "He never says anything, never makes a sound. But he does need sanctuary until we can find a way to be sure of having him safe away from Sir Reynold's men."

"So I've been told." Dame Perpetua sent a displeased glance toward the west door and granted, equally displeased, "Yes, of course he may stay. It's not as if it were a thing we can refuse, is it, if he needs it. Unless Domina Alys says otherwise," she added for warning. She looked at the madman with unconcealed distaste. "But he'll have to be washed somehow. We can't bear that in here."

Frevisse agreed with that readily enough. The madman's stench—still principally pigsty muck but with undersmells of sweating horse—was thicker with being indoors. It was only by fighting her own disgusted urge to keep her distance from him that she went to take him by the chin and lift and turn his head, to be sure of what she had glimpsed there on the side away from Joliffe: a wide brightness of blood beginning to ooze through the matted hair and encrusted filth above his ear and between his fingers clutched to his head.

"He's bleeding," she said.

"That fool with the dagger." Joliffe shifted so he saw it now, too.

Dame Perpetua made an annoyed sound and pulled a handkerchief from her sleeve, holding it out toward Frevisse without coming nearer, while ordering, "Lady Adela, go find Dame Claire and have her come. Tell her hot water and soap and a cloth and a towel are needed as well as her medicines. You bring them for her."

Swift despite her limp, Lady Adela curtsied and left while Frevisse took the handkerchief, pried the madman's hand enough away from his head so she could slip it under his fingers, and let him go so that whether he knew it or not, he was pressing it over the wound himself. Joliffe circled him, feeling expertly at his sides and back. The madman flinched and cringed but nothing else, and Joliffe said, "I don't feel anything broken but he's probably bruised from the kicks. We can't tell much more until he's been washed. Meanwhile." He hoisted the unresisting madman up to something like his feet. A stone bench ran along the nave wall, meant for the weak and ill to rest during services. There was no place else for sitting in the church besides the floor and the nuns' choir stalls, and Joliffe shuffled the madman aside to it, seated him with a twist and a push, and stepped back, wiping his hands on each other. The madman promptly slumped forward, hands still to his head.

Frevisse had followed, to be sure the handkerchief had not shifted, and when she saw that it was still firmly over the wound, stepped back willingly with Joliffe. Something definitely had to be done about the man's smell.

He was cold, too, shivering in the church's chill. Something better than the coarse-cloth tunic from the alms clothing would have to be found for him. After he was washed.

Behind her, Dame Perpetua asked, "And now?"

The side door slammed open. The madman cringed and huddled farther in on himself, and the rest of them jerked around toward it, to face Domina Alys, flushed with fury and triumph, standing there to judge them all with a single hard look before she swung around to Katerin, crowded close behind her, and said with that odd patience that Frevisse had heard her use before to the woman, "See? All's well. Everything's well. You can go back to your cleaning."

"The men?" Katerin asked worriedly.

"All gone. No one here to hurt me."

Despite Joliffe was plainly there and plainly a man, Katerin with her eyes set doglike to Domina Alys' face accepted that, curtsied with her unsteady bob, and drew back out the door, presumably to her cleaning.

Domina Alys heaved a huge sigh at being finished with that, turned again to survey them all with disapproval, then stalked along the nave toward the madman. Joliffe, skilled at being unobtrusive when he chose, drew smoothly back, giving her space to ignore him if she wished. She did, for now, and instead stopped in front of the unnoticing madman, glaring down at him, fists on her hips, in open disapproval of his existence.

Kept outside behind her and Katerin until then, Sister Amicia came in hastily, still wide-eyed at whatever had passed in the yard, stopped to see who was there and what was happening, then came aside to Frevisse and Dame Perpetua, asking questions with her eyes she did not dare to say aloud. Hardly noticed, Sister Thomasine came to stand on their other side as Domina Alys turned to demand at Frevisse, "He stinks. Where've you been lodging him, Dame? The pigsty?"

All day Frevisse had been praying to be rid of her anger at Domina Alys. The hatred had been strongly enough refused that she was safe from it, she hoped, but all she had been able to do with her anger so far was curb it. Now it started to rouse sharply into words that would have been a mistake to utter. It was Dame Perpetua who saved her, saying hurriedly, quick to appease, "Lady Adela is bringing water and soap for him. And Dame Claire is coming to see to his hurts."

"He's hurt more than his head?" Domina Alys looked with disapproval at the bloodied handkerchief. She had small use for people bothering to be hurt.

"His ribs are maybe bruised," Joliffe said, "but there's nothing broken, I think."

Domina Alys threw him a look that said she did not want to hear what he had to think and ordered at Dame Perpetua, "So have him out of here if that's all it is. Into the kitchen yard, I'd say. Some servant can tend his hurt, feed him, send him on his way."

Dame Perpetua looked at Frevisse, silently pointing out they had a problem now. Domina Alys caught the look and snapped, "What is it?" And when no one answered, "Dame?" dangerously.

Frevisse drew breath to say it, but Sister Thomasine,

aside and silent until then, spoke first, softly. "We've given him sanctuary."

Domina Alys looked in disbelief at—and did not conceal that she was smelling, too—the madman shivering on the wall bench all too near her. "Sanctuary?" she repeated. "Sanctuary to that dirty, stinking rag?" She turned on Frevisse and Dame Perpetua together, leaving Sister Thomasine out of it. "What do you mean, you gave him sanctuary?"

"Those men . . ." Dame Perpetua began, forced into defending what she had done.

Domina Alys was not interested. "I've settled with them. They won't give trouble again." She rammed a finger at the madman. "*That* is the trouble! He's lunatic and stinking and you'll see to his hurt yourself, feed him, and put him out the back gate, on his way before Vespers, and there's an end to it!"

"But if he's come to ask St. Frideswide's aid," Sister Thomasine said, "then we have to let him stay. If he wants to pray here, we can't put him out."

The madman lifted his head to look at her, out of the dirty mask of his face and tangled hair, his eyes staring directly, brightly at her; and she looked back at him, not wavering, repeating, "If he wants to pray here, we have to let him stay. We can't refuse anyone who wants to pray."

It was true enough but not something Domina Alys wanted to hear, and she began sharply, "He can't pray. He doesn't even know . . ."

The madman rose to his feet, the bloodied handkerchief clutched in his hand. "Pray," he croaked.

Frevisse gasped and crossed herself, and on either side of her, Sister Amicia and Dame Perpetua did likewise.

"Pray," the man repeated, more strongly.

"Yes," Sister Thomasine agreed. "Pray."

More quickly than anyone could have moved to stop him, he darted away at a stooping run up the nave. Domina Alys made a raged outcry and started after him, then caught herself back, apparently remembering that running after a madman was not part of a prioress's dignity or duty, and snapped at Joliffe, "You brought him in. Fetch him back here. *Now*."

"Not from the altar," Sister Thomasine said calmly.

The madman had reached it, gone up its steps, was crouched beside it, clutching at the altar cloth like a small child to a mother's skirts. A lunatic, filthy child and all too likely to pull everything down on top of him. Too impatient to wait for someone to obey her, Domina Alys started after him herself.

Dame Perpetua flung out a hand to stop her. "He spoke!"

Brought up short, Domina Alys stared at her.

"He spoke!" Dame Perpetua insisted.

Urgently Frevisse explained, "He's never spoken before."

Domina Alys turned on them both. "What?"

"He spoke," Frevisse repeated. "Even when the men were at him, he never made even a sound."

Domina Alys frowned, absorbing that, and looked along the nave toward the altar and madman. "He's never spoken?"

"Never," Dame Perpetua said. Her voice trembled.

"He didn't even cry out when the men were hurting him," Sister Amicia said, her voice trembling.

"That has to mean he couldn't," Dame Perpetua said, the beginning of awe in her voice. "Now he's crying out for prayers. He's praying at the altar!"

He was not. He was clutching the altar cloth, silent again, but he *had* spoken. They had all heard him. And although a paternoster while ago he had hardly had wits enough to hold his own head up, they had seen him go, run, of his own will, to the blessed shelter of the altar. They had *seen* him.

With the same willingness to awe as Dame Perpetua, Sister Amicia whispered, "A miracle."

# Chapter

## 15

A SHIVER OF possibility went up Alys' spine. A miracle. A healing. Here in St. Frideswide's. When word of it went out . . .

Dame Claire came in from the cloister, her box of medicines in her arms, and behind her was Aunt Eleanor with Margrete, and Lady Adela with a ewer and clean cloths, and behind her that girl Joice who was making so much trouble but being useful now, carrying a basin of steaming water.

Taking the matter in hand, Alys pointed them toward the altar. "He's there. Dame Perpetua, go with them. Sister Thomasine, stay with me. Sister Amicia, you stay by the door and make certain no one else comes in." Dame Claire and the others had surely been noticed crossing the cloister, and the curious would not be far behind them. Alys did not want the complication of them just yet, not until she had things thoroughly in hand here. She gave a sharp nod at the minstrel, letting her displeasure show, and said, "Dame Frevisse, see him out of the cloister and quickly." And as an afterthought: "Sister Amicia, send someone for Father Henry." Even if it were only Father Henry, it would not hurt to have a priest to testify to everything. Followed by Sister Thomasine, she followed the others to the altar to take over matters there, in time to hear Dame Perpetua exclaiming to them, "He's not mad anymore! He talks now. Sister Thomasine . . ."

"Dame Perpetua!" Domina Alys snapped her short. "There'll be time enough for that later."

She knew the questions that would have to be asked and answered: How long had the fellow been possessed? Who was he? Who knew him? The more important the people who knew him, the better the miracle, and if this proved to be a great enough miracle—or, better, if more miracles followed it—she would have no more worry over the tower or anything else. There would be pilgrimages to here, and pilgrimages meant offerings, gifts, money enough for the tower, for its bells, for a gilded weathercock if she wanted it. Money enough for everything she meant St. Frideswide's to have.

But for now she had to see to this miracle, such as he was, kneeling with one filthy shoulder leaned against the green damask altar cloth—probably dirtying it, but that did not matter now—one hand fisted into its hem, the other pressing a bloodied handkerchief to the side of his head while Dame Claire tried to gentle it away to come at the wound. Her box of medicines was set beside her and the girl Joice was near it, holding the basin of water and a soaked cloth ready for when Dame Claire would need it. Lady Adela hovered close behind them, but since she had set down the ewer and cloths beside Joice, she was not needed there, and Alys ordered, "Lady Adela, go to Lady Eleanor, out of the way." At least Aunt Eleanor, Dame Perpetua, and Margrete had sense enough to stand aside. Or maybe it was just the smell that kept them at bay. Well, if they wanted the odor of sanctity about the man, they were going to have to wait for it.

But the child had not shifted and Alys turned a hard stare on her. "Lady Adela, don't make me tell you twice."

Lady Adela's outthrust lower lip told she was about to be stubborn, but Dame Perpetua called, a little desperately,

"Come here now, child. You've been told. You'll be sent away altogether, you go on like this."

Lady Adela shared an unfriendly look between her and Alys and ungracefully obeyed.

Putting the thought away for later that Lady Adela was someone else who was going to have to be dealt with and probably soon, Alys moved in close on Dame Claire, who had the man's hand away from his head now and was beginning to wash the blood and dirt out of his matted hair so she could find where he was hurt.

"Keep him from bleeding on things if you can help it, Dame," Alys said for the sake of saying something. Dame Claire gave no sign of hearing her but just now that did not matter. Let her see to the hurt. Alys would see to the rest. She drew back, away from his smell. It would be better when he had been cleaned. They could see more clearly what they had then. "Dame Perpetua, go find some kitchen folk to bring a tub of water from the laundry, large enough to wash him in. Hot water, mind you, and soap and towels and plenty more rags."

Dame Perpetua momentarily stared at her, then exclaimed, "You're going to have him washed here? In the *church*? All else aside, it's nearly time for Vespers!"

Alys had forgotten Vespers. Dame Perpetua was right, there would not be time to have the fellow scrubbed like he needed to be before Vespers. But neither did Alys mean to pray with the smell of him for company. Either Vespers would have to go elsewhere or he would.

But that did not excuse Dame Perpetua speaking out at her that way, and she said coldly, letting her displeasure show, "You forget your place, Dame. No, not in the church. In the warming room. Give order for the fire to be laid there while the water is being brought and then stay to oversee it all."

Dame Perpetua flinched at the warning but still held back, seemingly unable to believe what she was being told, until Alys snapped, "Dame!" She flinched again at that, dropped hurriedly into a low curtsy, and fled, Alys calling after her,

"When he's clean and Vespers is over, I want him back here at the altar and no delay. You understand?"

"Yes, my lady," Dame Perpetua called back, not slowing. Good. Someone at least could learn their lessons.

Beside her, Aunt Eleanor asked mildly, "You mean to keep him in the church, then?"

From someone else that would have been too close to criticism, but Alys answered her readily with, "How much did Dame Perpetua manage to tell you about what happened?"

"Enough, I think. The man was lunatic and mute, and after Sister Thomasine spoke to him, he has his wits back." Aunt Eleanor glanced toward the limp, dirty figure letting Dame Claire do what she wanted to him. "A little," she amended. "Enough that he could speak and ask for prayers and go to the altar."

"But you see the rest of it?" Alys asked. "It's not going to matter anymore that all we've ever had here is one of St. Frideswide's fingerbones! It's never done aught for us anyway. What I have now is far better than it's ever proved to be." All of a saint's power to bless and protect was supposed to be as present in the smallest part of her as in the whole, but Alys had never seen any particular good come from their tiny bit of bone. She looked aside to Sister Thomasine, standing where she had stopped after following Alys up the church. As always, she was simply there, head bowed, hands folded, so lost in prayers she hardly heard anything that happened around her. A thin little nothing of a nun, that's what she looked like, but Alys had known what she was, had always known. She had thought Aunt Eleanor would realize it now, too, but her aunt's expression was more blank than comprehending and Alys leaned close to whisper, just between them—it was not something servant or child needed to know yet: "She's a saint. You see it? She spoke to a madman, and despite all the powers of the devil and demons inside him, he spoke back. He answered her and asked for prayers. He's her first miracle and if she can do one miracle, she can do more."

She drew back, to enjoy Aunt Eleanor's wonder, but what

there was of it was too slight, too questioning. "You really mean to keep him in the church, then?" she repeated.

"In the church. Here at the altar." Alys was beginning to be impatient. She had expected her aunt to grasp it easily, even if no one else did. "It's done in other places." The sick—and most particularly the lunatic—were allowed to stay at the altar or the saint's tomb through a night or even nights and days together while they prayed and were prayed for.

Aunt Eleanor nodded, understanding that at least, but then said slowly, "In the great pilgrimage churches, yes, it's done."

"And it can be done here!" Alys cried, forgetting to hold her voice down. That was exactly the point. Was she the only one who could see it? "This madman is the beginning for St. Frideswide's and he'll stay here at the altar for as long as it takes Sister Thomasine to pray him back to his full wits!"

Softly, without raising her head, Sister Thomasine murmured, "I won't."

Alys turned to stare at her, blank-minded with surprise, then jerked her wits back together. Aware that everyone else except the madman was staring, too, she demanded, "What do you mean, you won't? You won't what?"

"I won't pray for him to be healed," Sister Thomasine said as quietly, still without raising her head.

Anger began to overtake Alys' disbelief. Her voice rising, she demanded, "You're telling me you won't pray for him?"

She had thought after the lesson she had given on Dame Frevisse this morning no one would dare to cross her for a long, long while to come. For it to be Sister Thomasine—*Sister Thomasine* . . .

"Alys," Aunt Eleanor said, "she's saying she won't pray simply for him to be healed. She *will* pray for him. You will pray, won't you, Sister Thomasine?"

Sister Thomasine raised her head and looked with clear, untroubled eyes, first at Aunt Eleanor and then at Alys. "Yes. Of course I'll pray for him," she said simply.

Relieved, shaken, fighting the trembling that was always the aftermath of her rages, Alys accepted that with relief. But why did people have to drive her into these angers to begin with?

From the altar, Dame Claire said, "I've cleaned enough of the blood and dirt away to see the wound isn't much."

Willing to be distracted, Alys turned away from Sister Thomasine to ask, "He'll be all right?" Reynold's men had better pray he was.

"I've an ointment for it, and if the wound is kept clean, he should do well enough."

"We'll keep it clean enough," Alys promised grimly. "Is he hurt aught else?"

"He doesn't seem to be." Dame Claire set her hand under the man's chin and tried to raise his head. He resisted but she forced him with, "Let me see you." There had been only scrubbing enough yet to have the wound clean, but she had shoved his matted hair back while she did it, so that for the first time his face showed, and she made him look at her while she asked as impatiently as if he were just any patient resisting her help, "Do you hurt anywhere besides your head?"

"No," he said hoarsely, pulled free, and tucked his head low again.

Dame Claire forced the cloth she had been using on him into his hand. "Wash your face then while I find the ointment."

He tried to resist that, too, but she warned sternly, "There won't be prayers for someone as ungodly filthy as you are. Wash." Not straightening up, the man fumbled with the cloth and began to rub at his face, somewhat unpurposefully.

The girl Joice shifted away from Dame Claire to hold the basin where he could use it more readily. No, Alys saw she was doing more than simply that—she was kneeling so low she could look up into his face. And Alys felt the spur of another hope. The girl had proved to be nothing but stubborn since she had come, had shown small sign that

Alys could see of warming to Benet at all. Now here she
was, after hardly looking at Benet, all but worshiping this
dirty lump of a man. What if it turned out it had not been
Reynold's doing at all that brought her here, but God's?
What if she was meant to be here for this miracle, to be
changed by it, to choose not Benet but nunhood in St.
Frideswide's? If she had the dowry Reynold said she did
and she chose to become a nun . . .

"Alys," Aunt Eleanor said.

Alys turned to find one of the kitchen women standing a
respectful distance off, wanting to be noticed.

"Yes?" Alys said impatiently.

"The bath is ready," the woman said, making a quick
curtsy with the words. "Dame Perpetua said to tell you."

"Good. Stay. You can help see him there. Dame Claire?"

"Done for now," Dame Claire said, just smearing ointment on the cut. "I'll put more on when he's been bathed,
but this will serve until then."

She stoppered the jar and put it back in her box of
medicines while Alys advanced to the foot of the altar steps
and ordered, "Fellow, look at me."

He did, for what it might be worth. He was still vile to the
eye and nose and had mostly only smeared the dirt with the
little washing he had done, but at least he had responded to
her, and with the loud encouragement she would have used
on a dog she meant to grasp at least something of her
meaning, she said at him, "You understand what you have to
do now? You're going to have a bath. You're going to be
cleaned so you can stay here in the church. They're going to
take you away for your bath and then bring you back and
you'll be fed and seen to and Sister Thomasine will pray for
you. You understand that?"

She was nodding at him while she said it and he was
nodding back, nod for nod, so there was hope he understood,
and she gestured the kitchen woman forward, ordering,
"Help him up. See him out. Go with him, Dame Claire. And
send someone to see what's keeping Father Henry."

She drew back and left them to it. The kitchen woman

came readily, probably curious enough by now from what
she must have heard from Sister Amicia and Dame Perpetua
not to mind the smell. Between them, she and Dame Claire
helped the man to stand and brought him down the altar
steps. As they passed her, Alys, drawing back, saw he was
shivering and ordered, "See to it he's better clothed before
you bring him back here. A cloak or something."

"Yes, my lady," the kitchen woman answered, but Joice
quickly set aside the basin and rose, sweeping off her
yards-of-green wool cloak—Reynold had to have the right
of it; her people must be wealthy—as she followed them
down the steps. "Mistress Southgate," Aunt Eleanor said, in
a tone meant to warn her off, but Joice swung the cloak
around the madman's shoulders, filthy though they were,
enveloping him. Frightened or wary, likely, he jerked as if
to twist free of it, but Joice laid a hand on his back in
reassurance and even dared to meet his startled eyes in a
long look before she drew aside, leaving him to go on with
Dame Claire and the other woman.

"Joice," Aunt Eleanor said, calling the girl to her as Lady
Adela went to take Joice's hand, asking, "Couldn't we go
with him, too?"

"No," Aunt Eleanor and Alys said together. What Joice
would have said was cut off by the cloister bell beginning to
ring to Vespers. Sister Thomasine immediately turned away
toward her choir stall; and Aunt Eleanor, taking the bell for
cue, came to take Lady Adela's other hand, saying firmly,
"What we'll do is pray for him. That will do him the most
good. Come along."

Lady Adela's lower lip went out in sign of coming
stubbornness, but Joice said, "That would be good," and
held between them, Lady Adela submitted, going away
down the nave with her and Aunt Eleanor, Margrete
following, so that Alys was free to swing her attention
toward the cloister door where the incoming nuns were
making a confusion, more interested in having a look at the
madman that clearing the way for him. Alys advanced on
them, ready to give them both sides of her tongue and
enough of her mind that after this they would think twice

before having anything but prayers in their heads once the bell rang for an office. St. Frideswide's had finally been blessed like it deserved, and by blessed St. Frideswide, they were going to start being worthy of it, like it or not.

# Chapter

# 16

As FREVISSE LED Joliffe out of the church, willingly leaving Domina Alys to make whatever she would of the madman, Sister Amicia was already fending off Sister Emma and Sister Cecely's attempt to go in with, "You can't. I told you. She said no one. She'd be angry."

Probably reminded by sight of Frevisse what Domina Alys' anger could lead to, they passed quick looks among them and fell to an embarrassed silence that Frevisse gave no sign of noticing; nor sign that she saw their looks change again as Joliffe came out behind her, merely bent her head to them slightly as she passed. But behind her Joliffe said in a deliberately deepened, mellowed voice, "Good day to you, my ladies," bowing low without losing stride as he passed.

Knowing too clearly what effect that would have, Frevisse walked faster, leaving Sister Cecely's beginning giggles behind, saying at Joliffe without turning her head, "You're not helping things here."

"Of course I am. Now they'll have something new to talk on."

"They *have* something new to talk on. We have a madman in the church."

"A cured madman," Joliffe pointed out.

Frevisse was not ready to think about that yet. The complications that would come if it were true were too many. "I thought you were going to see him out of here and away yesterday."

"I did. I thought I had. He must have come back on his own." The protest was real, but then Joliffe shifted his voice to profound piety and added, "It has to be God's will he's here."

Goaded, Frevisse swung around to tell him what she thought of people who invoked "God's will" whenever they did not want the responsibility of dealing with things gone ill, but the sharp movement startled pain across her back and she went very still, waiting for it to subside.

Joliffe froze with her then said quickly, "I'm sorry. I shouldn't have done that."

She managed something toward a smile. "It was my own doing."

"Then is it safe to mention that I think I'd rather not go out this way?" He nodded ahead of him toward the door into the guest-hall yard. "There are likely to be men out there who aren't too happy with me at present."

Chagrined she had not thought of that, Frevisse said, "The kitchen yard instead," and started to go on around the cloister walk, meaning to let him out through the kitchen passage, but stopped short again—more carefully—to ask, "Your lute. Your other things. Are they somewhere the men could come at them?"

"There's nothing of mine they can come at," Joliffe said cheerfully. "Master Porter asked me last night if I would prefer his masons' company to Sir Reynold's, and the choice wasn't hard. My lute and all are in the masons' lodge and very safe."

"Then you'd do better to go out through the orchard rather than the kitchen yard," Frevisse said, thinking aloud.

"A quiet walk in an autumn orchard with a lovely lady," Joliffe said. "Yes, that will do well."

"I'll go so far as to take you to the gate and see you out,"

Frevisse said dryly, not to be drawn again. "You'll have to do your walking on your own."

They had come almost around the cloister to the slype, the narrow passage out to the walled path that ran along the gardens to the orchard gate. The other nuns' voices were rising shrill, with Sister Johane come from somewhere to join the excited talk outside the church door, and Frevisse turned down the passage with relief. Joliffe followed her without comment or question, still a few proper paces behind her, through the slype and along the path to the gate, where she turned to face him again, saying, "The gate is locked and Domina Alys has the key, but I don't suppose it will bother you to climb the wall."

"Not in the slightest," he assured her, his face alight with silent laughter. "Only tell me before I go, are those the women you're penned in with all the time? Is it always like this?"

"It can't be always like this," Frevisse pointed out. "We've not had a madman in the church before and it seems to me that that was your doing."

"But your prioress isn't. God's mercy, how did you come to vote her into office?"

"I didn't," Frevisse answered curtly.

Suddenly unlaughing, Joliffe agreed, "No. I don't suppose you did."

They regarded each other silently for a moment, before Frevisse said, "You'll take word to Mistress Southgate's people and our abbot when you leave here?"

"Assuredly."

"I've no way to pay you for it," she began.

Joliffe dismissed that with a hand over his heart and a deep bow. "I'll do it for nothing else than the pleasure of thwarting your prioress. And Sir Reynold, too, come to that." He eyed the wall, gauging its height. "This wall must be meant only for keeping nuns in, because there's hardly enough of it to keep anyone out." He stretched up a hand, easily reaching its top, then turned to her again. "If you need to see me before I've gone . . ."

"There won't be any way for me to talk with you after

this. Sister Amicia has to be with me whenever I leave the cloister, and after tomorrow I won't be allowed out of it at all, and from now on, for a time at least, Domina Alys will surely keep the church door to the yard barred to protect her madman. You won't be able to come in."

Joliffe dismissed all that with a gesture. "There's always the tower."

"Yes," Frevisse agreed. "There's the tower. I can go to its top and call across the rooftops for you. Except there's no way in for me."

For a grown man, Joliffe's smile could take on all of a small boy's mischief. "Secrets, my lady. There are always secrets. You know those boards covering the doorway into the choir? If you take good hold of them on one side, lift a little, and pull, they swing open just wide enough for someone not too broad to go through into the tower. Then all you need do is go up the stairs inside and down the scaffolding outside and there I am."

"Oh, yes," Frevisse said, covering her alarm and sudden speculations—who else knew that, had used it, for what, and how had Joliffe come to know of it?—with mockery. "I'm likely to do that. Why isn't there a secret door directly through the tower's outer wall, too, and save the trouble of stairs and scaffolding?"

"Secret doors through stone are so difficult to manage," Joliffe said, matching her mockery. "I gather the masons aren't being paid enough to take the trouble of making one."

"They weren't paid to take the trouble of making this one!"

"From what Master Porter says," Joliffe returned, turning away to gauge how much a scramble he needed to reach the top of the wall, "they're not being paid at all for anything."

"What?" Frevisse asked sharply.

Surprised by her surprise, Joliffe turned back to her. "You didn't know?"

"That they aren't being paid? No, I didn't know. Surely they haven't done all this building unpaid?"

"Assuredly they've been paid something or you'd not have as much of a tower as you do. But you're not going to have much more. Wages aside, they're nearly out of stone and your prioress doesn't seem inclined to pay for more."

Inclined—or able to? It was two Sundays since Domina Alys had allowed them their weekly afternoon walk in the orchard to admire how the tower went. It had been nearly to the church's eaves then, a bulk of stone crowned by a network of scaffolding, and Frevisse had understood the plan was for it to be finished and roofed before freezing weather could bring an end to the work. But they had not been allowed near it that day or out to see it since; and now that Frevisse came to think about it, Domina Alys no longer said anything about the work except when forced to it.

"If they're nearly out of stone and they haven't been paid," she said, inadvertently thinking aloud, "then—" She heard herself and stopped.

"Then you're going to end up with an unfinished tower and some very angry masons," Joliffe finished for her.

They regarded each other silently a moment, both of them considering what could come of that, before she said, subdued, "You'd best go."

He nodded, made a small leap to grab the top of the wall, and with a deft-footed scramble was over and gone.

Frevisse stayed where she was, trying to sort into sense what Joliffe had told her and what had happened in the church and everything else she was becoming afraid of in St. Frideswide's. But it would not sort to sense and finally, no nearer to quiet of mind, she walked slowly back along the garden wall and through the slype, into the cloister walk just as Katerin began to clang the bell for Vespers.

The day was almost finished. Vespers, supper, an hour's recreation, Compline prayers, and it was done.

It was a day she was desperately ready to have end, and her impatience stirred at finding her way into the church blocked by other nuns clustered just inside the door, apparently more interested in being in her way than going to their places in the choir. But beyond them Domina Alys' voice was raised, sorting them out in no uncertain terms, so that abruptly they were shifting aside, and Dame Claire and Bess from the kitchen were coming out, holding up the

shambling madman between them, on their way to somewhere with him.

Moving out of their way, Frevisse asked, "Where are you
taking him? Has Domina Alys given up on him? He can't
just be turned loose again."

The madman raised his loosely hanging head and looked
at her, the first time she had ever had chance to see his face
clearly. Its lack of the unnatural childness so many of the
wandering mad carried with them startled her. Instead, it
was the face of a man who had had some sort of life worth
living before the madness came on him; a young man's face
but marked by years lived, rather than wandered through
unthinkingly. And there was more sanity in the eyes that
looked out at her from under the strong-boned line of his
brows than could have been there an hour ago; but only for
an instant. Then they lost focus again, the brief sense in
them blurring, and his head fell loosely forward as Dame
Claire said, "Domina Alys has ordered he's to have a bath,
be fed, and cleanly clothed."

"And then?" Frevisse asked.

"Then he's to be brought back into the church."

She and Bess had kept him moving, were past Frevisse by
then, and she turned to go into the church. If he was to be
brought back here to stay, it had to mean that Domina Alys
was seriously thinking there had been a miracle. Frevisse
wished she could feel some warmth of pleasure at that
possibility, but just now all that rose up in her was a weary
contemplation of the complications there could be from it. A
miracle was not something simply to be accepted and
exclaimed over. A seeming miracle had to be judged,
considered, proven. There would have to be explanations
to the abbot, even to the bishop, if it went that far, and
then intense investigations by churchmen from outside St.
Frideswide's. Was Domina Alys seriously considering opening them up to all of that, particularly given everything else
that was presently so wrong?

She was following the other nuns toward the choir when
a smother of noise from the yard warned that Sir Reynold
and his men were returned. She shut her mind to it as

another thing she could do nothing about. Mercifully she was done with them for today, and after tomorrow she would not have to deal with them again. But as she passed Lady Eleanor, Lady Adela, and Joice, standing together with Margrete a little behind them in the nave waiting for Vespers, a heavy-handed pounding started on the west door and everyone swung in confusion to face it, with small shrieks among the nuns and Joice shrinking a wild step backward, except Domina Alys who stormed down from her choir stall, ordering, "Margrete, go open it!"

Used to being given orders, Margrete hurried to obey, with Lady Adela following her, as Lady Eleanor put a steadying hand on Joice's arm, and Domina Alys snapped, "The rest of you, into your places! Whoever's doing that had better pray he has a good reason or he'll still be sorry a week from now!"

The nuns were still sorting out their exclamations and not yet in their stalls as Margrete swung the bar aside and Lady Adela pulled open the door. A wide swathe of golden afternoon light swept down the nave, startling the church's shadows, then was broken as a man burst into the doorway, a dark shape against the light, crying out before Domina Alys could yell at him, "There's a man hurt! Sir Reynold wants your infirmarian!"

"Is it Sir Reynold?" Domina Alys demanded, starting for him.

"Sir Hugh?" Lady Eleanor asked with equal urgency.

"Not them, no." The man was short of breath with urgency. "It's Godard. They're taking him into the guest hall. He's bad hurt."

"Sister Amicia." Domina Alys chose the nun nearest her. "Go tell Dame Claire she's wanted." She swung to find Frevisse. "You, hie to the guest hall and see to what needs doing there. You." She pointed at the man. "Tell Sir Reynold we're coming."

The man was hurriedly bowing as he retreated. Frevisse, following him, heard Domina Alys say behind her, "There's still Vespers to do, the rest of you. Dame Juliana, see to it. And no scanting!"

There were fewer men and horses in the yard than Frevisse had expected, but the servants, crowded at the top of the guest-hall stairs, trying to see in or go in all at the same time, slowed her. She gave orders that cleared them out of her way, sending some for hot water and to be sure the kitchen fire was kept up for more, another for towels, another for rags, the rest simply to stand aside, and all the while she was hoping this was not as bad as the man had made it sound.

It was.

Inside the hall, near the hearth, a half dozen of Sir Reynold's men were gathered apart from Sir Reynold and Sir Hugh who were supporting a man between them more as if he were a deadweight than a live one. There was blood on the man's right side and on Sir Hugh holding him there, and as a hall servant dragged one of the straw-filled pallets that served as beds for the servants and lesser guests on the hall floor at night to lay it in front of them, Sir Reynold and Sir Hugh looked at each other over Godard's head, made silent agreement, and in a single concerted motion shifted their holds, Sir Reynold loosing him to bend and take him behind the knees and lift while Sir Hugh caught him by both shoulders from behind, so that together they swung him sideways and down onto the mattress. Godard cried out and his body spasmed with pain, but he was down and Sir Reynold let him go and stepped back, wiping sweat from his own face. Sir Hugh stayed where he was, kneeling with Godard leaning back against him, saying, "We have to have your doublet off. It's better we do it now before we lay you down than have to lift you up again."

Godard, his eyes shut, his face clay gray, groaned acceptance, and Frevisse turned away to find something, anything, that needed her across the hall.

Beyond telling Ela to have wine ready—"Dame Claire will want it to mix with what she'll give him for the pain"—there was nothing except shifting the servants with naught to do clear of the doorways and well aside from Sir Reynold's men and back from what was happening. There was no point in sending them away, but they did not need to crowd in on it.

By then Domina Alys was come, was standing with Sir Reynold away from his own men and the servants both, and Godard, with Sir Hugh holding his head, was stretched out flat on the pallet, the bloody leather doublet thrown aside but the wound still hidden by a wad of blood-bright cloth that had maybe been someone's shirt. Sir Hugh was bent over him, saying something that was lost under Godard's racked breathing, but Godard was still conscious enough to twitch his head in slight answer to it.

"Where's Dame Claire?" Domina Alys said at no one in particular, then looked around, saw Frevisse, and demanded, "Where is she?"

Frevisse went forward, about to answer pointlessly that Dame Claire was surely coming, when Dame Claire was there, flushed and short-breathed with haste, carrying her box of medicines. With heed for nothing else, she passed servants, Frevisse, and Domina Alys to kneel beside Godard who opened his eyes and turned his head toward her with a desperate look. She laid a hand on his shoulder as if in reassurance she was truly there, spoke to him, then to Sir Hugh, asking questions. As she began, still questioning Sir Hugh, to loose the wadded cloth from his side, Godard shut his eyes and turned his head away.

Domina Alys, not heeding or else not minding that Frevisse and probably the hall servants were near enough to hear, asked at Sir Reynold, "What happened? Was it a fall? His horse went down on him?"

Sir Reynold made a disgusted sound. "It was some fool of a villein with a shovel. His side is all smashed in."

"One of our people?" Domina Alys asked, sounding somewhere between disbelief and anger. "One of our villeins? Why? If it was one of ours, I'll make the fool sorry. . . ."

"There's no making him more sorry than I have," Sir Reynold said grimly. "I left him dead on his doorstep."

Frevisse's gasp was covered by Domina Alys', before,

too disbelieving for anger yet, Domina Alys demanded, "You killed him? You *killed* him?"

Sir Reynold shrugged. "He struck Godard and I struck him. He's dead."

Disbelief was going to anger now. "You'll have the crowner and the sheriff on your neck before you can turn around, if that's what you've done! You'll have them on *my* neck! And if he isn't one of ours, he'll have to be paid for!"

"No one is paying anything for his filthy carcass," Sir Reynold answered harshly. "I gave him what he had coming."

"He's maybe not dead." That Domina Alys was searching for a better side to it betrayed she knew exactly how much trouble this could be.

"He's dead. I laid his guts open."

Domina Alys tried a different way at it. "Why did he attack Godard? What was he doing? Where was this?"

"Some village. I don't know." Sir Reynold shrugged off the questions.

"One of our villages?" Domina Alys persisted.

Frevisse knew what she was trying for. St. Frideswide's had property in more than one place. If the dead villein belonged to the priory, the whole thing could maybe be handled without the worst that could come of it, so far as Domina Alys was concerned.

"Not one of yours," Sir Reynold answered impatiently. "Why would we be taking from one of yours? Where would be the sense of that?"

"Taking?" Dame Alys repeated blankly.

Sir Reynold flung a hand toward the outer door. "The carts are somewhere. They're coming. That's where most of the men are, guarding them. We brought Godard on ahead but they'll be here. Food. Fodder. What you've been asking for. What I promised."

Domina Alys grabbed his arm and jerked him around to face her. "What do you mean *'taking'*?"

Sir Reynold jerked loose from her hold. "They're not likely to *give* it, are they?"

"Nor sell it," said Master Porter from their other side,

"because what good is money if there's no food to buy with it once yours is sold?"

Frevisse had seen the master mason come in, sidling behind the gathered servants near the door and joining Sir Reynold's men without drawing anyone's particular notice. He was a short man, squared and solid as one of his own stone blocks and looking the shorter among the tall Godfreys around him, still wearing his coarse workman's apron and with stone dust graying his hands, hair, and clothing to set him more apart, but he showed no sense that he was less than anyone there as he looked assessingly at Sir Reynold and added with what came perilously near contempt, "Not that you likely offered to pay."

"There'd have been no point in my offering, would there?" Sir Reynold returned. Frevisse guessed that they had confronted each other before and not enjoyed the encounter. "And why pay when they give readily enough if they're left no choice? Besides, it was only the one fool that gave trouble. Fifteen armed men in his yard and he tells us no. What did he think was going to happen when he did for Godard?"

"Eh, well," Master Porter said, cocking his head, "people tend to take it badly when you go stealing from them when they don't have enough to start with."

"If they can't hold on to it, why should they keep it?" Sir Reynold asked back sharply.

"So they can be alive come next spring to grow you some more! The starved dead won't work. Or the unpaid," he added at Domina Alys.

She started to answer, chewed air a moment, bit down on whatever she had been about to say, and turned on Sir Reynold instead, snapping at him, "That's none of it to the point now. There's no way we can keep the crowner and the sheriff out of this, and once they're in it, the abbot will know and then the bishop, and what am I supposed to say about you being here and that girl and everything else?"

"There are ways around a thing like this," Sir Reynold said dismissively. "Money does it. Your crowner in these parts is fond of it and probably your sheriff is, too."

"Do you have money?" Domina Alys demanded. "I'd be pleased to hear it if you do, because I surely don't!"

"If you're so set on thieving," Master Porter put in, "why don't you thieve me some stone? Likely folk will part with that readier than food. As it is, this tower of yours is going no higher, that's sure."

Sir Reynold looked at him with sudden interest. "There's building going on in Banbury. We could maybe—"

"No!" Domina Alys cut him off. "No more thieving! No more killing! There's going to be trouble enough without more."

From where he still knelt with Godard's head in his lap, Sir Hugh said low-voiced, angry and showing it, "Take it outside if you can't keep it down!"

Godard groaned. Only the men's grip on him kept him from writhing away from Dame Claire. Domina Alys cringed and drew slightly back, looking away, then, as Godard subsided, she snarled at Sir Reynold, "There's no good my being here. I've things to see to elsewhere. Tonight, when this is done . . ." She looked sideways at Godard as if she were caught somewhere between resentment and being sickened—or maybe she was resenting the sickened feeling, Frevisse disconcertingly thought; disliking weakness in others, maybe she hated it in herself. ". . . you come see me. We have to talk."

"Alys, my girl," Sir Reynold started, not pleased.

"You come," Domina Alys said and left no space for him to answer by turning sharply around and shoving her way out among the men, giving them no chance to move aside.

Godard seemed only partly conscious now. There was blood at the corner of his mouth, and Dame Claire leaned back from him, holding up her reddened hands. In the white encircling of her wimple, her face was set with the tight-mouthed anger and grief she always had when someone in her care was beyond her help, when someone was going to die and she could not stop it. "Where's Father Henry?" she asked tersely. "We need him."

"Here, Dame," the priest gasped, short-breathed with hurry, his black robe tucked up into his belt to clear his

hosened legs, and the curls around his tonsure in more
disarray even than usual as he pushed in among the men.
They pulled aside to make way for him, going down on their
knees, one after another, as they realized he was carrying
cradled against his breast in his large hands the small gilt
box that held the pax and other things needful for the
safeguarding of the soul of a man closing in on the death.
"We were out hunting, Benet and I," he explained as he
came. "We're only just back." He was not listening to what
he said, too intent on reaching Godard to care whether
anyone heard. Frevisse glimpsed Benet behind him, rough-
dressed for hunting afoot, with a bulging game bag still
slung over his shoulder. He stopped at the inner edge of the
gathered men, carried that far in Father Henry's wake but
able to see now there was nothing for him to do except kneel
with everyone else. Someone must have found him and
Father Henry as they were coming in, and Father Henry had
turned aside only long enough to fetch the pax from his
room.

Already on her knees, Dame Claire was turned aside,
washing her hands in one of the waiting basins as Father
Henry joined her beside Godard. He looked at the torn
hopelessness of the wound and drew in his breath. Dame
Claire made a small gesture of helplessness and rose to her
feet, saying, "There's nothing else I can do except mix
something for the pain." She looked at Frevisse, who
understood and rose to her feet to go and give the necessary
order to Ela.

When that was done, there seemed no more purpose to
her staying in the guest hall; she slipped away behind the
servants and out.

Evening had come far on while she was inside. The yard
was shadowed and far colder than it had been. A rich smell
of distant fresh-turned earth told that the winter plowing had
been started in the priory's harvested fields, and she
breathed it in deeply, trying to find comfort in the thought of
harvest, of the year's end and quiet turning of the seasons,
each one bound around and through by work and prayers as
ordered and unending as God himself. That was the right

way of things. That was how a life should be lived and
ended, with simple inevitability.

Not in anger and on a sword's blade.

She bent her head in prayer. Not for Godard yet. What
could be done for his soul was being done, and Dame Claire
was readying what small ease there could be for his body.
For him, beyond that, there was only the waiting. It was the
other man who needed prayers, the man Sir Reynold had
killed, the man who had died with all his sins still on him
and no chance of priest or prayers.

Someone went past her, down the stairs, and she looked
to see it was Master Porter, headed back to his men, she
supposed. Without thinking, she called quietly after him as
he reached the foot of the steps, "Why did you goad Sir
Reynold and Domina Alys like that just now? You did it of
a purpose, didn't you?"

He faced around to her. They were alone in the yard;
everyone else was in the hall, but he glanced around to be
sure of it, then came two steps back up toward her and said
quietly, "You'd be Dame Frevisse then, wouldn't you?"

She nodded.

"Master Joliffe said you were too clever to be comfortable with and out-of-ordinary to be trusted."

How very like Joliffe to make what could have been a
compliment sound like something else, Frevisse thought.

"He says you'd no thought we'd not been paid this
while."

"No, none of us knew," she said.

Master Porter nodded grimly. "That sounds like what I
know of her. And that cousin of hers. I was goading them,
right enough, hoping one of them would turn angry enough
to order me gone. If she ends the contract, it looks better for
me than if I have to do it." He lifted his heavy shoulders in
a resigned shrug. "But it didn't work and I'm not waiting
around for the trouble that's coming next, that's sure. We'll
be out of here tomorrow if we can."

"Sir Reynold may try to stop you," Frevisse warned.

"Aye. He might," Master Porter agreed with a solidity

that suggested it would be better for Sir Reynold if he did not, and with a bow went on his way.

Thoughtful about a man who seemed to see Sir Reynold more as an inconvenience than a threat, Frevisse went on across to the cloister. She could hear that Vespers was not yet over, but rather than go in to it, she chose to sit on the low wall between walk and garth, waiting for Dame Claire, who came soon, carrying her box of medicines, and did not question Frevisse being there but crossed the walk to set her box on the garth wall beside her. Because there seemed nothing useful to be said about Godard, Frevisse asked instead, "How was it with the madman? Was he badly hurt?"

"Only a bare scratch that bled too much, in the way of head wounds. If it doesn't infect, he'll not have trouble with it."

"And his madness? How clear of it does he seem to be?"

Dame Claire made a weary movement of her head that meant nothing. "I didn't see him before. I don't know how he was."

"He was mute and near to completely witless."

"He speaks now and has at least some wits." Dame Claire slowly drew in and let out a deep breath. "Domina Alys thinks it's Sister Thomasine's doing, that she's made a miracle."

Frevisse did not want to hear that. To have to deal with the abbot, even the bishop, if it went that far, over a possible miracle as well as with everything else now so wrong . . . It was more than she wanted to think about just now. She could see why a miracle would well suit their prioress at present, but it would mean questionings, investigations, doubts, and—from the readily satisfied—passions and even hysteria—all of it turning on Sister Thomasine, and how would she, unworldly and forever lost in prayers as she was, endure all that?

"It's Sister Thomasine I don't understand," Dame Claire said, paralleling Frevisse's thought.

"She's frightened?" Frevisse asked.

"Not even slightly, so far as I can tell. But when Domina Alys told her to pray for the madman, she said she wouldn't."

"Sister Thomasine refused to pray?" Sister Thomasine was always praying. For her to refuse to . . . Frevisse found nowhere to follow that thought.

"Well"—Dame Claire sighed—"that's probably the least of our troubles at present. Prayers or no prayers, miracle or no miracle, we'll have the sheriff here before we have the abbot."

Frevisse shut her eyes and, in trying to avoid that thought, said aloud what she had only meant to think. "Besides that—or maybe it's part of it—she's lied to us about the tower."

"Lied? Who's lied? Domina Alys?"

"There isn't enough money to finish it. There was maybe never enough money to finish it. The masons are planning to leave because they haven't been paid in weeks."

"She wouldn't lie," Dame Claire said.

Frevisse opened her eyes and looked at her in unconcealed disbelief. "She wouldn't lie? Why not, with everything else she's done?"

"Lying is a sin. She wouldn't do it."

"She wouldn't sin?" Frevisse said sharply. "Wrath and pride are sins and she indulges in them readily enough, you've surely noticed."

"She doesn't see wrath as wrath. For her, I think it's rightful anger against our failings, the way God is angry at our sins."

Shying away from equating Domina Alys with God, Frevisse asked, "And her pride? What's that if it isn't pride?"

"Love," Dame Claire said simply.

"Love?" Frevisse stood up, her voice rising in protest. *"Love?"*

Dame Claire made a hushing motion at her. "You never try to see her without loathing anymore, but I do, if only for my soul's sake. I've tried to see her as she sees herself and she loves St. Frideswide's, she truly does. I think everything she does, she thinks she's doing for the priory."

"Sir Reynold is done for the priory?" Frevisse mocked savagely.

"She doesn't willfully sin," Dame Claire insisted. "She doesn't knowingly sin."

"And therefore she hasn't lied to us over the tower because lying is a sin and she wouldn't do that," Frevisse said bitterly. "So let's just say instead that she's managed to leave a great deal of the truth out of what she's told us!"

Before Dame Claire could answer, silence fell from inside the church, telling Vespers was ended, and with a shake of her head because there was no time for saying more, she took up her box of medicines and went away toward the infirmary, leaving Frevisse to go resignedly the other way and lie down, aching, beside the church door.

# Chapter

## ❧ 17 ❧

ALYS PACED HER parlor lengthwise, door to far wall to door to far wall. Katerin had lighted the fire because it was time to light the fire and now was standing beside it, shifting uneasily from foot to foot because it was time for Alys to sit and Alys was not and Katerin did not know what to do about it.

In a corner of her thoughts, Alys was sorry for that. Katerin's expectations were so few, it went hard with her when one of them failed. But she could not sit. She had to move, to force some kind of sense into her mind by making her body go somewhere, if only from door to far wall to door to . . .

What had Reynold been thinking of? He had to know he couldn't go thieving through the countryside and not be called to account for it. And killing a man. That was not something that would go by. He had been angry over Godard when he did it and she understood anger, but Reynold's had been wrong. When she was angry over a thing, then she was sure she was right, and her anger made others sure with her and saved her the need to argue a matter

out with folks too slow to see it the way she did. But killing
a man . . .

Reynold was supposed to help her. He had promised. She
had believed him. Now she could not even use what he had
brought, knowing it was stolen. Why had Godard been fool
enough to be killed? Except for that, she would have gone
on knowing nothing and everything would still be well.

No. Everything would still be ill, but she would be
ignorant of it while it went on to worse before she learned
of it too late. If it was not too late already. No. She refused
that possibility. It was not too late. She would not let it be
too late. There were still ways to make it right.

To begin with, Reynold had to go and take his men with
him. Now. Tonight. As soon as Godard was dead. That's
what she had to tell him when he came.

But that was not what she wanted him to do. She wanted
him to stay. She wanted him to undo what he had done,
explain it to her and make it right.

And she doubted that he could.

She swung aside from her pacing to slam her open hands
down on the tabletop. She rarely had trouble with uncertainty. She despised it as a weakness, a thing only weaklings
had, but she had it now, like a heavy headache, thickening
her thoughts, so they would not go the way she wanted them
to go. She slammed her hands down on the table again and
shoved away from it to pace to the window back to the table
back to the window and finally stand staring out.

Below her the yard was lost in darkness. At this hour folk
were expected to be settled for the night, no need for light
where no one was supposed to be. The thin trace of light
along the guest-hall shutters, and under the guest-hall door,
showed nothing except their shapes. Was Godard dead yet?

The guest-hall door jerked open and broom-yellow light
spilled out, down the steps and into the darkness of the yard.
Alys stiffened as Reynold came out, no more than a dark
shape against the light, but she knew him. Knew him by the
way he held himself, by the turn of his head as he looked
behind him. Knew him as surely as he would know her if he

looked up and saw her there, another dark shape, against the low glow of her firelight.

They had always been that near in knowing, in understanding each other. From the time they had been children, they had been that near. He *had* to make this thing right before it went worse between them.

He did not look up to see her but back over his shoulder. Hugh joined him and they started down the steps together, into the darkness.

So Godard was dead and Reynold was coming but bringing Hugh with him rather than face her alone.

More wearied than she could remember ever being, Alys turned from the window and the dark toward her firelight, crossed heavy-footed to her chair, and sat. Beside the fire, Katerin sighed and was content.

"Sir Reynold and Sir Hugh are coming to the cloister door," Alys told her, saying the words slowly to be sure she understood. "Go and let them in and bring them here."

Katerin watched her speak, then gave an eager head bob to show she understood, bobbed a curtsy, and scurried away.

Alys shoved up out of her chair, about to pace again, then dropped back into it. Better to face him with all her dignity. But she could not. Sitting still was beyond her and she stood up again, facing the door as Katerin opened it and stood aside for Reynold and Hugh to enter.

"Godard is dead," Reynold said without other greeting.

"You're still armed," Alys said back to him. All the men always wore their daggers but not their swords and particularly not in the nunnery, most particularly not in the cloister. Hugh was without his; Alys had a vague thought of him unbuckling it, handing it off to a squire to make it easier to kneel with Godard. Why did Reynold have to do yet another thing wrongly?

Reynold looked down at his hand, resting on his sword hilt against his hip as if surprised it was there, but kept on toward her, saying, "Given one thing and another, it's probably best for now." He held out his hands to take hers.

She turned away from him and circled her chair, putting it between them. "It's not best here," she said. "Katerin, light the lamps. All of them." She suddenly wanted more light, much more light. There were too many shadows. She wanted to see Reynold's face.

Katerin scurried to light a taper at the fire. While she carried it, carefully shielded in her hand, from lamp to lamp around the room, Reynold watched Alys a little, then sat down in her other chair and said, "It's been a hell of a day. Godard was a good man."

"So maybe was the man you killed," Alys said back. But that was not to the point in this, and because there was no easy way to come to it, she went on bluntly, "You and your men have to be out of St. Frideswide's before Tierce tomorrow unless you can find me a good reason why you shouldn't be."

Reynold looked at Hugh, who had gone aside to sit on a corner of the table, one leg swinging, his expression as grim as Alys felt. To Reynold's look he only shrugged, as if he did not have an answer. Reynold shrugged back, looked back at Alys, and leaned forward, hands clasped in front of his knees, to say earnestly, "If I go, Master Porter will have your masons out of here within the hour. I'm all that's keeping them here."

"You said you'd worked the matter out with him, that you'd persuaded him it was best he stay."

"And when I'm not here to go on 'persuading' him"— Reynold gave the word a different twist, broad with threat behind it—"he won't stay, let me promise you."

"You've promised me much, including help in paying him!"

"If I go, you still won't have the money for it and he'll be gone and you won't persuade him back or any other masons to come instead and where's your tower then?"

"Where is it now?"

Reynold spread his hands. "Say the word and you'll have stone here in a day or so."

"Stolen!" Alys accused. "You'd steal it in Banbury!"

"And why not?" Hugh asked. "He's stolen everything else he's brought you."

Reynold slid him a hard sideways look. "Be quiet."

Alys found her chest too tight for breath, had to fight for it before she could force out, "What?"

Reynold spread his hands, grinning wryly, asking her to share the jest. "How else could I come by it?"

"Pay for it, like everyone else!"

"The way you've paid your masons?"

"I'll pay them! I've never meant to steal from them. There'll be money for it and soon enough, too!"

"From where?" Reynold mocked.

He always turned to mocking when he thought he was going to win an argument without needing to lose his temper, but this time Alys had an answer and said triumphantly, "We had a miracle in the church this afternoon. Sister Thomasine cured a madman."

"So?" Reynold asked.

She knew he was being deliberately thick and said, wanting to make him admit to what she had, "He was mute and witless and now he's on his knees in front of the altar, praying." Or he had better be. She had given orders for it to be seen to.

"And?" Reynold asked.

"Don't be stupid, Reynold! Before Sister Thomasine touched him, he couldn't speak, didn't know where he was or what was happening to him. Now he's cured! When word goes out there's been a healing here and people start to come, there'll be money enough for the tower and whatever else I want."

"If they come."

"They'll come." Of that Alys was positive. To doubt it after she had seen the miracle with her own eyes would be the same as doubting God.

"They very well might," Hugh agreed.

"Be quiet!" Reynold snapped at him again.

"Reynold," Alys said, "the point is, the straightest way out is for you to go before you drag the priory into more trouble than you have."

"Than *we* have, Alys my girl," Reynold said. "You've had most of the profit from my thieving, when all's said and done and totaled up."

"But I didn't know until now that that was what was happening!"

"And so you'll say, but will you be believed?"

"I'm more likely to be believed if you're not still here when sheriff and crowner come!"

"And when the Fenners come?"

The constriction in her chest came back, worse than before. She could not always tell when Reynold was jesting, but she knew when he was utterly serious. "Fenners," she said.

Reynold shrugged. "At least a few."

*That* was a jest. There was no such thing as "a few" Fenners. They were like crows—seen solitary sometimes and even sometimes quarreling among themselves but flocking loud and fierce together at any outward threat to one or any of them. There were no "few" Fenners. She looked desperately at Hugh. "It isn't Fenners you've been raiding." Silently she pleaded for him to tell her that, to tell her that Reynold had not been raiding Fenners and bringing what he stole back here and that he had not killed on Fenner property today.

Hugh made no answer except a level stare directly back at her that was answer enough and too much.

She slammed her hands down on her chair, facing Reynold in a rage. "You fool! What were you thinking of?"

Reynold swung his scabbarded sword up to rest across his knees and leaned forward over it, not touched by her anger, saying earnestly, "Alys, Alys, think about it. It's a quarrel that's been shaping a long while. It was time to bring it to a head and be done with it."

What was he talking about? The quarrel they had with the Fenners had been in abeyance for years, with Godfrey properties finally left in Fenner hands when the legal fees looked to rise higher than the properties were worth.

"That was over years ago," she protested.

"Not over," Reynold said. "Only waiting to come to life again. It's been long enough. It's time they paid us back for all they cost us."

"I don't recall they ever cost you a penny," Hugh said.

"Neither you nor your father were ever the ones who took it to court." No, it had been Hugh's father had done that, Alys remembered.

Reynold ignored him, concentrating on her. "Alys, I've raided the Fenners and they haven't been able to do anything about it. I've shown what can be done against them, that they're vulnerable, and I've sent out word I've done it. In a few days more there'll be at least a score more Godfreys here, satisfied I can do what I said I'd do, and then we'll set a raid against the Fenners—one great raid that will pay back for everything and have back our lands for good measure at the end of it."

Alys shook her head, wanting to refuse what he was saying. "Why use me for that? Why use St. Frideswide's?"

"You're not a place anyone would come looking first when trying to find out who was doing this to Fenner lands. That was a way to buy us more time. And you're better walled than any of my properties, so a better defense when we're found out. And even when we are, whoever finds us will think twice about attacking a nunnery and that buys us more time, for more men to join the game. And they will. There'll be men in plenty and not just Godfreys who'll come for this sport."

Alys came around her chair and sank slowly into it, her legs not able to hold up the weight of pain in her head, the weight of pain in her heart. That was why he was here? Because he needed her nunnery. And he expected her to let it go on happening?

"Alys, listen." He leaned farther forward, reached out to lay his hand on hers. She drew it away from him, refusing to look at him, staring past him into a shadowed corner of the room. He rested his hand on the arm of her chair and went on, "You see how you've made it possible to come this near to having at the Fenners? I can't leave here now. It's too late to break this off."

"Of course the dead Fenner villein ups the stakes," Hugh said. "Thieving is one thing. Killing is another."

Reynold made an exasperated sound. "Forget the villein. If it ever comes to having to explain it, it was Godard killed him after he struck Godard, and now Godard is dead and there's an end to it."

"Our men will go along with that, but I doubt the villagers will," Sir Hugh said.

"They will if they're told what will happen to them if they don't," Sir Reynold snapped. "Don't make trouble where there doesn't have to be."

"You can't stay here," Alys said. She looked at Hugh. "Make him understand he has to leave."

"He won't listen to me either."

"Don't give me this!" Reynold said angrily. "You've been part of this every step of the way, Hugh. Don't try slipping out of it now."

"You've pushed the thing too far, too fast. I've been telling you that," Hugh answered.

"And if we pull back now, what happens?" Reynold demanded.

"If we don't pull back now, what's going to happen?" Hugh returned.

"What happens to me, whatever you do?" Alys cried.

"Nothing happens to you," Reynold said impatiently. "When it comes to it, just keep insisting you didn't know until it was too late and what could you have done then to be rid of us anyway? Have your nuns drive out my men? Set your nunnery folk to fight us?"

"They'll say I should have sent word the moment I knew what you were about."

"You didn't know until now."

Hugh made a rude sound and said, "Try making anyone believe that."

Alys glanced at him, a little wild with knowing he was right, no one would believe her, but Reynold said, ignoring Hugh, "You couldn't send word anyway. I've set guards. No one goes out or in from here without I know it from here on."

Alys started to rise, too caught between half-disbelieving outrage and outright rage to find words. Reynold, seeming not to notice except he put a hand on her knee to keep her down, went on easily. "No, you should be able to clear you and your nunnery readily enough."

"So long as it's only words, she maybe can," said Hugh, "but if it comes to us being attacked here . . ."

"If you've lost your stomach for it," Reynold said angrily, "leave."

"If I leave, my men go with me."

"All three of them," Reynold scorned. "You're a ways yet from being some great lord."

Hugh stood up from the table. "And so are you, cousin!"

"I'm nearer to it than you are and at least I've the guts to try for it!"

Beside the door Katerin whimpered, understanding the anger if nothing else of what was happening, and Alys could almost have whimpered with her, for once not seeing how she ought to go, afraid—unbelieving, she found she was afraid, a thing that, like uncertainty, she had no use for—afraid of what would happen if Reynold and Hugh broke and openly went for one another.

Then Hugh gave way, drew back from both Reynold and his anger, and said, "Play it your way, Reynold," sounding as if they had come to this end between them before and he no longer much cared. "I'm going to bed. You have this out with her on your own." He started toward the door, then paused, looked back and said, "But, Alys, don't let him talk you into this. From here on out, the way things are, you're better off without him."

# Chapter

# 18

IN SUMMER THE difficulty of rising at dawn came from the too few hours of night and rest. By late autumn, when the nights had lengthened and there were more hours for sleep, it was the cold waiting for her beyond her blankets that made Frevisse wish she could deny the dawn. In her young days as a nun, she had taken pride—God pardon her—and pleasure in making the sacrifice of rising at midnight and again at dawn for prayers; but although she thought—she prayed—that she had long since overcome the pride, lately she had noticed that her bones at least were taking less pleasure in the sacrifice. The spirit was still willing, but the body's wish to cling to bed a little longer was becoming a problem.

And yet once it was done, once she had forced her body out of bed's comfort and hurriedly dressed in the darkness by feel and familiarity, warm woolen gown over the linen underdress she wore to bed, feet into soft-soled leather shoes to be off the chill rush matting, white wimple over her hair and throat and around her face, black veil pinned carefully into place over the wimple, then she was near enough to what she wanted to gladly leave her sleeping cell,

join the others at the head of the stairs at the near end of the
high-roofed dormitory, and go down in silence except for
the hush of their skirts, shadows moving through shadows,
their way lighted only by the small lamp kept burning
through the night at the head of the dormitory stairs, into the
cloister walk and along it by starlight or moonlight or with
no light at all if it were cloudy, to the church, where, for
Frevisse, the joy of prayer, of greeting God's day as dawn
began to fill the eastern window, more than balanced the
discomfort of rising in the dark and cold.

But this morning, at last, she would have no reluctance.
This morning she was awake and waiting for the morning
bell to release her from bed and her back. Dame Claire's
ointment had eased the pain to aching and she had managed
to sleep, but in the throes of a dream she no longer remembered, she had rolled over on it and now was widely
awake, lying very carefully still, willing the roused pain to
subside, and hoping it was near dawn because she doubted
she would be able to sleep again.

The pain at least was easing to a separate throbbing of
each welt across her back and she was able to turn her mind
away from it, to begin repeating silently into the dark the
psalms for this morning's Prime, for her own comforting in
their beauty and to make the dark less endless.

*Caeli enarrant gloriam Dei . . . Dies diei effundit
verbum* . . . The heavens tell the glory of God. . . . Day
pours out the word to day. . . .

Not that she was much looking forward to what this
particular day was likely to entail.

*Quis ascendet in montem Domini, aut quis stabit in loco
sancto eius?* Who ascends into the mountain of the Lord, or
who stands in his holy place? *Innocens manibus et mundus
corde, qui non intendit mentem suam ad vana.* . . . The
innocent in hands and clean in heart, who does not strain his
mind toward things empty, toward things vain, useless,
false, conceited, unreliable, cruel. . . .

Frevisse clamped off that run of bitter words, taking her
exactly back to where she did not want to go—to Domina
Alys and Sir Reynold.

She thought of rising and going to the church to pray. It was allowed and Sister Thomasine frequently did it, but thought of the madman—the once-mad man—held her where she was. He had been given a straw-filled pallet and blankets on the floor behind the altar and he was probably asleep there now. Or maybe he was awake and waiting for what the day would bring him, maybe wondering at the movement of thoughts in his mind where there had been only chaos or emptiness before. What must that be like?

When the nuns had gone into the choir for Matins at midnight, he had been a featureless heap, huddled in the blankets on his bed, only the top of his now clean head and the glint of his eyes to be seen at the edge of the choir candlelight. He had not stirred while they were there. He had watched but made no move or sound and probably would do no more if she went in to pray; but even his simply being there made her uneasy. There were too many questions about him. How cured was he? Was the cure momentary or would it last? How much would he be able to tell them when Dame Claire said he could be questioned? Had it truly been Sister Thomasine's doing? Did she even know whether it was or not, and what did she think of it? No one had been able to bring her to talk of it yesterday.

Apart from all of that, what did Domina Alys mean to make of this seeming miracle laid into her hands? Because make something of it she surely meant to do. If nothing else, she was foreseeing pilgrims with money and gifts that would pay for that miserable tower of hers. . . .

Frevisse forced her mind away from that. Whoever ascended to the mountain of the Lord, it was not likely to be someone who interspersed her prayers with bitter thoughts against her prioress. *Domini est terra et quae replent eam, orbis terrarum et qui habitant in eo.* Of the Lord is the earth and that which fills it, the circle of the earth and those who live on it.

Better to give herself over to prayer and God's praise, as Sister Thomasine did, than sink into bitterness over things beyond her power to mend. Leave to God how the world would go.

Unless, her mind suggested, the Lord meant for his faithful to see to his world the way worldly lords expected their men to see to their lands, with the lord holding sovereignty but his men responsible and answerable for how well or ill things went in their keeping.

If that were the way of it, it was sin to leave things to go which way they would, and she . . .

Frevisse shoved off the blankets. Lying there with her aching back and her thoughts for company was doing her no good at all. Madman or no, she would go to the church to pray. It could not be that far to Prime now.

In fact, she saw as she arose that the small square of sky through the high window under the dormitory's gable was pale with early light. That meant it was past time for the bell to have rung to Prime, and she began to dress with a haste pressed by curiosity. Being late was not Katerin's way. Given any task that she could understand, she did it faithfully for always afterward.

It crossed Frevisse's mind to wonder why, if miracles were being done, it hadn't been that poor woman's wits that were given back instead of a stranger's.

She shook away that thought as yet another run of speculation that would do no good. There were stirrings now in the other cells as others began waking out of habit despite there was no bell. Dressed, Frevisse pushed aside the curtain that shut her cell off from the dormitory's aisle as Sister Emma from behind her own set to murmuring increasingly loud questions about where the bell could be; and as Frevisse started down the stairs Dame Perpetua said back impatiently, sleepily, "We don't know, do we? Just dress. We'll go see."

Frevisse was nearly at the stairs' foot when the bell broke into the morning's stillness but not with Katerin's evenly paced clanging. Instead it smashed into the quiet, clashing and banging. Frevisse startled to a stop, then flung herself forward, off the last steps and out into the cloister walk, where there was light enough now to see shapes if not colors clearly. Light enough to see it was Katerin at the bell pentice in the midst of the cloister garth, frantically jerking the bell rope with both hands.

"Katerin!" Frevisse cried. "That's enough! We're up. You can stop!"

Katerin looked over a shoulder at her, hearing her despite the clanging but not stopping. Frevisse crossed into the garth and to her, exclaiming, "It doesn't matter you were late, Katerin! You can stop now. We're awake!" Then she saw the terror on Katerin's face and changed to urgent comforting, trying to lower and even her voice with "Katerin, stop it. There's no harm done. You're only a little late. It's well enough. Stop now." She caught her by the wrists, careful to be gentle but surprised at Katerin's strength. "You can stop now, Katerin."

Words always took time to reach Katerin's wits and she struggled to go on ringing, pulling against Frevisse's hold, until abruptly, of her own will and not Frevisse's force, she stood still and silence clashed down around them, momentarily as startling as the noise had been. The only sound was Katerin's panting in the stillness, before Frevisse, making an effort to speak soothingly, said very quietly, "It doesn't matter you were late, Katerin. It doesn't matter. No one is angry at you."

"Dead!" Katerin sobbed.

Frevisse stared at her, trying to guess what she was trying to say. Katerin wrested a hand loose and pointed across the garth toward the stairs to Domina Alys' parlor. "Dead!"

Suddenly cold around the heart, Frevisse let her go and started across the garth toward the stairs, not wanting to. Katerin could only think in simplicities. It had to be no more than that Domina Alys was ill. It was surely only that, not death.

Domina Alys loomed out of the darkness of the narrow stairs to her parlor, dressed but still pinning her veil into place as she came, demanding at full voice, "Katerin, what do you think you're doing? You're supposed to ring the bell, not smash it to pieces!" Finding Frevisse instead of Katerin in front of her, she stopped on the last step, momentarily wordless, then shifted her attack. "And you! If you're here, why didn't you stop her sooner?"

Frevisse, abruptly stopped at the edge of the cloister walk, hardly heard the question. Her hand shaking from more than the ice-edged morning air, she pointed aside to the passageway to the outer door.

"What?" Domina Alys demanded and turned to look.

The passage's length was in deeper darkness than the cloister walk where the gray dawnlight was winning against the night. What lay there was as yet only a shape stretched out and lost in shadows except for one booted foot thrust a little into the walk and the beginning daylight. That would have been what Katerin saw when she came down the stairs—a booted foot and then a shape lying in the darkness where no one ought to be. And terrified of something unfamiliar, she had done the one thing already in her mind to do—she had rung the bell for people to come.

Now she was edging around Frevisse, whimpering; and when Domina Alys put out an arm toward her without looking away from the foot, Katerin went to crowd against her like a frightened child to its mother, pleading, "Don't be angry. Don't be dead. Angry. Dead." Beginning to wail.

Not heeding her, Domina Alys whispered hoarsely at Frevisse, "Who?"

Frevisse went a step nearer, forcing herself. The light was steadily growing. She could see him now, enough to know him and what had been done to him. Enough that she shifted to block him from Domina Alys' view before she answered. "Sir Reynold."

Domina Alys started forward, shoving Katerin aside, but Sister Amicia, Sister Cecely, and Sister Emma came rushing across the garth, dressed but bareheaded, their veils and wimples in their hands, exclaiming over each other as they came, "Why was Katerin . . ." "The madman, has he . . ." "Fire? Are we on fire?" Domina Alys swung around on them in fury, yelling "Cover your heads! Are you gone wanton? Cover yourselves!"

Their tumble of words cut off, they crowded backward into each other, snatching their wimples over their heads, and Domina Alys, her fury as suddenly gone as it had come, swung back on Frevisse, demanding, wanting to be told no, "Sir Reynold?"

Frevisse could only stand, looking at her, not able to give her the answer that she wanted. But when Domina Alys moved toward him, Frevisse held out a hand, saying warningly, "Best not."

More of the nuns were coming, and servants from where they slept in the kitchen, and Margrete down the stairs from Lady Eleanor's room. For all Domina Alys heeded them, there might have been no one there but herself and Frevisse as she kept on, ordering harshly, "Let me see him."

Frevisse moved aside.

Between them, she and Domina Alys had blocked anyone else from seeing what was there but someone caught glimpse enough now, gasped, and a hurried whispering spread from nuns to servants, with more exclaims and hurried crossings of breasts and murmured bits of prayers.

Domina Alys stood with her back to it all, staring down at Sir Reynold's body, at first not seeming to understand what she was seeing. Then a soft moaning began far down in her throat and she drew back a slow, uneven step, her head beginning to twist from side to side in refusal of what was there. Frevisse tried and could not put out a hand to her or find anything to say. It was Dame Claire who came, took light hold of her arm, said, "My lady, come away. Don't see . . ."

Domina Alys flung her hand harshly aside, roughly pushed her into Frevisse and both of them out of her way, and still with that low and terrible moaning in her throat, lurched past them toward the stairs.

No one followed her but Katerin, huddled in misery and maybe fear.

Her going left a silent gap, but only for a moment. Then servants and nuns together crowded forward, some still not sure what they were trying to see but not willing to miss whatever it was. Dame Claire and Frevisse swung around to face them, keeping Sir Reynold's body from their view as Sister Johane demanded, "Who is it? Is he dead?"

"It's Sir Reynold," Dame Claire answered tersely. "Yes, he's dead."

Sister Johane stared at her, and belatedly, as Sister Cecely began a soft wailing that promised to grow louder, and Sister Johane's face crumpled to tears, Frevisse realized that Sir Reynold was as much kin to the two of them as to Domina Alys. Dame Juliana and Dame Perpetua set to trying to comfort them and Sister Emma, who had joined in the wailing, while Sir Reynold's name ran among the rest of the nuns and servants in exclaims and agitation. Some of them tried to pull back. Others tried to crowd closer. Frevisse held where she was and Dame Claire went forward, trying to persuade everyone away, nuns toward the church, the servants toward the kitchen, but no one was heeding her.

Frevisse had not seen Margrete leave, but she was coming back now, following Lady Eleanor down her stairs, Lady Adela and Joice behind them, all of them wrapped in cloaks, the girls with their hair loose over their shoulders, but Lady Eleanor's and Margrete's fastened back and veils pinned quickly on for decency's sake. The crocus flame of the lamp Lady Eleanor carried was bright in the soft-edged dawn light as with a quick word to the girls, she left them on the stairs and advanced with Margrete on the coil of nuns and servants, adding her orders to Dame Perpetua's and Dame Juliana's with the calm expectation of being obeyed, telling the servants, "That's enough. You don't need to see more. Go back to the kitchen. We'll all be wanting breakfast. Go on. You've seen enough for now. Move out of my way."

Under her assurance and orders the servants sorted themselves out from among the nuns and drew back, almost convinced they wanted to go, while Dame Juliana and Dame Perpetua drove the nuns the other way, toward the church, Dame Juliana saying, "There now, we're late for Prime as it is. That isn't right. Come, we'll pray for him. He needs that more than your staring at him and wailing. Go on now."

Only Sister Thomasine went readily. The others followed less willingly, still weeping and exclaiming, so that when the church door finally shut behind them, with the servants already herded to the kitchen by Margrete, there was a sudden silence, even from Lady Adela and Joice still on the stairs, holding on to each other. Only Lady Eleanor was left, now facing Frevisse who still stood with Sir Reynold's body mostly hidden behind her skirts; and very quietly she asked, "It's indeed Reynold?"

Frevisse nodded.

Lady Eleanor briefly closed her eyes, drew in and let out a shaken breath, and ordered, much as Domina Alys had, "Let me see him."

# Chapter

# 19

Sir Reynold was sprawled forward, his head canted carelessly, gape-mouthed, staring, his body slightly twisted to one side, arms and legs loosely out as if he had made no attempt to stop what must have been an utterly graceless fall. If there had been spasming once he was down, it had been slight. Lady Eleanor's small lamplight cast the shadows back to the passage's far end but made no change to the darkness of the wide wound, the black, dried blood across his back.

"From behind," Lady Eleanor said and drew back the lamp, letting the shadows take him again, for which Frevisse was grateful. The blood and the mingled smells of death, even subdued by hours and the night's cold, were as much and more of mortality as she wanted just now.

"Margrete." Lady Eleanor spoke without looking around, knowing she would be there. "Bring Father Henry and Sir Hugh."

Come silently back, the servants dealt with, Margrete asked, speaking as evenly as her lady, "Tell them what's happened or just tell them to come?"

"Tell them what's happened, and tell Hugh to bring some men. We'll need to move him."

Lady Eleanor drew back as she spoke, away from Sir Reynold and the passage. Frevisse and Dame Claire moved with her, making room, and Margrete edged past them and past the body with her skirt and cloak carefully gathered in to keep from touching it. Once clear, she hurried on to the outer door, opened it, and went out—not needing to unlock or unbar it, Frevisse noticed. That meant that all night there had been nothing to keep anyone from entering that way.

"Lady Eleanor, you had best come sit," Dame Claire said, and Frevisse turned from the passageway to realize that the day had gone on growing, that sunrise was swelling up the sky above the eastern roofline and the cloister shadows had thinned to blue, the lamp flame faded to pale primrose. Their breath showed in the cold dawn air now, and so did Lady Eleanor's face, sagged into lines of grief, betraying how much her level voice and outward calm were an act of will and how much the effort was costing her in strength. She made no protest to Dame Claire taking her by the arm, a little supporting her, or Frevisse taking her by her other and the lamp out of her hand. Together, they helped her the little way across the cloister walk, to sit on the low wall between it and the garth, enough aside from the passageway so she would not see Sir Reynold's body unless she chose to turn that way.

She kept turned away from it, and as Lady Adela and Joice came down the stairs and toward her in worried haste, she looked at Frevisse and said, "Don't let them see," then while Frevisse moved so that her skirts again hid Sir Reynold's body, raised her voice to say firmly to the girls, "I'm not ill. It's only that this is overmuch to face so early in the day and unexpected. No," she added to Lady Adela who was sidling aside to see past Frevisse. "Stay there. You don't need to see."

Lady Adela stopped but could not hold back from asking, "Is it Sir Reynold? And he's dead?"

"He's dead," Lady Eleanor said quellingly.

"And I can't see?"

"No!" Dame Claire and Frevisse said together.

But Lady Adela had already known; and it passed through Frevisse's mind that Lady Adela's life was overly full of things she could not do.

Joice, with no wish to see Sir Reynold, dead or otherwise, had gone directly to Lady Eleanor and said now, anxiously, "Should you come back to bed awhile? It's been too sudden for you."

Lady Eleanor straightened, willing herself past her weakness. "I can't. Not yet. There's too much to be seen to."

"We can see to it," Dame Claire said.

Lady Eleanor refused the possibility. "Hugh will take orders best from me."

"He can take them from someone else if this is going to be too much for you," Dame Claire insisted.

"I'm well enough." She looked to Joice. "Take Lady Adela back to my room and have wine ready, warm and well spiced, for Margrete and me. I won't be long at this." And when Joice hesitated, said to her, "I've seen to worse than this in my time. I'll be well enough."

"And we'll keep with her," Dame Claire put in. "Dame Frevisse and I both."

"Nor should you be here when the men come for him," Lady Eleanor added, and Joice's hesitation gave way. She held out her hand to Lady Adela, who took it reluctantly and dragged a full step behind her all the way to the stairs; but they were well up them when Father Henry, his robe unbelted, his curls uncombed, his brass-bound box clutched in his arms, hastened to the passageway from the yard, hurrying in the obvious hope that despite what Margrete must have told him, there was still a chance to protect Sir Reynold's soul before it was gone.

His first clear look at Sir Reynold told him the hope was useless. There had been no life in Sir Reynold longer than a single breath after the blow was struck. For a silent moment Father Henry stood staring down at him, slack-shouldered with misery, then straightened, knelt down, and began to do what could be done now in the way of prayers.

Across the cloister the nuns' chanting of one of the morning's psalms, distant through stone wall and heavy door, seemed to have nothing to do with the morning Frevisse was in. There was where she wanted to be—in the church, in her choir stall, deep in prayer. Not here and facing this.

Loud, hurrying, angry, Sir Hugh and his men burst in at the outer door. Lady Eleanor stood up from the wall and took a few steps back toward Sir Reynold's body, and Frevisse and Dame Claire, without need of word between them, moved to either side of and behind her, hands tucked into sleeves and heads bowed, leaving it to her because it was what she wanted, but there if they were needed.

Sir Hugh was first in. She had sent him word to bring only a few men but seemingly all Sir Reynold's men were there behind him, crowding, most only in their shirts and quickly flung-on cloaks, still rumpled from sleep but every one with their weapon-hung sword belts in their hands. Frevisse saw Benet, close behind Sir Hugh, give a swift look around to be sure Joice was not there and trying, too, to Frevisse's eye, not to see Sir Reynold's body before he moved well aside from the others, past Father Henry who had shifted himself and his prayers into the cloister walk as the shove of men came in on him.

Sir Hugh, the only one among them unarmed, gave Sir Reynold's body a single swift look but was more intent on Lady Eleanor, crossing to her to take her by the arms and stare worriedly down into her face, asking, "How is it with you? Should you be here?"

Lady Eleanor laid a hand over one of his hands and said gently, "I've seen dead men enough in my days. I'm well enough."

Sir Hugh studied her a moment longer, then let her go and turned back to his men and the body.

"Send the men away," Lady Eleanor said. "They don't all need to be here."

"They had to see him," Sir Hugh said grimly. "We all had to see him."

The men were crowded and jostled around the body, some grimly silent as they looked, most loud with exclaims and swearing. Hands moved in the sign of the cross and among the oaths were mutterings of "Lord have mercy," but they all cleared out of Sir Hugh's way as he came back to them, subsiding to silence around him as he stood for a moment, looking down at his cousin's body before saying bitterly, "It was ill done."

Someone among the men, down the passage and out of Frevisse's view, snarled, "It was done from behind and in the dark. It was foully done!"

"It had to be one of those damned masons," a man said, at Sir Hugh's shoulder. Another Godfrey, by the look of him, "It had to have been one of them."

"That's talk we don't need," Sir Hugh said coldly. "We'll find out who did it in good time, and when we do, we'll deal with him, but we won't start trouble until we're sure."

"We're not the ones who started trouble," the man beside him said. "I say we wring some necks until we have the truth out of someone."

"I'd wring your neck, Hal, until I'd put some sense in your head," Sir Hugh snapped back, "but likely all I'd be left with is a wrung-necked goose. I'll say what's done here and what isn't." He swung his gaze around to include them all in that and added, "Take yourselves back to the hall and stay there until I come."

Hal pointed at Sir Reynold. "What about him?"

"Lady Eleanor and the nuns will see to him."

From where she stood apart from them, Lady Eleanor said calmly, grief and authority both in her voice, "We'll see him cleansed, shrouded, coffined. Everything that's right. Then you can take him to keep vigil over. Until then there's no use in your being here."

"So go," Sir Hugh said in clear expectation of being obeyed. They were used to obeying him and Frevisse saw with relief that they would now, too, beginning to shift toward the outer door.

"Except you, Benet," Sir Hugh said. "You stay to help with him. And Lewis, you," he added to the white-faced boy, younger than Benet, kneeling at Sir Reynold's head. He was Sir Reynold's squire and looked up, taut-faced with holding back tears, to nod to Sir Hugh's orders.

As the last of the men jostled out the door into the yard, Margrete pushed in past them. Again avoiding Sir Reynold's body with both skirts and gaze, she hastened through to Lady Eleanor, ignoring everyone else, complaining and explaining, "They clotted up the way, so I couldn't pass. I tried to go through the church, but the west door is barred and I had to come back." And then anxiously: "How is with you, my lady?"

"Well enough," Lady Eleanor assured her crisply. "This won't be the end of me." She looked to Dame Claire. "Where would be best to take him?"

"The lower parlor here." A room immediately to hand here along the cloister walk, meant for the nuns to receive such friends and relatives as did not need the prioress' attention. It might have been better to have taken the body on to the infirmary, but to Frevisse's mind and apparently Dame Claire's, too, that was too far into the priory for the coming and going of so many men as there would be in this. Better that everything be kept here, as near the outer door as might be.

"Dame Frevisse, can you bring sheets?" Dame Claire asked. "And Margrete, the other things?"

Shears to cut the ruined clothing off. Basins of water. Soap. Cloths. Margrete would know as well as Frevisse what was needed. They had all of them seen to other dead in their years of life, had readied for their graves people they knew, just as, God willing, they would all be readied for their own graves by those who knew them when their own times came. It did not matter that this time their work was for Sir Reynold. What mattered was that it was for the dead, as someday they would be.

But Frevisse noticed that in all of this there was no word said of sending for the crowner, the King's officer who was supposed to be called in whenever there was any violent death, to determine where the wrong lay and collect the fines due to the King in the matter. Another thing that would be laid against the priory, to keep company with all the rest, when this was over.

# Chapter

## 20

It took surprisingly little time to sort matters into order. When Frevisse came back from the infirmary with sheets, Benet was standing outside the parlor door, waiting to take them from her, but though she gave them to him, she followed him in anyway, to find the scant furnishings of a bench, small table, a few stools, a chair had all been moved back to the walls now and Sir Reynold's body laid out in the middle of the floor with Lewis waiting beside it, stiff-faced and pale.

Lady Eleanor was sitting, composed but equally pallid, on the bench, hands folded in her lap, her eyes closed as if she prayed. Dame Claire stood near her and answered Frevisse's questioning look with a shake of her head that said Lady Eleanor was as well as might be and there was nothing more to do for her just now.

"Father Henry?" Frevisse asked.

"Someone had to see how it was with Domina Alys," Dame Claire said; and neither she nor Frevisse would have been welcome, nor Lady Eleanor fit to do it just now.

"Sir Hugh?" Frevisse asked.

"Gone to be sure the men are making no trouble," Benet

answered. He had spread the sheet out on the floor and he and Lewis were readying to move Sir Reynold's body onto it.

Not needed there, Frevisse willingly left. The first numbness was wearing off; her mind was beginning to move more clearly and she did not like where her thoughts were going. Nor was she pleased to find Prime had ended and Sister Cecely and Sister Emma approaching her in a rush of black gowns and veils along the walk, with Sister Johane more slowly in their wake. She moved to intercept them, saying, to forestall their flurry of questions, "Go on to breakfast with the rest," so firmly that they stopped, momentarily silenced, until Sister Cecely burst out, "He's our cousin! It's our right! Where's he been taken? What's happening?"

Dame Juliana was leading the rest of the nuns, except for Sister Thomasine, of whom there was no sign, along the far side of the cloister walk toward the refectory, and Frevisse guessed these three were to be left to her, and with the barest of sympathy, since there was more avid curiosity than grief in their eager faces, she said, "He's been moved into the parlor and is being seen to by Lady Eleanor, Dame Claire, and some of his men. There's no need of you here." And added, "Nor is Sister Emma his cousin."

"That's no matter," Sister Cecely said. "She's with us. We should go to him."

"No, you shouldn't," Frevisse said, deciding patience was no use. "You're not needed there. If you truly want to be of use to him, go back to the choir and pray for his soul."

"Yes, but—" Sister Johane began.

"Or if you're that eager to see his blood," Frevisse interrupted, pointing into the passageway where it was spread and darkened on the floor where Sir Reynold had lain, "there's a great deal of it. Maybe you'd like the task of scrubbing it away."

"Oh no!" Sister Johane shrank back, not looking. Sister Cecely and Sister Emma had less sense, looked where Frevisse pointed at the spread and mess of Sir Reynold's blood, gasped, grabbed each other for support, and went on staring. Frevisse, out of patience, took them each by an arm, pulled them apart, and pushed them along the walk, shoving them on their way when they were past the parlor door.

"Go to breakfast," she ordered disgustedly. "You're not wanted here."

Compelled, they went, and belatedly it occurred to Frevisse that she could go to breakfast, too, that maybe she ought to rejoin the others in making what they could of the day, since she was no more needed here than Sister Cecely was.

Instead, she turned the other way, toward the church, wondering about Sister Thomasine and whether she should be there alone with the madman, despite she had an endangered soul to pray for and no matter how harmless he had seemed until now.

Walking quickly, her own head bowed, she was nearly to the church door before she realized Joliffe was there, outside the door, in the cloister walk, where he had no business being, standing at ease and as if he had been waiting for her. Startled, annoyed that he must have used the door out of the tower and come through the church, she asked him without other greeting, "You know?"

"You think I'd come in here otherwise?"

She gestured past him toward the church. "Is it well in there with Sister Thomasine?"

"She's praying at the altar," he said, and then answered what she had not asked. "And your madman is tucked into his blankets and not looking likely to stir out of them for any reason."

"He's not my madman. Listen, there was talk among Sir Reynold's men against Master Porter that you'd better warn him of."

"He's heard. Word of it came right along with the word Sir Reynold was dead. It took the edge off our mourning for him, you can guess."

Frevisse ignored that. "Sir Hugh warned them off, but he's not Sir Reynold and they may decide not to heed him."

"Master Porter already has Sir Reynold's man off the tower, and on the chance the masons have to retreat into it, they're readying the scaffolding to go over at a push if need be. Preferably with a few of Sir Reynold's men on it, come to that."

"Wait," Frevisse said. "Sir Reynold had a man on the tower? Why? Since when?"

"Since yesterday, after they came back from the raid. A watch to warn if anyone was coming. Or trying to leave," Joliffe said, grimly enough to show he saw the implications as clearly as she did. Sir Reynold had been afraid trouble was so close behind him, or at least that it was closing on him fast, that he had set watch against it. Had Domina Alys known that or was this something else he had kept from her?

Just now what Domina Alys had known or not known did not matter. A trouble closer than any he had thought of had overtaken Sir Reynold, and Frevisse asked, not even trying to make it casual, "Where did you spend last night?"

Joliffe understood exactly what she was asking and answered readily, "With the masons. From when I left you, on through supper and all night. But," he added thoughtfully, "I slept near the door. I might have gone out after they were all asleep without anyone's knowing."

"Did you?"

"Go out? I'm not likely to say I did, am I?"

"Not if you have any wit at all. Did anyone else?"

"The nights are long and many bladders small. Some went out, as usual, but no one in particular or for overly long. Not Master Porter with a particularly heavy hammer—"

"Sir Reynold was stabbed," Frevisse said.

"Not Master Porter carrying his dagger in his hand and snarling about vengeance. Of course I seem to recall that I slept a great deal of the time, it being night and all, so I probably missed some comings and goings, but no, I didn't notice anything in particular."

"And might not tell me if you had?" Frevisse suggested.

Joliffe tended to be unpredictable in what he took seriously and what he did not. He grinned at her question. "You're not a very trusting woman, are you?"

"No. I'm not. You wouldn't tell me, would you?"

"Probably not," he said lightly. Then the lightness dropped away and he said, altogether serious, "There's something I *will* tell you. Sir Reynold was being an obvious idiot for a long while before yesterday. You know about the Fenners and the Godfreys' quarrel?"

"The Fenners," Frevisse said with new alarm. "What about the Fenners?"

"There's been word out for half a year and more that Sir Reynold meant to reopen the quarrel, so when things began to happen to various Fenner properties and Fenner followers these past few months — small things, nothing like yesterday's raid but enough — there were suspicions, and when Sir Walter Fenner heard Sir Reynold was moved in here, he thought it was time to find out more of what Sir Reynold might have in hand. Do you know anything about Sir Walter?"

"A little." Enough that she did not want to know more or have him in St. Frideswide's again. The last time he had been there he had been trying to find his mother's murderer among the nuns and not been greatly concerned with legalities while doing it.

"He's somewhat more subtle in his ways than Sir Reynold was," Joliffe said. "Before stirring trouble up, he decided to send someone to find out for certain, secretly, what Sir Reynold was about."

"You," Frevisse said.

"Me," Joliffe agreed. He made her a graceful, mocking bow. "A simple minstrel, seemingly wandered into your fair priory by chance and therefore suspected of nothing."

"Why you?"

"I was to hand when Sir Walter needed someone and he offered enough money it was worth my while to do it."

"But you haven't sent him word yet. There hasn't been time," Frevisse said.

"I sent it yesterday morning."

Yes, he would have known enough by then to tell Sir Walter his suspicions were justified, even without the raid and killing afterward, but: "How?"

She did not expect him to tell her, but he did. "A peddler

came into your village the same day I came here. He wasn't a friendly sort and settled for bedding down alone in someone's byre instead of someplace better, with no one to notice if he slipped out and spent a while near onto moonrise in the deep shadows of the church's doorway, doing nothing. No more than anyone noticed me go out over your orchard wall—no great trick, let me tell you—and meet him there, tell him what I knew, and come back the same way. He was away yesterday morning to pass word to someone in Banbury, who's sent it on fast to Sir Walter by now."

"And when Sir Walter hears it, he'll come in force against Sir Reynold here."

"Yes," Joliffe agreed.

"How soon?" Frevisse demanded. "If you went now and told him things had changed, that Sir Reynold is dead . . ."

"Sir Reynold's men aren't. Nor Sir Hugh. After yesterday's work, Sir Walter won't be satisfied with anything short of being sure no Godfrey can strike at him again."

With St. Frideswide's caught in the middle.

Not trying to hide her anger, only the fear that was goading it on, Frevisse asked, "How soon is he likely to be here?"

"Tomorrow, I would guess."

"When you meant to be gone, well out of it before he ever came but here long enough you wouldn't be suspected of being the one who told him, even if anyone bothered to think of you at all."

"That was what I had in mind, yes."

"Leaving us to face it all unwarned!"

"No!" Joliffe denied that forcefully. "Before I left, I would have told *you* and trusted you not to betray me."

She would not have, he was right about that, but: "What good would that have done?"

He shrugged, confident. "There are only three doors into the cloister. You would have found way to have them barred when Sir Walter and his men came. With Sir Reynold and his men shut out and the nuns shut in, you'd all have been safe enough."

"But our priory folk wouldn't be, or our villagers!"

"I suspect I would have passed a word of something like warning along to your villagers as I went through, and they'd see your priory folk heard in time, and I doubt they would be passing it along to Sir Reynold's folk."

"Wouldn't that risk you being found out if anyone asked questions afterward? Exactly what you've tried to avoid?" she said caustically, too angry to believe him willingly.

He answered caustically back, "I doubt Sir Reynold and his ilk—your prioress among them—would bother with questioning their peasants afterward. Aside from despising them too much to think it worth their while, they'd likely be too busy answering questions themselves by then from sheriff and crowner and abbot and all to care what any villagers might have to say."

Beyond the fact that he was probably right, Frevisse was annoyed to find she believed he would have done exactly as he said.

Improbably, as if there had been no taint of anger between them, he grinned at her. "Unfortunately, it doesn't look like I'll be going anywhere for a time, as things are now."

"It would be a great pity if you wandered off at this point," Frevisse agreed. "Because if you did, suspicion of Sir Reynold's murder would very likely turn on you."

"But now that you know Sir Walter is coming . . . ?"

Joliffe left the question unfinished but she knew what it was. What was she going to do with what she knew?

"Nothing, yet," she said. Joliffe would be in danger as soon as she warned anyone because they would want to know how she knew. But neither could she keep it secret for long, for everyone else's sake.

She sat down on the garth wall with a suddenness that acknowledged how tired she was, in mind and body both. Joliffe joined her, leaning back against a pillar the way her back would not presently let her, with one leg crooked under him, at ease. The morning was still cold, but the sun had cleared the roof of the east range, spilling thick gold light into the cloister; Joliffe held out his hand into the brightness, cupped as if the light were something he could hold.

"The simplest way to handle it," he said, "is of course to find out who Sir Reynold's murderer is. Then I can go, warnings can be given, all is well."

"*Well* is not the word I would have chosen," Frevisse said. "Nor *simplest*."

"Ah, words," Joliffe said airily. "Such feckless things."

"But supposing you aren't the one who killed him . . . ?"

Joliffe bowed his head to her without looking away from his hand. "Thank you for being willing to suppose that."

"You're welcome. So supposing it wasn't you, who else could it have been?"

"For choice, your Domina Alys."

"For choice, your Master Porter," she answered back.

Joliffe regretfully agreed. "Sir Reynold had both of them furious with him before yesterday was over."

"But he was Domina Alys' kinsman. She'd be less likely than Master Porter to turn to killing him."

"I've always found myself more inclined to loathe those I know best, rather than strangers," Joliffe observed.

Ignoring that, Frevisse said, "And she's likely to lose whatever she hoped to gain by him being here, now he's dead, besides that she knows better than most, being nun and prioress, how she's damned her soul if she's killed him, while for Master Porter killing him might seem no more than a straightforward way to be rid of the threat Sir Reynold was to him."

"Except now Sir Reynold's men are a danger to him. He would have likely foreseen that."

"He's maybe counting on the clear fact that Sir Hugh is not so short-headed as Sir Reynold, that he'll see better than to turn them loose on anyone."

"Of course there could be reasons Sir Hugh would want Sir Reynold dead," Joliffe said. "One at least. He'll likely take over the men for his own and have the profit of what Sir Reynold started, now Sir Reynold is dead."

"There's that," Frevisse granted. "He's hardly to know how ungood a thing that is at this point. Though, again, this is hardly the time to unbalance things, even not knowing that. Wouldn't it serve him better to wait until Sir Reynold had fully succeeded?"

"Who knows?" Joliffe said. "What we have is somewhere to start, three possibilities to find out about." He stood up. "I'll go learn what I can about Master Porter and anyone else among the masons last night. You'll do the same for your prioress and Sir Hugh and anyone else inside the cloister who may look likely once you've started?"

Frevisse nodded and stood up. She did not see how she would be able to do much, but it was better than waiting for what might happen, with a murderer somewhere among them. Oddly, that had been a thought she had been keeping clear of, concentrating on Sir Reynold being dead. But Sir Reynold was dead because someone had killed him, and she had to gather her thoughts to face that. "Meet me in the church after Tierce," she said. It was not much time, but they did not have much time, nor maybe many chances either, to exchange what they might learn.

"One thing," Joliffe said. "About how Sir Reynold was killed. You said he was stabbed. Where?"

"In the passage from the cloister out to the yard."

"I meant where, on him, was he stabbed. How was it done? With what?"

"In the back with a sword."

"Not a dagger?"

"It was a wide wound. I'd think it would have taken a sword to make it."

"Where?" Joliffe turned his back toward her. "Show me."

Frevisse drew her finger in a line below his left shoulder blade, from midway across that side of his back toward his spine. Joliffe's shoulders twitched and a shiver ran up him. "There."

Joliffe turned around. "Did it go all the way through him?"

Frevisse remembered the blood had spread from under the body and answered, "Yes. Why are you asking all this?"

"I don't know. It's just I've always found it better to know too much than too little. Haven't you? Ask questions while you can, for what you might need to know later."

She had found that true, too, though probably on different sorts of occasions than he had. They regarded each other in considering silence a moment before Joliffe said, "I'll see you after Tierce," and turned back toward the church.

# Chapter

## 21

FREVISSE HAD THOUGHT to go to Domina Alys first. Since it could not be avoided, it would be best to have it done. But Joliffe's questions about the wound took her back to the parlor. She had seen Sir Reynold's gashed flesh and dried blood but not looked closely. Had not wanted to look closely. It had seemed sufficient to know the wound had surely caused Sir Reynold's death. But there was never a sufficiency of knowing, not about anything, only an end to where the mind could reach. Or to where it *wanted* to reach. And now Frevisse wanted to know more.

And wished she did not have to.

She rapped lightly at the parlor's closed door, and after a pause Dame Claire opened it. Her sleeves were pushed up above her elbows; she had probably helped to strip off the befouled clothing that lay in a heap by the door and then with washing off the filth and blood that came with violent death. She had the strained look of someone who had been concentrating too long on a thing they did not like, but she and Frevisse had dealt with death together before now and saying calmly, "I thought you'd be here to see him sooner," she stood aside for Frevisse to enter, leaving the door open behind her for more light than the rushlights they had been using.

Sir Reynold's body was laid out on a sheet in the cleared center of the floor with Benet and Lewis kneeling beside it, rinsing cloths out in basins of reddened water. They looked up briefly as Frevisse entered but were too absorbed in enduring what they were doing to care that she was there.

Lady Eleanor was still sitting where Frevisse had last seen her, eyes shut, Margrete beside her now. Margrete nodded to Frevisse without speaking and Frevisse nodded silently back, but Lady Eleanor stayed behind her closed eyes, sitting very upright and very still. Her help had not been needed with the body, but there should be kin present while the last worldly things were done for the dead, and although Benet was kin, Lady Eleanor held memories of Sir Reynold for more years of his life than anyone else at the priory and so she had kept him company through this last while, despite what it had obviously cost her. Frevisse looked to Dame Claire, silently asking how it was with her, if anything should be done; and Dame Claire as silently answered with a shake of her head that there was nothing.

Knowing that Dame Claire would on the instant leave the dead to fend for themselves if there was aught she could do for the living, Frevisse accepted that and went to stand over Sir Reynold's body.

Her first thought was that there seemed to be so much less of him than there had been when he was alive. It was something she had thought before when faced with the dead, but used though she was to the diminishing of death, it still disconcerted her. The soul was incorporeal, but the body was reduced to such irrelevance by its going. Did the soul, when it went free in death, come to forget the body that had belonged to it? Was that something of how it was with Sister Thomasine? Were her austerities of prayer and fasting not so much a denial of her body as simply that her soul had begun to forget her body too soon? Poor body, forgotten while it still lived.

With Sir Reynold it was the other way around—poor soul, driven out of the body before it was ready.

Benet and Lewis had nearly finished cleansing the body,

the task more awkward because of the stiffness still in it.
Benet was wringing out a cloth into one of the basins; Lewis
was pressing another cloth, dripping wet, to Sir Reynold's
lower left chest, over what Frevisse presumed was the
wound there, soaking loose the blood, she supposed. She
gestured at it and said to Dame Claire, "The blood was
dried."

"Dried. Darkened," Dame Claire agreed.

"He's been dead all night?"

"Allowing for everything, the body's stiffening and the
cold and the blood, yes, I'd warrant he was dead most of the
night."

"May I see the wound?" Frevisse asked.

Lewis and Benet both jerked up their heads to stare at her.

Dame Claire, with quiet authority, bid them, "Let her see
whatever she wants."

Lewis uncertainly drew back his hand, removing the
cloth and uncovering the wound.

Frevisse took a closer look than she wanted to at the gash
with its curled lips of darkened flesh reaching from beside
Sir Reynold's breastbone around almost to his side, a
narrow slash but four or five inches long. A desecration of
flesh.

"The wound in his back," she said, holding her voice
steady. "Let me see that, too."

Benet and Lewis looked at Dame Claire who again
nodded and carefully they rolled Sir Reynold's body to its
side and almost over, holding it for her to see the other
wound.

It was much like the one in the front but with the sliced
flesh dragged outward by the withdrawing blade. She had
been assuming he had been struck from behind because of
how he had been lying and because it was unlikely he would
have gone down so silently, so easily as he must have, if he
had known the blow was coming. Now she could be sure.

But she could also see now that he had not been killed by
a simple sword thrust. Front and back, the wound was too
wide for that. He had been run through the body, and
probably through the heart in the same stroke, by a long

blade, that was certain; but then the sword must have been wrenched sideways hard enough, far enough, that the spine was probably at least partly severed in the bargain. If it was, it meant someone with a great deal of strength had wanted to be very sure of Sir Reynold's death.

"His spine, is it cut through?" she asked.

Dame Claire knelt and felt into the wound. Benet jerked his head away to stare at the wall. Lewis looked at the roof beams.

"Not completely through," Dame Claire said, withdrawing her fingers, "but it's deeply cut, yes."

"You can lay him down now," Frevisse said and Benet and Lewis gratefully did. "Thank you," she thought to add, her mind already away to what else she might learn here.

Behind her in the doorway Domina Alys asked hoarsely, "He's not shrouded yet?"

Frevisse faced her as Dame Claire moved toward her, saying, "No, my lady. We—"

Domina Alys cut her off, turning away. "Call me when it's done."

Not wanting to, Frevisse followed her into the cloister walk. She had to question her sometime; sooner would be better and it might as well be now, before she found another reason not to do it.

Father Henry and Katerin were waiting outside uncertainly, but Domina Alys was walking past them without word, back toward her stairs, moving heavily, unsteadily, as if her mind were paying too scant attention to what her body did.

"My lady," Frevisse said.

Domina Alys turned around. In the parlor her back had been to the light and Frevisse had not seen her clearly. Out here, with daylight now fully come, her face showed haggard, hollow, as if both anger and excess words were presently drained out of her. Coldly, unencouraging, she said, "Dame."

There was no subtle way to go about it, no way that would make it easier on either Domina Alys or herself.

Frevisse asked bluntly, "Sir Reynold came to see you last night?"

Domina Alys stared at her dully, without any overt feeling before answering, "You're after who did this to him, aren't you? You. Still alive while he's dead." Frevisse, chilled, stood still, not knowing what to answer, more chilled as Domina Alys' look deepened to a dull glare. "But better you than some fool of a crowner. Yes, he came after Compline, when Godard was dead."

Father Henry shifted uneasily. Domina Alys swung her head and fixed him with a stare, and he pointed uncertainly at the nuns just now leaving the refectory. Almost apologizing, he said, "It's time for Mass." And past time; breakfast had taken far longer than was necessary over what was always very little food, and now they were hesitating in the walk, seeing their prioress, not sure which way to go. She twitched an uncaring glance toward them, jerked a hand to send them on toward the church, and said at Father Henry, "So go. Do it."

Not hiding his relief, Father Henry went. Frevisse wished she could go with him. Domina Alys' coldness of control where there should have been a rage of grief was worse to face than her familiar rage would have been, and to have it over with, Frevisse asked straight out, "Was it only you and Sir Reynold last night?"

"Don't be a fool," Domina Alys said as if it hardly mattered whether she was or not. "Sir Hugh came with him. And Katerin was there."

Katerin bobbed a little in pleasure at hearing her name. How much she grasped of what had happened, either last night or this morning, Frevisse could not be sure but asked her carefully, not to startle her, "Katerin, do you remember last night?"

Katerin stopped bobbing to stare at her, mouth a little open, then said, "Yes."

"What do you remember?"

Katerin thought again.

Frevisse prompted, "About last night."

"It was night. We slept," Katerin said. She nodded, more certain of it. "We slept."

"Before you slept, do you remember anything? Do you remember what happened before you slept?"

It took a moment, but then Katerin's face clouded. "They were angry."

"Who was?" Frevisse asked.

"We all were," Domina Alys said. "Before it was done we all were. Don't set her off on it. She frightens when folk are angry. She'll lose what wits she has if you make her think about it."

"Angry," Katerin said mournfully. "He was angry and then he went away."

"Who went away?" Frevisse asked.

"Sir Hugh," Domina Alys interrupted curtly. "She means Hugh went away angry. He was quarreling with Reynold. We were both quarreling with Reynold. Everyone quarrels . . . quarreled with Reynold."

Katerin wailed softly, "Angry."

"Be quiet," Domina Alys said. "Nobody's angry now."

Katerin went quiet.

"Quarreled about what?" Frevisse asked.

"About what?" Domina Alys said, contemptuous of her ignorance. "About what he's been doing. I said he couldn't stay here after what he'd done, that it would bring too much trouble down on us, and Hugh agreed with me, and he and Reynold quarreled over it. He was even purposing to bring in more men, no matter that I said he couldn't."

"And Sir Hugh was against that? They were quarreling about it?"

"Don't you listen, Dame? Yes, they were quarreling. I was quarreling. We'd have had open war with the Fenners on our hands, the way Reynold was going."

So she had known about the Fenners. For how long? Frevisse wondered.

But Domina Alys, lost in a strange mixture of grief and rousing anger, was going on, "Hugh at least could see it. He understood. He's not the fool Reynold is. Was."

The twitch of tense distracted her. She paused, the thread of her anger lost. "Was," she repeated slowly, with a denying shake of her head as if she could not make it real, and went on, the anger gone, "So Reynold turned all arrogant and set to insulting him. Once Reynold starts that, there's no reasoning with him until he's worn it out, so Hugh left, thinking I'd have a better chance at bringing him around alone."

"And did you?" Frevisse asked.

"Bring Reynold around?" Domina Alys made a small, sad sound that might have been, sometime, a laugh. "There's never been any bringing Reynold around. He was set on his Fenner baiting. So I told him to take his men and be out of here. Today. I told him I didn't want him in St. Frideswide's any longer."

"He agreed to that?"

"Agreed?" Domina Alys bit down on the word with distant bitterness. "No. He didn't agree."

"And then?"

"He left. He just left."

"And you didn't see him again."

Domina Alys shook her head, her mind somewhere else. "No," she said. "No. Not alive." Careful in her persistence, Frevisse asked, "How long was it between when Sir Hugh went and Sir Reynold?"

"A while. Not long." Vaguely, Domina Alys said, "Or it might have been. Who tells time when they're arguing?" Her eyes focused, narrowed, as she finally heard what she was saying, what she had been asked, and with something of her familiar sharpness said, "Listen, Dame, don't go trying to make out Hugh for Reynold's murderer. The quarreling is nothing. They always quarrel. Reynold is . . . Reynold was—" She stopped again, tangled, then swept a hand at the air in front of her as if to push away something there and went on, "That's all there was. Just that and no more. Now leave me alone."

She moved toward the parlor door, back to Sir Reynold, as she spoke, and Frevisse stepped out of her way but asked as she did, "Why wasn't the outer door barred last night?"

Domina Alys stopped, baffled a moment, then said, "That's Katerin's task. To see them out and bar the door."

"But she didn't last night."

"She was too frightened by all the anger. I didn't make her go."

"Angry," Katerin said unhappily.

"So the door was never barred last night," Frevisse persisted.

Domina Alys started forward again. "She didn't want to go and neither did I and I told her it didn't matter. Now nothing matters," she said and was gone into the parlor, her head sunk heavily between her shoulders as if she were facing a fight she expected to lose. Katerin, with a whimper, scurried after her, and Frevisse let them go, hesitant over what she could ask next and with no questions just now for Lady Eleanor either as she came out of the parlor a moment later. With the slightest of weary nods, looking as if she had no strength for more, she acknowledged Frevisse was there but did not speak and Frevisse nodded back as silently and let her go on toward her room, Margrete following her.

Benet coming out with his arms full of Sir Reynold's ruined clothing and Lewis after him, carrying Sir Reynold's sheathed sword and sword belt, were a different matter. Intent on what they carried, they went past with small bows of the head but Frevisse followed them, stopped them before they reached the passageway, and said, "You're finished, then."

They faced her and Benet nodded. "He's shrouded now. Dame Claire said there's a coffin somewhere, that someone in the guest halls will know where it is."

"The loft of the carpentry shop for a guess," Frevisse said. There was always a coffin ready. Death came so very easily for so many reasons—illness, accident, old age—that it was well always to have one to hand.

"Before you go, I need to talk to you, to both of you."

He and Lewis exchanged looks, to see if either of them knew why she wanted that.

"About Sir Reynold," she said, and went on before they could realize they could refuse her. "After Sir Reynold and Sir Hugh came to see Domina Alys last night, did Sir Reynold come back to the guest hall?"

They both looked puzzled and Lewis answered, "No, he was killed."

"He didn't come back to the guest hall and then return here later?"

"Why would he do that?" Lewis asked blankly.

Frevisse could think of no reason he would, but she had wanted to be rid of the possibility that he had left the cloister after quarreling with Domina Alys and come back later, been followed and killed. If that looked to be the way of it, it would have complicated things more than they already were, but it seemed he had not and she asked, "You didn't wonder why Sir Reynold didn't come back to the hall last night?"

"Why are you asking all this?" Benet demanded.

"Someone killed Sir Reynold. We have to find out who it was."

"It was that mason," Lewis said bitterly.

"But best to be certain past doubt," Frevisse said. "If we can find when people were where, then maybe we can find who wasn't where they were supposed to be when Sir Reynold died, and likely that will be our murderer."

Benet and Lewis exchanged looks again but said nothing. In hopes that meant acceptance, Frevisse repeated, "You didn't wonder why Sir Reynold didn't come back?" and Lewis answered, "Before he left, he told me I could go to sleep if I wanted to. He thought he'd be a long while because he was going to have to argue her around, he said, and when he didn't come back soon, I went to sleep."

He said it miserably, as if there were some sort of guilt in it, but he wanted no comforting from her, and Frevisse turned her questioning to Benet. "Sir Reynold and Sir Hugh came here together from the guest hall and then Sir Hugh went back to the guest hall by himself. Do you know if anyone saw him come back?"

"Everyone, I suppose," Benet said. "We were all still up."

"Did Sir Hugh come back soon or long after he and Sir Reynold had gone?"

"I hadn't been sitting there long," Benet said, "but I don't know how long they'd been gone before I came outside. Everything was confused in the hall after Godard died."

"Where were you sitting?" Frevisse asked.

"On the guest-hall steps." More in answer to Lewis' look of surprise than to Frevisse, Benet said a little defiantly, "After Godard died, I wanted to be away from them awhile, out of the hall. Away from how it was in there. No one needed me. I came out and sat there in the dark until I could face going in again."

"You saw Sir Hugh come back from the cloister while you were there," Frevisse said.

"Yes."

"Did he go to the well in the yard?"

"To the well? To wash off the blood, you mean? Because you think he killed Sir Reynold? No! He didn't go to the well. There wasn't any blood on him."

"It's dark in the yard by that hour. How could you tell there was no blood?"

"Why do you think he killed Sir Reynold?" Benet threw back at her.

"I don't think he killed Sir Reynold," Frevisse answered as curtly. "I don't think anything, except that I have to learn all there is to learn about how and where everyone was last night or Sir Reynold's murderer may go uncaught."

Where Benet might have gone with that was cut short as the door from the yard opened. They waited, instinctively silent, for whomever was coming, until Sir Hugh came out of the passageway. He looked at them incuriously and said to Frevisse as she made a small curtsy and Benet and Lewis small bows to him, "My lady mother?"

"Gone to her chamber," Frevisse answered.

He nodded thanks, said to Benet and Lewis both, with a nod back toward the passage, "Have someone come clean the blood up. The nuns shouldn't have to do that," and went on.

Benet and Lewis immediately started for the outer door, skirting the blood dried on the stones. Frevisse followed them, doing the same and saying low-voiced at their backs, "Sir Hugh isn't wearing what he wore yesterday." That had been a brown doublet with close-fitted sleeves. Today he had on one of dark blue, the sleeves cut more fully. "He's changed his clothing since yesterday."

Benet and Lewis both stopped and faced her. "He had Godard's blood all over him yesterday, remember?" Benet said sharply. "He changed after Godard died, before he and Sir Reynold went to see your prioress."

"What he's wearing now is the clothing he changed into then?" Frevisse persisted.

"Yes!" Benet said, and Lewis nodded in agreement.

"You're sure of it?"

"He has the brown doublet. He has the blue. That's all he has." Benet was very sure of it.

"And he wore the blue one to see Domina Alys last night."

"I saw him when he was going out with Sir Reynold," Lewis said. "That's what he was wearing."

"How long did you stay out after Sir Hugh went in?" she asked Benet.

"I don't know." He was impatient now. "The moon wasn't up and I wasn't heeding the stars. Awhile."

"Did you see anyone else while you were out there?"

"No. No one. Whoever did it must have gone in through some back way. Or come later."

"And you didn't hear anything? No outcry? Nothing?"

"*No*. We have to go."

She wanted to ask him if anyone had likely noticed when he returned to the hall but there seemed small point to it. Even if they had, they would likely have no more certainty about when it was than he had about when Sir Reynold and

Sir Hugh had gone or Sir Hugh had come back. No one would have been turning an hourglass on it.

She nodded that she was done and they went, leaving her standing there looking at the door that had not been barred last night, thinking on what she had learned so far and wishing she could see she was near to an answer. But she was not, and she should go, while there was chance to question Sir Hugh.

# Chapter

## 22

UNEASY WITH DISLIKE of everything that she was doing, Frevisse went up the stairs to Lady Eleanor's room. Its door was shut, but the heavy wood was not enough to keep in Lady Eleanor's angry voice and Frevisse paused with her hand raised to knock. She had never heard Lady Eleanor close to anger before, over anything, but in what sounded like a cold fury she was demanding, "And you'll just go, like that, with everything undone? Is that all this has come to?"

Sir Hugh's answer was less clear, his voice low, hurried, but without obvious anger ". . . later . . . see that . . ."

Frevisse knocked at the door. There was instantly silence but hardly a pause before Margrete opened it. Lady Eleanor and Sir Hugh stood facing each other near the foot of the bed. Across the room Joice and Lady Adela were seated at the window, each holding a dog and both looking toward the door with open relief. If they were there, then whatever Lady Eleanor and her son had been arguing over, it had not been murder, Frevisse thought. And was disconcerted at how easily the thought came.

"Dame Frevisse," Lady Eleanor said crisply. Her face, so

pale when Frevisse last saw her, now had the bright flush of anger. "It's good you've come. He means to take the men and go, now, today."

"He can't go! None of them can!" The protest burst out before Frevisse could stop it.

Less patiently than he had spoken to his mother, Sir Hugh said back, "I can. I'd better, unless you want more bloodshed here than there's been already."

"Surely you can hold your men back from doing anything against the masons," Frevisse said.

"Hah!" Lady Eleanor exclaimed. "It's not the masons I'd fear for if this lot of sword draggers went against them."

"Mother," Sir Hugh said, tight-lipped with control. "If we're here when this abbot comes—and my guess is that someone has talked too much and he's coming in force, by what it says here—" He jerked up his hand with a paper that looked to have been a sealed letter but was open and unfolded now. "He'll see too much, and if he does, he'll likely try to keep us from leaving at all. I can't afford to have him seeing things or keeping us here!"

"Abbot?" Frevisse said, going toward them. "Which abbot? Lady Eleanor, does he mean our Abbot Gilberd?"

"Yes," Lady Eleanor answered. "Someone has stirred him up, it seems. The letter says he means to be here this afternoon at latest, and that letter is a nice balancing between giving word he's coming and not leaving time for much to be done about it!"

Frevisse turned on Sir Hugh. "How did you come by the letter? It surely wasn't to you. When did it come?"

"It came this morning. No, it's for Alys. I took it from the messenger," Sir Hugh said impatiently.

"It wasn't yours to take!"

"She'll have it in good time."

"She should have had it from the messenger's hand! Unopened!"

"She'll have to settle at having it from mine," he said coolly, and turned his attention deliberately away from her. "Mother, I haven't time for this. I'll let you know where we settle. It won't be so good as here, but we'll make do. This isn't finished."

"Then you're not calling off the Fenner matter. You're only out of here for safety's sake?" Lady Eleanor said.

*"Yes!"* Sir Hugh's patience was suddenly thin. "You don't think there can be any calling off of it now, do you? After what Reynold's done? Even if I wanted to, I couldn't."

"But you don't want to," Lady Eleanor insisted.

Unexpectedly Sir Hugh half laughed and leaned down to kiss Lady Eleanor on the forehead. "No," he said, quietly certain. "I don't want to. Not any more than you do. Set your mind to ease on that."

Lady Eleanor reached up and laid her hand along his cheek, smiling, saying fondly, "That's my good son." She patted him lightly, briskly, affectionately. "Then you'd best be off. If it were me, I'd choose a place and time to meet and send the men off by different ways. Don't bother with taking more than you can carry yourselves. Carts are only a bother. The priory can use whatever you leave."

"Already considered and decided. Only I won't tell you where we'll be because then you can swear you don't know." He stepped back, took one of her hands, and kissed it. "You'll hear from me."

He gave a brief bow of his head toward Lady Adela and Joice, another to Frevisse, and would have gone with no more than that, but Frevisse said, disbelieving she had understood, "You mean you're taking your men and going? Now? Before anything has been settled over Sir Reynold's murder?"

Sir Hugh gave her a cold look. "You have it, my lady."

"But Sir Reynold's murder . . ."

"We'll maybe find out who did it and we'll maybe not. Right now it's more important to have us away from here before your abbot comes."

"If you leave, it will be said you did it."

"If I stay, it may very well not matter whether I did it or not. If we're kept here long enough for the Fenners to find us out, I'll likely be dead anyway."

He was moving for the door as he spoke. Quickly

Frevisse asked as he went past her, "When you left Domina Alys and Sir Reynold last night, did you go directly back to the guest hall?"

"Where else would I go? Yes, I went directly back to the guest hall."

He was to the door now, ready to forget her if she would let him, but Frevisse demanded at his back, "Did you see anyone else out then?"

He turned, letting her see she annoyed him but answering, "I saw Benet on the guest-hall steps. And, no, I didn't see anyone else. And, no, I didn't kill Reynold. Mother, take care, stay well." He clipped a bow of his head toward Lady Eleanor and was gone.

Margrete shut the door behind him but was looking at Frevisse while she did. They were all looking at her, Frevisse realized. Joice, for whom it was essentially finished, the threat of Sir Reynold gone and Benet unlikely now to push any claim on her, so that all she need do from here on was wait. Lady Adela, never any part of it except in curiosity. And Lady Eleanor, whose part in the Godfreys being here seemed to have been far more than Frevisse had ever had reason to guess.

Silently she and Frevisse regarded one another across the room, Frevisse with no words for what was in her mind, until finally Lady Eleanor said mildly, not offended, only curious, "What are you doing? Suspecting Hugh of killing Reynold?"

"I don't know what I'm doing," Frevisse said. And then because that was a lie, said, "Yes, I'm suspecting Sir Hugh of killing Sir Reynold. I'm suspecting everyone and asking questions I'd rather not be asking, because someone has to and no one else is."

"And now you've found out something you'd rather not have known. About me," Lady Eleanor said calmly.

"*Yes.*" Frevisse threw all her anger into that, glad to have it said. "You knew Sir Reynold was attacking the Fenners, didn't you? Not just the other day but for months now. You've known about it and you want Sir Hugh to keep on with it."

Lady Eleanor bent her head in quiet acknowledgment. "Yes. Exactly so."

"Yes to all of it?" Frevisse asked a little desperately, wanting her denial.

"To all of it," Lady Eleanor said.

"It was because of you Sir Reynold came here, wasn't it? All the years Domina Alys has been here, he never came until now. It was you who thought how he could use St. Frideswide's and told him."

"I wrote to Hugh about it," Lady Eleanor answered, undisturbed by the anger behind Frevisse's accusation. "My husband, his father, paid most of the costs of the court matters that came to nothing against the Fenners. Hugh and I had talked of having our own back from the Fenners somehow, and this seemed a good chance to do it. He brought Reynold in on it."

"Is this why you come to St. Frideswide's? To use it against the Fenners?"

"Oh, no!" That, at least, roused Lady Eleanor to strong denial. "I came for exactly the reasons I gave. It was only after I was here that I began to see the possibilities." She smiled, wanting Frevisse to understand. "We needed somewhere not readily thought of when raids started against the Fenners, but somewhere defensible if we were found out too soon."

"But why?" Frevisse asked. "Why any of it at all? The Godfreys and Fenners have let whatever it was between them go by for years. Why start it up again? It was over."

"It was never over," Lady Eleanor said in gentle explanation, expecting her to understand. "They still have what's ours. We fought it through the courts, hired lawyers, clerks, met the cost of paying judges off to hear the matter fairly when the Fenners were paying them to hear it otherwise. Years of that, all cost and no return, until we couldn't afford to go on with it, particularly after my husband died, and had to let it lie, but, no, it wasn't over, only at a standstill for a time."

"But this raiding of them," Frevisse said. "Why?"

"Partly as a way to have back a little of what they owe us.

They've gone unhurt too long. But more than that, now that we've shown how vulnerable they are, men enough will join us so we can go against them openly. Men enough we can take back our properties the same way the Fenners have held them. By force."

Frevisse stood still, bringing herself to accept that all of this thus far—the thieving, at least two deaths, and possibly Sir Reynold's—was, at the most, because of Lady Eleanor. Carefully keeping her feelings from her voice, she asked, "Did Domina Alys know any of this?"

"None of it," Lady Eleanor said unhesitantly. "She would never accept her priory being used this way. You know that."

Frevisse had thought she knew it; but she had thought she knew other things—thought she had known Lady Eleanor—and was finding she had been very wrong. "Why not have Sir Hugh do it alone, instead of giving it over to Sir Reynold?"

"Partly because Reynold could always bring men to follow him more easily than anyone I've ever known, no matter what he asked of them, and partly because Alys would believe whatever Reynold told her, never look past it, nor tire of him being here as soon as she would have tired of Hugh." Despite she had been speaking calmly, reasonably, tears shone in Lady Eleanor's eyes and she broke off, pressing a hand to her lips to stop their trembling before going on a little brokenly, "You see, when Reynold set his mind to it, he could charm a bird out of a tree, a badger out of its holt, a man or woman into doing anything he asked of them, and Alys more quickly than most."

"And never mind that every word of what he said was likely a lie," Margrete put in, handing her lady a handkerchief for the tears now sliding down her cheeks.

"An utter lie," Lady Eleanor agreed. "He was bound to be killed for it sooner or later. But there was no way to change him. The most that could be done was find a use for him."

"Bound to be killed?" Frevisse asked, trying to come back to the point. "Why?"

"Because with Reynold the only thing that ever counted

in the long run was having his own way. He'd say and do whatever he had to, to have it."

"And make everyone else pay whatever price they had to so he could," Margrete said.

"Knowing all that about him, you thought you could use him, trust him?" Frevisse asked.

Lady Eleanor smiled faintly, fondly. "I've known him since he was a little boy. He couldn't lie to me. I knew how he always dimpled in beside his mouth when he was lying." Her tears were more for the boy maybe than for the man. "I'd tell him to his face when he was lying to me and he'd laugh and admit it, so we did well enough together when we wanted to. And in something like this against the Fenners where our purposes ran together, yes, I thought I could use him."

"Only he decided to play the fool with this last raid and ruined it all," Margrete said bitterly.

"We expected he'd play the fool sooner or later, being Reynold," Lady Eleanor said, "but I'd hoped it would be later. I'd hoped Hugh could sway him long enough. But it's likely that Hugh will be able to manage it from here. Things aren't ruined, only made more difficult."

Frevisse forebore to point out that "things" had been made more than merely difficult for Domina Alys, and by no knowing consent of her own; and that unlike Sir Hugh and his men, neither she nor the nuns were going to be able to ride away from the trouble coming.

Lady Eleanor dried the last of her tears, done with them for now, and said, "But even given what a fool he could be, Reynold shouldn't have died this way. Not like this."

But then neither should he have been the kind of man he was, Frevisse thought; and without the apology she would have made a few minutes ago, she said, "I need to ask questions about when and where everyone was last night. Even you."

Lady Eleanor considered that a moment, then nodded. "Yes. I can see why."

Choosing to take that for permission, Frevisse asked,

"Did any of you leave the room last night after Compline? You or Margrete or Joice?"

"Or me," said Lady Adela. "I slept here, too."

"You did," Lady Eleanor agreed, "but this is one of those times you're not to speak until you're spoken to, my lady. No, none of us left that I know of, and I would have known, I think. I slept only fitfully and never deeply."

"Rheumatic pains," Margrete said. "She won't take enough of her medicine to let her sleep soundly."

"It makes my head thick all the next day when I do."

"And so does not sleeping well when you don't," Margrete returned.

Lady Eleanor ignored her, following where Frevisse's question led instead. "No, none of us went anywhere, but someone was where they shouldn't have been, weren't they? That's what you're trying to find out. It wouldn't have been one of Reynold's own men who killed him, that's certain. But if it was someone from outside, come on purpose to kill him, how could they have counted on happening on so good a chance?"

"It was maybe someone come from outside who wanted to kill just anyone," Lady Adela suggested happily. She crossed the room to Lady Eleanor's side, the dog tucked under her arm. "And it happened to be Sir Reynold and they've gone miles away from here by now and we'll never know who it was." Her eyes widened with another thought. "Or they're still here somewhere. In the priory. Hiding."

"Lady Adela, go and sit and be quiet," Lady Eleanor ordered, sharply enough that after a startled hesitation Lady Adela went back to the window bench to join Joice, who was sitting with the other dog cuddled to her breast, her face hidden against his furry back, surely listening but not interested enough to join in. Her green cloak had been returned to her last evening, cleaned, and she was wearing it against the room's morning cold. The night's airing had probably been enough to rid it of any lingering smell, and so she had everything that she had brought to St. Frideswide's, and when the time came, she would probably leave without a backward look or thought, even for Benet. It was not going to be so simple for the rest of them, and Frevisse said carefully to Lady Eleanor, "You don't think it was one of his own men, then, or that it was likely to have been someone from outside."

"No. It had to have been someone already here. Someone still here, most likely. Or someone who *should* be here but isn't."

She was watching Frevisse as she said it, and Frevisse was watching her, but there was nothing wrong with the logic of what she had said, and Frevisse agreed, "Yes."

"You'll ask about all the servants, of course, and there are the masons," Lady Eleanor went on consideringly. "The master mason in particular, I think, from what I've heard. And there's the minstrel. And the madman, of course. It would be none so bad if it were either of them."

Not saying she was unready yet to discount Sir Reynold's men, Frevisse said, "There are others to consider, too. Domina Alys, for one. She'd found out what Sir Reynold was doing and was angry at him. And Benet. He was outside the guest hall and unseen last night. And Sir Hugh. It seems he wasn't happy with Sir Reynold last night, either."

Lady Eleanor lifted her head. "Not my son," she said, meeting that possibility with flat refusal, as if that were enough to settle it.

Joice spilled the dog onto the bench beside her and stood up. "I'm going to the church," she said. "I need to pray."

Lady Eleanor started, "Do you think, Joice, that's . . ." but Joice, moving quickly and with only a shadow of a curtsy to her and Frevisse, repeated, "I need to pray," was out the door and gone. Belatedly, Lady Adela slid the dog she held to the floor with an ungracious bump and said, starting for the door, "I'll go, too!"

"You will not," said Lady Eleanor. "Sit down."

Lady Adela hesitated.

"Sit," Lady Eleanor repeated.

"But—"

"Mistress Joice does not need your help in prayers, and this is not a day for everyone to be wandering anywhere they want to around the nunnery. Sit!"

Lady Adela sat, unhappy with it, and Frevisse took the
chance to say, "I must needs go, too."

Lady Eleanor began to say something to that, thought
better of it, and said instead with her familiar gentleness,
"Best let things simply go what way they will, Dame.
There's naught that we can do to make them better."

Not after some of us have done so much to make them
worse, Frevisse thought bitterly, but schooled her face to
what might be taken for agreement and merely curtsied and
went out.

No one was in the cloister walk, and Frevisse stopped at
the corner of the garth wall near the foot of Lady Eleanor's
stairs, a hand on the pillar, her forehead resting against the
stone as she listened to the quiet, deep even for the cloister.
By the emptiness, the stillness, the nunnery might have been
deserted; the loudest sound seemed to be the throbbing of
her back, and she wondered briefly what Dame Juliana and
Dame Perpetua had done with the other nuns for now. In a
usual day it would have been time, or nearly time, for
Tierce, but the day had lost all the familiar shape of days in
St. Frideswide's. The sky was unabated blue and sunlight
filled the cloister; by midday there might even be a passing
warmth on the stones; but the gray ash of fear was lying
over everything, even her thoughts. What had she learned so
far? Nothing that helped, so far as she could tell.

She tried to say a prayer for Sir Reynold's soul. Death—
and fear—should not be more real than prayers, but for now
they seemed to be, distracting her from what should come
easily.

She went along the walk, toward the church, seeing as she
passed the parlor that Sir Reynold's body was gone. Was it
at all possible that it had been someone from outside who
killed him, someone come seeking revenge, finding it and
gone now?

She wished she could believe that had been the way of it,
but she did not. Whoever the murderer was, it was someone
here.

She went into the church, expecting to find Sir Reynold's

body coffined and vigil being kept, but the church was empty except for Sister Thomasine kneeling on the altar's lowest step, far gone in prayer, as usual. Sir Hugh must intend to take the body with them, out of Fenner reach. That would not go down well with the crowner either when the time came he learned of all this.

In the familiar shadows and quiet, Frevisse closed her eyes as she sought to gather her feelings and her thoughts into something coherent, but what came was another question.

Where was Joice?

Frevisse opened her eyes, looking for her. St. Frideswide's was a plain church; there were few places in it to be out of sight, and Frevisse circled quickly behind the farther choir stalls, to the door into the tower. The boards closing it looked solidly set, just as always, but when she took hold and lifted from one side, they shifted, just as Joliffe had said. Not much but enough that a slender person would go through. But how could Joice have known? And even if she did, what would be her purpose in going out of the nunnery now?

Frevisse shut the boards again and turned away toward the altar, more from habit than purpose, not thinking of the madman until she came past the end of the choir stalls. From there she could see both the altar and behind it, where he had been bedded. Obscure in the shadows, he was sitting up on his pallet now, instead of huddled into his blankets. And Joice was kneeling in front of him, her green cloak spread out around her as she leaned toward him in what looked to Frevisse like familiar, earnest talk.

The madman was leaning toward her, too, their heads close, but he looked suddenly sideways to Frevisse and jerked back at sight of her. Joice looked and jerked back too; and as Frevisse went toward them, she stood sharply up and moved to hide the madman behind the full swing of her cloak, saying quickly, "I came to pray, then thought it would be . . . wonderful to talk to someone who . . . the miracle . . . I wanted to ask him . . ."

Frevisse stopped almost near enough to push Joice aside

if she wanted. Whatever else she was, the girl was a poor liar; and Frevisse, trying to hold her growing anger of disbelief behind an outwardly calm voice, said accusingly, "You know him."

"No!" Joice answered a little desperately. "It's that he's not mad anymore! It's safe to talk to him. Sister Thomasine cured him. He . . ."

Behind her the madman rose to his feet.

Joice turned quickly on him, exclaiming, "Edmund, no. Don't!" grasping his arm as if to force him down again; but he took hold of her hands, refusing, saying, "Joice, she's not a fool. She knows."

"Quite probably." Unhuddled, standing straight, he was tall. His hair, dark golden now that the mud was washed out of it, was combed back from his face, which had been scrubbed clean, too, and as if it had been washed off him with the dirt, there was no sign of madness in him as he met Frevisse's look. "My deep apology for our deception, my lady."

Momentarily ignoring him, Frevisse said accusingly at Joice, "You recognized him yesterday. You put your cloak around him not from pity but because you knew him!"

"Of course I knew him!" Joice said angrily. "I should have let him freeze!"

"Joice," he tried again.

"It might be best," Sister Thomasine said gently from beside the altar steps, "if you went on seeming mad awhile. Things being as they are," she added hesitantly, looking from one to another of them as if to be certain she had it right.

Frevisse stared at her, blank-minded with surprise. Joice, frozen, stared, too; but Edmund, after a moment, collapsed back into a crumpled heap on the pallet behind him, gone useless again to all appearances except for the long look of understanding between him and Sister Thomasine.

Half disbelieving, Frevisse managed to say, "You know that he was never mad?"

"Oh." Sister Thomasine pushed her hands a little farther up her sleeves and ducked her head shyly. "Yes. I knew."

"From the very first?"

Sister Thomasine ducked her head lower. "Yes," she said softly.

"And you let us think he was? Let us think you'd made a miracle?"

"I knew you'd find out it wasn't a miracle," Sister Thomasine said in almost a whisper. "It was just it seemed he'd be safer if everyone thought he'd been mad and that he'd been cured for a while."

"But you know he wasn't, that he hadn't been," Frevisse insisted. "How did you know he wasn't?"

Sister Thomasine turtled back into her wimple as if she would have altogether disappeared if possible. "It was just . . ." She hesitated, then said with surprising firmness, considering she was still whispering, "It was just he didn't *feel* mad."

He had not *felt* mad.

Frevisse had been worrying at the back of her mind over Sister Thomasine's hurt when she found she had worked no miracle. Apparently it was not Sister Thomasine she needed to worry over, and she was distractedly trying not to follow the implications of that as Edmund said warmly, "She was protecting me."

"You *need* protecting!" Joice said. "What did you think you were doing, coming here like this?"

That told Frevisse they had not had much time for talk before she came, and Edmund's edged answer said some of that time had been spent in Joice being angry at him.

"I told you. I was trying to find out how it was with you. Word had gone to your father of what had happened before someone came to your uncle with rumor of where you were, and then it seemed well for me to find out if you needed help sooner than the sheriff could be here."

"Oh, yes," Joice said scornfully. "How great a help did you think you'd be, drooling and filthy and stinking?"

"I didn't drool. And the filth and stench were to keep people at bay."

"It did do that," Joliffe agreed from the corner of the choir stalls behind Frevisse.

Frevisse startled around as Joice exclaimed in alarm and Edmund jerked up to his knees, a hand going to his waist for a dagger he was not wearing. Only Sister Thomasine looked toward Joliffe with no particular alarm, and he gave her a small bow before he strolled toward the rest of them, making a general bow and saying to Edmund, "You did the madman very well. You fooled me along with the rest."

Edmund settled back onto his blankets. "Thank you, and more particularly my thanks for your help yesterday."

Joliffe sat down on his heels to come head level with him and said cheerfully, "A pleasure. So besides being Edmund and an occasional madman, who are you?"

"Edmund Harman, a clerk to her uncle." Edmund nodded at Joice.

"A merchant's clerk?" Joliffe grinned with delight. "But come knight-erranting to save the lady. What you ought to be is a player, you did your madman so well."

"What he ought to be is locked away," Joice snapped, then demanded at Edmund, "What do you think will happen to you if Sir Reynold's men find you out? What were you thinking of, coming here like . . ."—she gestured at him in a frustration for words—"like that?"

"How should I have come?" Edmund asked back. "What chance would I have had if I'd just come knocking at the gate with inquiries after your welfare? None of us were even sure you wanted help. At least this way I could wander off again, no harm done, and no one the wiser except me if that was the way of it."

"Knew if I wanted help?" Joice exclaimed indignantly. "You think I asked to be grabbed in the street and carried off?"

"How should I know? Knowing you, you might very well have!"

Joice gasped, momentarily driven beyond words.

"So," said Joliffe, still cheerfully, "with that settled, what do we do next?"

"You might begin with taking all this somewhat more seriously," Frevisse said curtly. She had neither prayed nor eaten yet today, and she wanted, suddenly, simply to sit down for a while and cope with nothing. "For one thing, someone besides me has mentioned you as possibly Sir Reynold's murderer."

"Ah, yes." Joliffe stood up. "Who better to blame for any new ill than the passing player, the wandering minstrel, the lordless, landless nobody? Always the favorite for anything gone wrong." His tone was slight but his eyes were bleak and unjesting. He knew as well as she did how much danger he was in. "In other words, the question is not, am I suspected, but have you learned anything that might save my neck? And I hope you have because I haven't. Or Edmund's neck either, come to that, because an unknown madman who, it turns out, isn't mad, will be first choice after me when they're looking for someone to hang."

"You found out nothing from the masons?"

"Only that if they're lying, they're better at it than I am."

"You're sure of all of them for all of last night?" Frevisse insisted.

"One way or another they're all answered for."

"Including Master Porter?"

"Seemingly."

"Seemingly?" she questioned quickly.

Joliffe spread out his hands. "I'm always open to possibilities, but right now he doesn't seem to be one. That leaves us all of Sir Reynold's men, Edmund, myself, Mistress Joice, nunnery servants, nunnery nuns, your Domina Alys, and you, to be thorough about it. Have I missed anyone?"

Only if she cared to believe Lady Eleanor and Lady Adela should be suspected, too, and she did not. She slowly shook her head and said regretfully, "There's something else that complicates matters, too."

"Oh, good. We needed complications."

Frevisse chose to ignore that. "Word has come that Abbot Gilberd will be here this afternoon at latest." Sister Thomasine made a small, glad sound and clasped her hands at her breast. The others looked only puzzled. "Abbot Gilberd?" Jolliffe asked.

"St. Frideswide's is answerable to him."

"Thank all the saints your Domina Alys is answerable to somebody," Joliffe said.

"But Sir Hugh means to be out of here with Sir Reynold's men before he comes, and that takes a good many of our possible murderers away," Frevisse pointed out.

"Always supposing it wasn't Edmund or I. Or Domina Alys."

"Or Joice or I or Sister Thomasine," Frevisse added caustically. "If we don't find out the murderer now, we may never be able to."

Joliffe grasped her point without difficulty. "So did you learn anything of use? Did you see the wound once it was cleaned?"

"Yes."

"Did it go straight into him or at an angle?"

"Straight into him. Straight in and all the way through."

Joice made a small, sickened sound. Sister Thomasine crossed herself and bowed her head. Joliffe merely looked interested.

"Straight through. And just below the left shoulder blade, you said. And from the back."

"From the back," Frevisse agreed.

"Then it wasn't done by Joice or Sister Thomasine. They're neither of them tall enough. You are, of course. Or nearly."

"Tall enough?" Edmund asked.

"Tall enough to drive home the kind of blow that killed him." Joliffe stood up. "Directly through him, not at an upward angle. Then there's the matter of strength enough for a blow like that. Dame Frevisse has the height, but I doubt she has the strength. The inclination probably, but not the strength."

Frevisse refrained from answering that, instead said only, "So we can let go suspecting anyone below, say, your height."

"Unless someone was seen carrying a joint stool as well as a sword around with them last night, yes," Joliffe agreed. "Which brings us back to Domina Alys and most of Sir Reynold's men."

"And you and Edmund," Frevisse said.

From behind Sister Thomasine, Benet asked, "Edmund?"

# Chapter

# 23

HE STOOD AT the corner of the altar steps behind Sister Thomasine, looking at all of them with a puzzlement that said he had not been listening out of sight. "Edmund?" he repeated. "Who's Edmund?"

Joice moved toward him, saying warmly as if glad he was there, "Benet, were you looking for me?"

Become a little wary, his gaze going from her to Joliffe to Edmund, slumped in on himself again, to Frevisse, to Sister Thomasine, and back to Joliffe and Edmund, he said, "I needed to see you. Lady Eleanor said you'd come here to pray?"

He made that too much a question and Frevisse tried desperately to find something to say to divert him from whatever he was starting to wonder, but it was Joliffe who said in apparent delight, moving between him and Edmund, "My lord! We're trying to work out who could have killed Sir Reynold and who could not."

"What? Here?" Benet asked, all the unacceptability of that answer plain in his voice.

"Where better? It's out of the way and quiet. And your sword is exactly what we need. Thank you."

He reached for the sword hung at Benet's side—Sir Hugh must have given order for the men to go armed now, Frevisse thought—and Benet immediately stepped back from him, clapping a hand to the pommel, asking, "Why do you think you need a sword?"

"It had to be someone fairly tall who killed Sir Reynold," Joliffe began, his hand still out for the sword.

"How do you know that?" Benet asked, making no move to give it.

"Because of how the blow went in."

Benet's other hand came around to grip the hilt, white-knuckled and ready to draw. "How do you know how the blow went in?"

Joliffe seemed not to notice, going on easily, "Dame Frevisse told me. She saw it."

"Yes," Benet agreed, glancing at her, his suspicion not allayed but spreading to include her. "She did."

"To put a blow straight through a man that way," Joliffe said, moving toward Benet as if still expecting him to hand over his sword, "it had to have been done by someone near Sir Reynold's height. If we have a sword and someone's back, we can maybe judge how tall the murderer was and that would limit who to be suspicious of."

Benet fell back another step, giving himself enough to draw his sword, and countered, "Who's Edmund?"

So much for diverting him.

"He's no one," Joice said.

Looking at all their faces guardedly, Benet held out his free hand to her. "Come away from here."

"No! Not with you," Joice said, beginning to draw back from him, and Benet moved suddenly forward, pushing Joliffe aside, reaching for her. Hampered by her cloak and skirts, Joice tried to avoid him but stumbled, and he caught her by the arm, saying, "There's something wrong here. Come away." She jerked to be free of him, and Edmund sprang up, ordering, "Leave her alone," as he started for Benet, who swung Joice behind him in the same movement of drawing his sword, to bring it point up to Edmund's throat, stopping him in mid-stride.

Unarmed, clad in only a rough tunic and hosen, Edmund froze where he was. They all froze, because the smallest movement of Benet's sword could be Edmund's death, until Sister Thomasine said quietly, "There's no need." Benet's gage flickered her way; she came nearer to him, to lay her hand on his wrist above where he held the sword and say, "Truly. There's no need. And this no place to shed anyone's blood."

Trying to sound as calm as Sister Thomasine, Frevisse said, "You're in a church, Benet. And the man isn't even armed."

Benet jerked his head at Joliffe. "He is." Joliffe promptly held his hands well out from himself, away from the dagger hung from his belt. Benet glanced at him but kept the sword at Edmund's throat. "And this man's been all a lie from the start. He's not witless. He was never witless, was he? Were you?" he added at Edmund in direct accusation.

Before Edmund could answer, Frevisse said, "No. You're right. He was never mad. He pretended to be so he could reach Joice, help her if she needed it. He's here for Joice's sake, the same as you are. He's a clerk to her uncle, that's all."

Gently, her hand still lightly on his wrist, Sister Thomasine said, "You're in a church."

Benet hesitated, then lowered his sword from Edmund's throat, turned the blade aside, but kept his gaze on him. "He could still be the one who killed Sir Reynold."

"Yes," Frevisse agreed. "But so could others. That's what we're trying to learn."

"I still say him for choice. Or you," Benet added at Joliffe.

"Indeed? Me?" Joliffe said, as if the thought took him completely by surprise.

"Or you, Benet," Joice said fiercely. She pulled free from his slacked hold impatiently and moved to stand well aside from both him and Edmund. "Why not you instead of them?"

"Because I had no reason to!" Benet protested.

"How do we know that?" Frevisse countered. "How do

we know that for certain about any of us or anyone else?"

Benet was momentarily without answer to that, but Sister Thomasine said quietly, "He's not tall enough." All of them, including Benet, looked at her questioningly, and she nodded toward him. "See? He's not tall enough," she repeated.

"She means you're shorter than Sir Reynold by almost a head," Frevisse said, catching up to her thought.

"Here," Joliffe said, turning his back on him. "I'm near Sir Reynold's height. Take your sword and see if you could give me the kind of blow that killed him. Straight through below the left shoulder blade."

Benet hesitated, looked around at all of them watching him, and raised his sword; then raised it higher, to bring its blade parallel to the floor, its point level with Joliffe's back below the left shoulder blade. In that position the hilt was nearly level with his chin and his elbows were thrust awkwardly out to the sides. "This won't work," he said.

Joliffe craned his head around to see. "You couldn't put much force into a blow from there," he agreed.

Benet dropped his elbows, cramping them together below the blade. "Nor if I held it this way either." He changed his grip to one hand above the hilt, one below. "Or this way either. My shoulders are too cramped." He shifted his hold and dropped the hilt below his waist, the blade angled up at Joliffe's back. "If I were striking a man from behind, it would be this way."

"Try it one-handed, as if it were a lighter, shorter sword," Frevisse suggested.

Benet shifted his body to an angle with Joliffe's back and raised the blade again and thrust. Although he pulled the stroke up short, it was clear there could have been enough to drive it in if he had chosen to, and lowering his arm and blade, he said, "I could probably thrust from there strongly enough." But he was frowning, dissatisfied over the thought. "The difficulty would be in thrusting true, to strike cleanly enough for a quick kill, there in the dark and with Sir Reynold moving."

"There's something else," Frevisse said slowly. "Even if

you had the skill or luck to put the blow just that way, why didn't Sir Reynold cry out? He would have, wouldn't he, even dying, from a blow like that?"

"He would have," Joliffe said grimly. "Very likely. Likely enough I wouldn't have cared to risk giving him the chance, risk someone hearing him if I was trying to do a murder."

Tentatively Joice said, "He might have been knocked over the head first, knocked down, unconscious."

"And if he were lying flat on the floor, driving a sword down into him would have been no problem," Edmund said, then added more hesitantly as he realized the complication that caused, "For almost anyone."

"I handled his head when we were readying him," Benet said. "There were no signs of any blow. Not to his head or anywhere else on him."

That could be checked with Lewis, Frevisse thought, or on the body itself, if she had the chance, but she did not think it mattered because: "Judging by the wound, the blade went fully through him," she said. "The gash in his chest wasn't a slight rip made by a sword's point. It was as wide as the one in his back. It looks as if the blade was thrust all the way through him, then wrenched sideways with enough strength to partly cut into his spine. The tip of a sword blade grounded on the floor wouldn't have done the kind of damage there is." She held out her hand to Joliffe. "Give me your dagger and turn around."

With a wry look but not questioning what she meant to do, Joliffe gave her the dagger and turned his back on her. Shaking back the loose sleeve of her outer gown to clear her arm, she moved up close behind him. "If it were done to Sir Reynold this way, it was done swiftly but I'll do it slowly, so please just stand still."

Joliffe nodded, and rising a little on her toes to compensate for his greater height, Frevisse reached around to clamp her left hand under his jaw, forcing his mouth closed and his head back as she drove the dagger toward just below his left shoulder blade, turning her hand aside so it was her knuckles instead of the point that she shoved against him. If she had not, the dagger would have gone straight into him, between the ribs, through the muscle and lung and heart. And moving slowly but with strength, she followed through on the blow, shoving her fisted hand against him, so that his body bowed out away from her and he would have staggered forward except she kept her grip on his chin, dragging his head back beside her own, holding his mouth shut against any sound beyond a strangled grunt.

Neither of them were using full strength. She could not have held him if he had tried to pull away from her; but it would have been difficult between two well-matched men, one of them with his death wound in him. Joliffe, playing Sir Reynold's part, sagged back against her, as a dying man would have, and they held where they were for a moment, making sure of what she had done, before she let him go and stepped back, flipping the dagger around to hand it to him hilt-first, wanting the thing out of her hand as soon as might be, as he turned to face her.

Joliffe took it, his face grim as she felt hers was, and said as he slipped it into the sheath on his hip, "That looks to have been the way of it. A sure blow and a simple one, with hardly a chance of any outcry."

Benet, looking sickened, said, "A coward's blow. Sir Reynold hadn't even the smallest chance of defending against it."

"A practical blow," Joliffe said. "Quick, certain, no chance of outcry and small likelihood of being caught of it."

More steadily than she felt, Frevisse said, "That means we can guess it was done with a dagger, not a sword, by someone Sir Reynold's height or very close to it. Someone strong enough to have held him like that long enough for him to die."

"Then flung him down and left him," Benet said bitterly.

"Which brings us back to Edmund and me," Joliffe said. "And Sir Hugh, Domina Alys, and the three or four among Sir Reynold's men who matched him in height."

"Or one of the masons," Benet said. "Master Porter first."

"Master Porter was never gone from the lodge last night between supper and dawn," Joliffe said. "Nor any of the others long enough to have come into the cloister, lain in wait on the possibility they'd have a chance to kill Sir Reynold, and come back."

"Before anything else," Frevisse said, "there's the matter of the blood. There had to have been blood on whoever did it."

"Yes!" Joice saw the point immediately. "Whoever did it, they'd have to change their clothing and wash off the blood. Without being seen."

"And neither would be easy to do," Frevisse said. Not in the cloister or the guest halls. For one thing, water would not be readily come by. Servants slept in the cloister and guest-hall kitchens, so there would be no having any water from there without being noticed. The wells were in the open in the kitchen yard and courtyard. The risk of being seen using either one was high. A desperate man might take the risk, but even then, even if he managed to wash clean his hands and body, what about his bloodied clothing? Wash it perfectly clean in the dark and have it dry by morning so no one would notice? Even being rid of it where it would not be found would be difficult to manage in the confines of the cloister and guest halls. Aside from that, someone wearing different clothing from what he had worn the day before would be remarked on after Sir Reynold was found, when anything noticed out of the expected would draw suspicion.

She had started on that line of thinking earlier but not followed it far enough. For whoever had done it, killing Sir Reynold had not been the end of it; and she said slowly, "Domina Alys."

"Yes," Joliffe agreed. "She was with him, already in the cloister, no problem there and no problem at being at his back if she was seeing him to the door and out. Afterward she would have had her own rooms to wash in, change her clothing, and who's to know a nun is wearing something different than the day before?"

The stairs to her rooms were beside the passage where Sir Reynold had been killed. She could have come down with him, killed him, gone back up with little chance of being seen. And she would have had Katerin to help her wash the blood off both her and her clothing, with her fire to dry her dress at afterward so that she might even be wearing it today, come to that.

And Katerin would likely have forgotten all about it by now, or shortly would. Only things that happened over and over again seemed to stay any length of time with her. Passing happenings drifted out of her mind within hours: by now she had likely forgotten there had been any anger between Domina Alys, Sir Reynold, and Sir Hugh last night.

"But it could as well have been him," Benet said suddenly, looking at Edmund with dislike. "He was alone in the church all night and wouldn't have to worry about changing clothing if he stripped off and went about it naked. If he was seen before he killed Sir Reynold, it wouldn't matter. We all thought he was mad. If he wasn't seen and he made the kill, he only had to wash the blood off to be in the clear, and he had water." He pointed to the jug and basin left for Edmund's necessities along the wall beyond the pallet and his blankets. "Any water he bloodied, he could dump out in the cloister garth and no one the wiser."

Before Edmund could answer, Joice exclaimed, outraged, "He never would!"

"I might," Edmund said more reasonably, "but where did I lay hands on a dagger? Everything I had was taken away to be burned when Domina Alys had me washed. I had no weapon of any kind."

Benet glared at him, visibly casting through his mind for an answer, before saying, "You might have had one when you first came to the priory, hid it somewhere, and went out after it last night."

"Before or after he stripped naked?" Joice asked scornfully.

Still reasonably, Edmund asked, "Where would I have hidden a dagger among those rags I was wearing when I came?"

"A small one, strapped to your side or thigh."

"It wasn't a small dagger killed Sir Reynold," Frevisse said. "It had to be one of the larger kinds to do the damage it did."

"A basilard for a guess," Joliffe said. "It would have to

be, to go completely through a man and be strong enough to cut sideways into his spine afterward."

"How would Domina Alys come by one of those?" Frevisse asked sharply. "Or Master Harman hide one in his rags?"

"A shorter way to go," said Edmund, "might be to ask if there's anyone we already know who has one."

Both Joliffe and Benet were suddenly, completely motionless, until Joliffe slowly turned his head and looked at Benet, who still did not move but stayed staring off into the air in front of him as if he were seeing something he very much did not want to see.

"Benet," Joliffe said gently.

"Sir Hugh," Benet said, hardly above a whisper. "Sir Hugh has one."

# Chapter

## N **24** Z

"HE MAY HAVE such a dagger," Frevisse said, "but you said he had no blood on him when he left the cloister last night, and I've seen him this morning wearing what he was wearing then."

Relief made Benet slump and almost laugh. "Yes!"

Edmund was not so easily done with Sir Hugh. He had begun to shiver lightly and wrapping his arms around him for a little warmth, he said, "He and your prioress could have worked together. He could have given her the dagger to use, she killed Sir Reynold, and then Sir Hugh carried the dagger away."

"That would leave her able to deal with the blood but with no weapon, while Sir Hugh had the weapon and no blood!" Joice said eagerly, going to pick up one of the blankets from the bed and handing it to Edmund who took it with a look of thanks that lingered on her, Frevisse saw; saw, too, that Joice's look lingered on him and their hands were together on the blanket a moment longer than was necessary. To increase the trouble, Benet saw it, too. Frevisse could tell by the frown tightening between his eyes, and she said, "No, I can't think they'd work together that way."

"Why not?" Joliffe reasonably asked, and added, "It would solve a great deal," meaning more than Sir Reynold's murder.

Ashamed that somewhere in her she would not have minded accepting Domina Alys' guilt for true, Frevisse said slowly, forcing her feelings aside, "Because that isn't . . . like her. She might kill in a fury, on the instant, but to plan out a thing like this . . . and against Sir Reynold . . . She doesn't plan."

But she had planned Frevisse's punishment yesterday. Frevisse's back was still too aching, too hurtful when she moved uncarefully, for her not to remember that Domina Alys had thought that out in detail ahead of time. But to kill Sir Reynold . . .

"It would have been more possible for them, that way, than it would have been for anyone else," Joice insisted.

"And if they did it, they can't be rid of all sign of it yet," said Edmund. "Isn't your prioress' gown made of wool? It won't dry quickly, even with the fire. It could still be damp, still show signs of just being washed. Anything like that would make a certainty."

"And we have to be certain," Joliffe said quietly, his gaze fixed on Frevisse. Unwillingly she nodded, agreeing. More quietly, understanding what he was asking her to do, he said, "It will have to be you who finds out. If there's anything to find, it will be in her rooms. A damp gown. Some trace of blood."

Frevisse lifted her head with a thought aside from what he was saying.

Blood.

There had been blood in St. Frideswide's yesterday, too. And yesterday, if not today, there had been bloodied clothing.

She looked at Benet.

Alys tried to rise to anger. Anger would at least be something she was used to, something better than this dead drag of grief that seemed to be all she could feel since seeing Reynold dead. Dull, aching, heavy grief that weighed down every thought she tried to have, every move she tried to make. The abbot's letter was in her hand, and she said at Hugh, standing in her parlor doorway, refusing to come farther in, "You had no right to read this. It was to me, not you."

"Alys, I haven't time for this. You sent to know why we were readying to go." He pointed at the letter. "There's why."

"Reynold wouldn't have left," she said dully. "Reynold would have stayed to help me face it out." But Reynold was dead.

"If it wasn't for Reynold, it wouldn't have to be faced at all," Hugh said coldly.

"And you," Alys said. "You, too. You're in this as much as he was."

"And you before any of us," Hugh returned, and turned to go, not interested. "I have to have the men out of here."

"I didn't know what he was playing at!" Alys said desperately, trying to be angry but only aching—aching as if something had broken in her that she could not find or mend. Forcing the desperation because she needed to feel something more than pain, she cried, "I didn't know how he was using me!"

Hugh swung half around to look at her and said disgustedly, "Maybe not, but you knew full well how you were using *him*."

She had known, but it had not mattered. What had mattered was that she had been glad of him being here. Using him had been only part of it, and so it had not mattered.

But if he had not been here, he would not be dead now. Dead without time to repent or be absolved of his sins and maybe gone to hell because of it.

She tried to drag her mind away from that, from the aching circle it had been in all morning now. Reynold was dead. He had no business being dead, leaving her only Hugh to be angry at, and she said, "You're using the abbot's letter for excuse, nothing more. You want to be gone without promising me you'll carry out what Reynold said he'd do."

"I'm not promising you anything," Hugh said impatiently. "I've told you that."

"Reynold promised—"

"I didn't and I won't."

"He swore he—"

"It doesn't matter what he swore! It's odds to evens whether he would have kept his word anyway, being Reynold. At least with me you know where you are. I'm swearing to nothing and you can expect nothing. Grasp it, Alys. Whether Reynold lived or not, you would have been on your own before long, and he wouldn't have cared that he'd played you for the fool along the way."

"He wasn't playing me for a fool!"

Reynold would never have played her for a fool. They had understood each other. No one had ever understood them except each other.

Hugh made a contemptuous sound. "Reynold played everybody for a fool."

With her aching rousing toward outright pain, Alys flung back at him, "Including you?"

"Including me. The only difference was that I *let* myself be played for the fool. That gave me a choice in when it stopped. Unlike the rest of you."

A shout and confused sounds from the yard below jerked him around toward the window. "Now what?" he said and came back, past her to the window. Leaning to look out, he swore and turned for the door again, saying, "It's your damned abbot. He's here before his time and some fool has opened the gate to him."

Alys had followed him to the window, was still there, looking out, seeing what he had not; and with laughter sickened behind her words, she said, "It's more than 'my' abbot. That's Walter Fenner with him, if I know anything."

Hugh spun and came back to her side, swearing.

"No going now, Hugh." She did not try to keep her great, grim satisfaction hidden. "There are Fenners and abbot's men together down there. You're going nowhere."

Hugh threw her a savage look. "Your people were told to keep the gates shut!"

"By Reynold," she answered.

"And by me this morning!"

"But not by me," Alys returned sharply, still looking at the mounted men now crowding full the yard. She could guess that the man foremost among them, richly dressed in Benedictine black with fur-edged sleeves and collar and a man behind him bearing an abbatial crozier the way a lay noble's man would carry his lord's banner, was Abbot Gilberd. Sir Walter Fenner, riding close beside him, she knew all too well by sight, and . . . she made a raw sound that was as close as she could come to open laughter. "There's why they opened the gate. That's Roger Naylor there." Her erstwhile, cursed steward. He had gone and betrayed her to the abbot, the first chance that he'd had.

"Fenners! A score and more besides your damned abbot's men," Hugh snarled. He stepped back from the window, rigid, considering possibilities and discarding most of them before he grabbed her arm. "You come with me. We'll face this out together. We blame it all on Reynold."

She went unresisting. Reynold was dead, and everyone and everything was turning against her, except for Katerin, who came out of her corner behind the door, a little crouched with fear, but following as Hugh pulled her down the stairs, ordering as they went, "We can blame it all on Reynold. Everything. I'll back you on how you knew nothing of what he was doing and you'll back me that I was against it all the way and set on having his men out of here as soon as he was dead, because, like you, I didn't think that they should be here. They may not believe us, but they can't disprove it. If we can find a way, too, to lay blame for his death on that madman you've in the church, that will be better yet. He's likely, so why not use him?"

Alys tried to say the madman was not Reynold's murderer because with Reynold dead, the madman was all she had left for hope; but they had reached the foot of the stairs, were just into the cloister walk, Hugh still holding her by the arm, still drawing her along with him, still talking as he turned toward the outer door and came, suddenly silent, to a stop, staring at—of all unlikely things—her madman standing on the low garth wall not far away along the walk. And beyond him, at the next pillar holding up the walk's roof, the minstrel. Both of them stretched as far up as they could reach and groping in the narrow wedge of space where roof beam and roof slanted together.

The beams of the cloister walk's roof were the only place that had come quickly to Frevisse's mind where something could be readily hidden in the cloister. Impelled by sounds of men and horses outside in the yard as she came out of the church, she had said urgently to Joliffe, Benet, and Edmund, "Hurry! They're leaving!"

Benet protested, "They can't be. I'm not with them," and started past her toward the outer door; but Joliffe went past her and leaped onto the low wall to start searching where she had told them to, at the pillar and roof beam nearest the stairs to Domina Alys' rooms, while Edmund took the next one. As Benet hesitated, half-turning back to them, Joliffe finished with the first, dropped down and circled past Edmund to leap up onto the wall again. As Sir Hugh and Domina Alys came from the stairs.

Frevisse froze and so did they, staring, before Sir Hugh started forward, drawing his sword as he came, ordering, "Down! The both of you. Down!"

Joice said urgently, "Edmund!" and moved toward him as if that would be some defense, while Frevisse without thinking stepped in front of Sister Thomasine. Benet, more practical than either of them, drew as Sir Hugh did, his sword out and in Sir Hugh's way.

"Benet . . ." Sir Hugh began.

In a voice hollowed with anger and grief, Benet answered, "No. It's done."

And behind Frevisse, Joliffe said, "It's here."

Sir Hugh made a spasmed move to go forward. Benet jerked his sword to hold him where he was, while Joliffe tugged and the thing came loose, a dark bundle, tightly rolled, that had been wedged into the angle of the roof and roof beam. He held it out toward Sir Hugh. "Yours?"

"No." Hugh bit the word short.

"No," Frevisse agreed. "Not yours. Godard's. You merely made use of it."

"When you killed Sir Reynold," Benet said with bitter certainty.

"What are you talking about?" Domina Alys asked, strangely unforcefully. "What do you mean, killed Reynold? What is it?"

"Godard's leather doublet," Frevisse said. Joliffe shook it out. The leather, stiffened with dried blood, only partly gave up its folds but there was no doubting what it was. "Godard was wearing it when he was hurt. They took it off him in the hall after they brought him back here. Remember? By then the wound had been covered and the blood on the doublet was dried. It was thrown aside. No one bothered with it. Everyone forgot about it. Except Sir Hugh. Benet remembers he took it to his own room after Godard died, saying he would see that Godard's things were given to his family when there was time."

Domina Alys shook her head, holding now to Katerin's arm as if she could not otherwise stand up, looking at Sir Hugh with a bewildered emptiness as she asked, "What's she saying, Hugh?"

Sir Hugh did not answer. It was Benet who said, raw with angry pain, "She's saying Sir Hugh took Godard's doublet and wore it under his own doublet last night when he and Sir Reynold came to see you. She's saying that after he left you, he put it on over his own doublet and waited here in the cloister walk, in the dark, for Sir Reynold to come down and then killed him." Benet's voice broke, leaving him wordless somewhere between grief and rage.

"It's leather," Frevisse said. "He needed to kill Sir Reynold close, to keep him from crying out, and the leather kept his own clothing from being bloodied. No one was going to miss a dead man's doublet. All he had to do with it afterward was hide it here and go out clean in his own clothing."

"Hugh?" Domina Alys asked. Tight-lipped with held-in rage, he threw her a harsh look and said nothing.

Joliffe picked up a dark blood-stiffened cloth that had fallen to the pavement from the unfolded doublet. "He'd even thought to bring a rag to clean his dagger with and left it here, too. The weather is too cold for flies to come to the blood and nothing else would give away its hiding place."

"Hugh?" Domina Alys asked again, wanting him to say something, not that.

Sir Hugh lowered his sword away from Benet's with a deep, impatient breath and said at her, "Don't be a greater fool than Reynold thought you were. That's exactly how it was."

Domina Alys tried to answer. Her mouth moved, but nothing came, as if there were nothing left in her to make words out of; as if anger and hope and everything else words came from no longer existed in her; until finally, faint in the cold morning air, she whispered, "Why?"

Hugh looked at her disgustedly. "Because I had no more use for him. That's why."

# Chapter

# 25

IN THE WARM midst of the afternoon the cloister lay quiet again, as if there had never been other than sunlight and peace inside its walls. Standing beside the church door, gazing at the frost-killed garth and trying to empty her mind of anything but stillness and prayer, Frevisse whispered, "*Exaudi, Domine, preces servi tui.*" Hear, Lord, the prayers of your servant. Prayers for peace, however momentary; for sanctuary, however brief; for mercy, however undeserved.

Behind her the door opened and closed so gently there was hardly sound from it, and Sister Thomasine came with barely a hush of skirts to stand beside her.

"Is she still there, the same?" Frevisse asked.

Sister Thomasine made a small nod.

"And Katerin?" Frevisse asked.

Again the small nod.

To Sir Hugh's answer, made as carelessly as if he were unguilty, Domina Alys had stood staring, only staring, not at anything, even him, only at nothing, at a terrible nothing bare of anything that should have been there—rage or grief or disbelief—and then had said to no one, out of that nothingness, empty of any feeling, "I have to go pray," and gone past them all as if no one was there, along the cloister walk and into the church.

Katerin had followed after her and there they still were, Domina Alys stretched out face down on the floor in front of the altar, silent, motionless, her arms spread out straight from her sides, with the small movement of her breathing the only sign she was alive, while Katerin crouched nearby, drawn up into as small a ball as she could manage, arms wrapped around her updrawn knees, as silent as her lady and rocking slightly, very slightly, back and forth.

No one had chosen to disturb them, not even Abbot Gilberd. He had come into the cloister as Sir Hugh was giving his sword over to Benet, and to Frevisse's relief Roger Naylor had been with him. That had meant there was less need of explanations than there might have been, though explanations enough were needed. Less welcome was the sight of Sir Walter Fenner crowded among the men behind him, ready to make a fight of something if he could. But Abbot Gilberd had proved to have a quick way with facts. He had sorted through what he needed to know just then and sent Sir Hugh away under guard of some of his men and Benet, refusing Sir Walter's offer to take him in charge and to the sheriff with, "No, Sir Walter. My thanks, but it will be best, I think, if I see to my men taking Sir Hugh to the sheriff. For now all the present wrongs in the matter have been done to the Fenners. I'd like to keep it that way."

That had been blunt enough that Sir Walter had had no quick reply, and Abbot Gilberd had given him no time to think of one but went on briskly with, "This is all secondary to what's brought me here. I'll see to it being given over to civil law as soon as may be. Sir Hugh can be conveyed directly to the sheriff by my men for a beginning, as soon as they can be horsed and gone. The rest of the Godfreys I'll bind over to keep the peace until the justices can deal with them, and then they can take themselves home. Today for preference. Sir Walter, you and your men shall be my guests here tonight and leave tomorrow." When the Godfreys would be well gone, he did not add but did say, on the chance Sir Walter missed the point, "I trust I will not have to bind you over, too, to keep the peace? You understand the matter is now for the law to see to?"

It required little acquaintance to know Sir Walter's character; it required a great deal of confidence to handle him with the assurance that Abbot Gilberd did. Sir Walter had darkened an unbecoming shade of red but said, grudgingly, that he understood.

"And so you don't mind swearing to it, do you?" Abbot Gilberd had said, and Sir Walter had sworn and been dismissed to see his men kept his oath along with him.

Abbot Gilberd's questions after that to those of them still there in the cloister walk had been short and few and left him in full enough understanding of how things were to say, "Tell—it's Dame Juliana who's presently cellarer?—tell her the nunnery is in her charge until I've finished with the Godfreys and made sure of the Fenners giving no trouble. I'll speak to you all after Vespers, before Compline. Matters outside should be well enough in hand by then to leave me free for it. But first your prioress."

Sister Thomasine, her head bowed, had said gently, "She's praying."

"Well, she should be," Abbot Gilberd had said in a tone meant to curb tongues that had no business wagging.

Sister Thomasine had lifted her head to look at him and said softly, "It might be best, my lord, to leave her there for now."

And Abbot Gilberd had paused, looking back at her, then said, "It might be, yes. Let her stay then until I'm ready for her."

He had left then, taking Master Naylor, Joliffe, Edmund, and his men with him. Joice had gone to Lady Eleanor who must know something from watching from her chamber window and now would have to know the rest. Frevisse and Sister Thomasine had gone to the gardens where Dame Juliana had had the nuns at work clearing the last of the beds for winter, having given up all hope of bringing the day back into line; and explanations had gone on until dinner. Even then, before they could eat, Frevisse had had to tell it all

again, to everyone—nuns and cloister servants gathered
together in the refectory—along with Abbot Gilberd's
warning he would talk to them later. That had given rise to
talk that had seen them through the meal and would see
them through the afternoon, so that when they had finished
eating, Dame Juliana—wide-eyed with the strain of responsibility now officially given—had set the servants to
scrubbing the kitchen and taken the nuns into the gardens to
walk and talk themselves into exhaustion.

Exhaustion was something of which Frevisse already had
enough, and when she had seen Sister Thomasine slip away
from the others, toward the church, she had quietly followed, not to the church but simply into the cloister walk to
be alone awhile.

Now she had been alone that while and was glad of Sister
Thomasine's coming, of something more than silence and
her own thoughts, even though now she had asked her
useless questions about Domina Alys there seemed nothing
more to say.

It was Sister Thomasine who offered quietly, "The
minstrel wants to see you."

For a moment, bound up in other thoughts, Frevissse did
not follow where she had gone, then said, "Joliffe? Where?
In the church?"

Sister Thomasine nodded.

"He spoke to you?"

"He asked if he could see you."

"Come with me," Frevisse said and turned to go inside.

Domina Alys still lay before the altar and Katerin was
still near her, unchanged, unmoved, from the two hours and
more ago that Frevisse had last seen them. When she had
crossed herself to the altar, she paused, looking at them,
and then said low-voiced to Sister Thomasine beside her, "Is
there anything to be done for her, any help we can give?"

"Our prayers," Sister Thomasine said simply, sounding
surprised she had needed to ask.

But, yes, she had needed to ask, Frevisse realized to her
shame, because prayers and Domina Alys did not go
together in her mind, except to pray for patience to endure

her, and that was not going to be enough now. Prayers for Domina Alys—possibly the hardest thing she could be asked to give and therefore the most necessary—for her own sake as well Domina Alys'.

Bowing her head, she made the first of what would have to be a great many, for both of them.

Joliffe was where she thought he would be, behind the choir stalls, sitting on the wall bench near the door into the tower. He rose to his feet as she and Sister Thomasine approached, bowed to them, then smiled at Sister Thomasine and asked her, "Here for propriety's sake?"

To Frevisse's surprise, Sister Thomasine smiled back at him, a small smile but warm, agreeing with him.

"On the chance that if Abbot Gilberd hears she's been talking with a man," Joliffe went on, "she can say she wasn't alone with me."

Sister Thomasine made a small nod. That was exactly why Frevisse had asked her to come but she did not much care to be discussed as if she was not there and said, "Your Sir Walter was here before his time."

"A matter I mean to mention to him when I collect my pay," Joliffe answered. "The word I sent him and Sir Reynold's yesterday raid together moved him faster than planned. It was only good luck your abbot was on the move, too, thanks to Master Naylor, and crossed his path in Banbury."

"God's will," Sister Thomasine murmured. When Joliffe and Frevisse looked at her questioningly she said, "God's will our abbot was there. Not luck."

"God's will," Joliffe amended. "Your pardon, my lady."

"My prayers," she said and smiled at him again, her small, shy, rarely seen smile now given to him twice.

He smiled, too, but then another look came into his eyes and he shifted from merely looking at her to something more intent and said, "You're fasting too much."

"Oh, no!" Sister Thomasine seemed shocked at the thought. "It's only been for penance, for . . ."

She hesitated, seeming not to know how to say it.

"For what?" Frevisse asked. "Penance for what? You've done nothing to need penance for."

"For all of us," Sister Thomasine said. "For everything that's been so wrong. For Domina Alys because she . . ."

Again she could not find the words.

"Because she couldn't do it for herself?" Joliffe asked.

Sister Thomasine nodded gratefully. Frevisse, suddenly seeing something she should have known before, asked, "And your praying for so many hours beyond . . ." Sense, was the word that came to mind. She changed it to, more simply, ". . . what you used to do, is that for Domina Alys, too?"

"Because of the offices," Sister Thomasine agreed. She looked down as if admitting it embarrassed her. "They've been so spoiled of late. We say them so wrong. I've been saying them again afterward."

Frevisse drew in a shocked breath. According to the Rule, a mistake made in the offices was to be corrected then and there by whomever had made it, but that was all. For Sister Thomasine to take on all the failed offices Domina Alys had brought down on them, to say them all over again, alone, when none of it was ever her fault. . . .

Sister Thomasine was looking at her anxiously, explaining, wanting her to understand, "It's so the perfection of prayer won't be broken, you see."

And suddenly Frevisse wanted to cry for how far she was, herself, from that entirety of heart and mind and soul.

Joliffe, holding to the point where he had begun, said, "But the fasting. How far do you mean to take it?" Too far? he did not say aloud. To the death, the way some holy women did—

Sister Thomasine turned her gaze to him in open dismay. "Oh, no! That would be wrong!" Refusing the possibility more strongly than Frevisse had ever heard her speak of anything since she had taken her vows. "I'd be no use to anyone here if I were dead. God let me come here to pray and be of use. I can't go until he says so."

"Nor drag your body toward death with hunger in hopes he'll take you sooner than he wants to?" Frevisse asked.

"Nor that either," Sister Thomasine said, sounding almost impatient at their doubting.

"I'll hold you to that," Joliffe said but lightly now, teasing her. Unexpectedly, she started to smile back at him again and ducked her head to hide it, as if as taken by surprise at it as Frevisse was. Joliffe turned back to Frevisse. "As for you, besides saying farewell"—which was more than he had done the last time he had left St. Frideswide's—"I wanted to warn you it looks like your Abbot Gilberd is going to scour your priory from top to bottom. You'd best be braced for it."

Frevisse had already feared as much but it was worse to hear it said. "You're saying that our 'rescue' is going to be as bad as our trouble has been?"

"Very likely."

"What about you? Are you going to be able to leave here clear of any trouble? Sir Walter won't give you away?"

"I told him my fee was double if he did. So far as everyone is concerned, he came here on a chance report from a chance peddler, nothing to do with me. I'm a mere wanderer who happened into this in all innocence and proved of noble use to Edmund in his peril. He's already told in great detail how much a help I was to him, bless the man, and it's planned I'm to ride out with him—the abbot is loaning us horses—when he leaves in maybe an hour to see Mistress Joice back to her loving family."

"Who may reward you further for the help you gave him?" Frevisse asked dryly.

Joliffe laid an earnest hand over his heart. "I can only hope. For just now, I'm going to go suggest to Master Porter what manner of agreement he might try to make with your abbot over wages and unfinished towers and things. Supposing it's possible to make agreement with your Abbot Gilberd. He seems to have come with a great many decisions already made." He bowed lightly and was turning away toward the boarded doorway as he spoke, adding over his shoulder for parting, "I don't envy you the next few days."

"I doubt you envy me anything," Frevisse said after him.

Joliffe turned back, with a look on his face that was disconcertingly like too many of Sister Thomasine's—deep and quiet and with nothing hidden in it and yet nothing there that Frevisse could clearly read. "Oh yes," he said most quietly after a moment. "There are things I envy you. Believe me."

Then his laughter flashed up across his face and he fell back, made them both a deep, elaborate bow, swung around and was gone into the tower, the door dragged shut behind him.

Carefully gathering her mind back to itself, Frevisse turned to Sister Thomasine and slowly, finding her way, said, "You didn't mind talking to him. To Joliffe. A man and a stranger."

"Oh, no," Sister Thomasine said simply.

"Nor mind the madman being in the church, when we thought he was a madman." Another man, another stranger, when ever since she had come to St. Frideswide's, Sister Thomasine had kept from any dealings with any man that she could possibly avoid.

"I knew he wasn't mad." That was what she had said before—that he had not *felt* mad to her. Then what had she *felt* of Joliffe that she had accepted him, too?

And almost Frevisse asked, how *she* felt to her, then knew she did not want to know and said instead, "We've let go two offices so far today. Do you think there's time for us to say them now?" Now, in the silence and the waiting before Vespers and whatever Abbot Gilberd would bring down on them. Here, with Domina Alys lying stretched out below the altar in what Frevisse hoped, for her soul's sake, was the deepest of prayer.

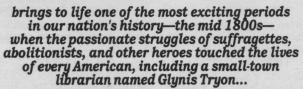